"You're sure?" asked Mahlo.

Tran shrugged. "As sure as I can be without seeing her. They even call her an alien. What are we going to do?"

"Sh-h-h!" Mahlo glanced around apprehensively. "I thought I heard someone." They were in a deserted corridor near the servants' quarters. At this hour of the day it was seldom frequented.

For a long moment the two men stood still, their eyes searching the shadowy corridor, their ears straining for a sound. Then it came again: a scuffling sound as of someone, improbably, dancing, just around the corner and out of sight. After a moment a thin, high voice began to hum tunelessly, and Tran relaxed. "It's only the Prince."

As if on cue, Prince Hawke emerged from a side corridor, moving backward in one of the slow, graceful folk dances of the People. He turned toward Tran and Mahlo without any indication that he saw them, and continued dancing till he was distracted by a portrait on the wall. He paused before it, head cocked. "Do you think it will rain?" he asked suddenly.

Tran and Mahlo stared, transfixed.

"Oh, no, I think snow is most unlikely this time of year," said Hawke.

"He doesn't even know we're here," Mahlo said, studying the youthful Prince. "He is truly mad."

Also by Melisa C. Michaels
published by Tor Books

FIRST BATTLE
FLOATER FACTOR
LAST WAR
PIRATE PRINCE
SKIRMISH

MELISA C. MICHAELS

FAR HARBOR

A TOM DOHERTY ASSOCIATES BOOK
NEW YORK

FAR HARBOR

Copyright © 1989 by Melisa C. Michaels

A TOR Book
Published by Tom Doherty Associates, Inc.
49 West 24 Street
New York, NY 10010

Cover art by Maelo Cintron

ISBN: 0-812-54581-8   Can. ISBN: 0-812-54580-X

Library of Congress Catalog Card Number: 88-50996

First edition: June 1989

Printed in the United States of America

0 9 8 7 6 5 4 3 2 1

This one's for my agent
Sharon Jarvis
and my editor at Tor
Wanda June Alexander—
friends indeed

1

Ugly Starling shifted on the cave's rock floor, trying to ease the pain of old bruises and the hot welts of a recent beating, and opened pale lavender eyes. The icy wind that had howled all night outside her cave had died at last, leaving behind a world ominously still and silent. The velvet dark of moonless night was familiar and comforting, but she couldn't sleep in the silence. Straining to hear something, anything beyond the hoarse sound of her own breathing and the thudding of her heart, she could hear only echoes: "What is the *matter* with you? You're a waste of food, a monster. How could anyone be so clumsy?"

The memory jerked her upright, blinking, dully aware that she must have dozed in spite of the silence. She shivered, hugging herself and moaning a little as stiff joints creaked in the cold. There had been sparse snow in that wind through which she had fled last night. With any luck, it would have covered her tracks well enough that they couldn't follow her if they tried.

Of course they would try. Even a waste of food couldn't be allowed to get away with murder. She blinked again in the darkness and turned her face toward the mouth of the cave, her pale eyes seeking any tiny sliver of light through the ragged storm clouds outside, wanting some true vision of *now* to block out the horror of memory. But there was no light.

In the awkward grasp of Ugly's clumsy hands the delicate crystal bowl had shattered, casting broken rainbows across Ugly's arms and face. Her foster father had shouted, his face twisted with rage: "Can't you do anything right? What is the *matter* with you?"

Ugly, conditioned since infancy, could only whisper

despairingly, "I don't know." It was no surprise to her when he lifted his ever-present staff to beat her. But what happened when the blows began to fall had startled her almost as much as it had startled her foster family. They were all there: old Mrs. Starling, grinning, with a stiff wanderwood switch in her hand to "discipline" Ugly; the two boys Karn and Joel, weaponless except for their fists and their feet, but ready enough to use both when the opportunity arose; and the girl Megan, her brown eyes gleaming, whose weapons against Ugly had always been more subtle and more devastating than all the others', because she was as small and beautiful and graceful as Ugly was not. . . .

It wasn't just that Ugly's cuts and bruises from the last beating weren't yet healed; she couldn't remember a time in all her life when she had fully healed from the last beating before they delivered the next, and it had never before provoked her to strike back. She didn't really mean to, this time. It was as if her treacherously powerful body had suddenly undertaken to act on its own. She didn't direct it. She didn't even know what it would do.

Her hand had caught the old man's wanderwood staff in a grip so powerful that the dark wood splintered beneath her fingers. The others saw—and understood—what was happening even before Ugly herself understood. Perhaps they had always secretly feared that her awkward strength might someday be turned against them. They attacked her like animals, as fierce and ruthless as if she had never shared bed and board with them and docilely accepted their alternate indifference and hostility.

Mrs. Starling flailed viciously with her switch; the boys kicked and hit with brutal efficiency; and Megan, despite her frail elegance, attacked with painted nails like claws and sharp white teeth like an alley cat's. She spat and hissed like an alley cat, too. And Ugly, who had throughout her life submitted miserably to the entire family's abuse without even questioning their judgment that she deserved it, had this time, at long last, fought back.

In the musty dark of her cave she shuddered again. She could not recall exactly what she had done; the scene in memory was a muddle of light and noise and pain. She remembered lifting an arm to fend off Mrs. Starling's switch, and slapping Megan to loosen her tooth-grip on Ugly's arm. The boys she must have hit with the broken stick she had wrenched from Mr. Starling's grip. And Mr. Starling . . . She was sure that all she had done to Mr. Starling was to shove him, almost negligently, aside.

As with the crystal bowl, her strength had betrayed her. Mr. Starling had gone sprawling away from her, across the glistening hardwood floor that Ugly herself had daily hand-polished with wanderwood oil under Mrs. Starling's critical eye. And his head had crashed so hard against one leg of the big oak table that the whole table shuddered. Two more crystal dishes that had been left on its surface shattered with little pinging sounds like spring ice on the river singing its way to the sea.

They had all been silent for one long moment while they stared first at the old man, lying slack-jawed on the gleaming yellow floor, and then at Ugly Starling, who had put him there. Outside, wind had begun to tug branches up against the walls and windows, scratching and tapping like creatures wanting in. The generator hummed in its eternal electronic madness. The tame birds talked in harsh, low mutters and a gecko scolded somewhere, briefly. The room smelled of fresh-baked bread and the sharp, clean scent of wood polish. A trapped fly buzzed against a window, startlingly loud in the silence.

Mrs. Starling was the first to recover. Shouting, she lifted her switch again and struck Ugly a solid blow across shoulder and head that left her dizzy, with blood from a new cut trickling down past her eye. "You've killed him! Monster! Useless garbage! You've killed my man!"

The others took up the cry and the beating. And Ugly, terrified and guilty, fled outside, into the amber light of the gathering storm. She was unaware, at the time, of the pelting rain that later turned to sleet and then to sparse, wet snow. Her mind was numbed with horror and despair; and instead of the rain-splattered dust beneath her feet, she had seen only the blank-eyed face of the old man who had been her foster father.

Now she sat shivering in the cave, her childhood retreat, hiding this time from the hunting parties that would have been sent out after her as soon as her crime was made known to the community of Gods-grace. She had slept uneasily, but long: with her face turned toward the mouth of the cave she could just detect the beginning of light through the clouds. Dawn could not be more than an hour away.

Even if the villagers had waited till dawn to start after her, they would wait no longer than that. And while the cave had been a safe refuge for a child hiding from malicious siblings, it might not serve so well a murderer hiding from hunters intent on executing her. Crouching, she crept to the mouth of the cave to peer out into pale misted darkness. The silence outside was complete. She shivered. A gecko scolded nearby; and in the distance a cat screamed once—hunting or mating—and fell still. The thick fog muffled both sounds, making them directionless and eerie.

Ugly sighed uneasily and turned back into the cave, feeling her way along the familiar cold stone till she found a shelf at the back where throughout her childhood she had stored her stolen playthings. There was a shred of gray blanket, rough and badly worn, that she had used last night as her pillow; it wasn't big or thick enough to keep her warm, but tied at the ragged corners it made a passable bundle in which to carry her other possessions.

An old kitchen knife with a broken tip went in first; the sturdy six-inch blade was good, sharpened on stones at the mouth of the cave. There was a cracked wooden bowl, a collapsible water jug without its lid, and a stained plastic cup in which she had collected shiny pebbles. Without even taking them to the growing light at the mouth of the cave to examine them one last time, she emptied the pebbles onto the shelf and thrust the cup into her bundle.

Besides those few items, there was little left of any value to her now. A shard of mirror in which she had often and despairingly examined her startlingly lavender-eyed face, and cried; the fragile halves of a crystal bowl she had broken years ago and desperately hoped to mend—that was before she had come to understand that they gave only the worthless bowls into her care anyway, because they *knew* she would break them; a broken string of orange beads that Megan had discarded; and the worthless metal token they said the Rangers had found in her baby hand when they rescued her from Freehold.

When she was younger she had imagined that token to be something precious, by which her real kin would identify her someday. It bore the image of a cat, and she had pretended the cat was the totem of her real family: maybe secretly she was a princess on some far planet, and the cat token would prove her identity so she could go and take her place among royalty.

She laughed at the thought: a bitter, broken sound, harsh in the morning silence. Megan had caught her dreaming over the token one day, and had badgered her till she admitted her fantasy. She could still hear Megan's incredulous laughter. Only then, after she had led Ugly to reveal her precious dream, did Megan tell her what they must all have known all along, and never told her: the token represented a lifetime pass to the Far Harbor Zoo and Botanic Gardens. Nothing more. Ugly's cherished "identity token" was only a bit of rubble that must have caught the attention of a wandering baby in the time between the death of her parents in the earthquake that all but destroyed the two major settlements on the planet Freehold, and the arrival of the Rangers who carried her away to a foster family on Paradise. Moreover, if the baby had been important to anybody at all, whoever it was would have sought for her among the Rangers' reports and would have come after her. Nobody had come. Nobody would come, except the hunters after a killer.

When she looked outside again, the mist had paled and thickened till she could barely see a few meters away from the cave. It would slow the hunting parties, but it might slow her as well; and she wasn't far enough from Godsgrace. She needed distance between her and those hunters before she would begin to feel safe.

She had seen hunting parties go out after criminals; and she had seen them come back, weary and satisfied, with blood on their clothes. She remembered the way their eyes had looked, and shuddered. From illicit reading she knew a little something about the world outside Godsgrace; enough to know that almost anywhere else on Paradise their prompt death sentences for even minor offenses against their many laws would be forbidden. But she hadn't been anywhere else, she had been in Godsgrace; and her offense wasn't minor, it was murder.

At least she was familiar with the ways of the wilderness. It was another thing for which her foster family had mocked her: her love of the wild, and her eager excursions into the forest whenever she was granted rare moments of free time. No one else on Paradise seemed to have any interest at all in the planet's deep wilderness beyond a desire to push it back, away from the Terran settlements, and then to forget it as best they could. That would work in her favor now. Paradise was really a wilderness planet: there were only ten small settlements and one large town on the whole equatorial landmass, and the settlers stayed in their villages or traveled between them by aircar, avoiding the unexplored areas below with its mysterious—and dangerous—natives who did not always remain docilely on the vast reservation granted them by Terran law. As long as Ugly stayed clear of the settlements, she would be safe from the hunters; and she was willing to take her chances with the natives if she met any. At this point, Terrans seemed a greater danger.

The first step toward freedom was to get well clear of Godsgrace. She was too near it still. Dragging her small bundle behind her, she crouched low to creep out of the cave and straightened outside, resting one hand on the smooth rock where so often in past she had sat in the sun, imagining what her life would be like when her true family found her. Those memories brought a twisted smile to her lips now. Hoisting her bundle, she looked one last time into the dark cave mouth and turned away.

The mist was spiced with the faint, sweet odor of herbs and flowers clustered around the mouth of the cave. It was still penetratingly cold, and Ugly wished again as she had wished several times during the night for a jacket or at least a warm shirt. On her way out of the house she had passed the coat rack, and she could have taken one; nobody would have stopped her. But she had not understood, then, what she was doing or where she was going, or that she would never return to the polished wood house where she grew up.

She shrugged. Last night's storm was probably the last for a long while; summer was very near. She would manage. Resolutely she shouldered her bundle and stepped out across rocks furred with dark moss under the melting snow, headed away from Godsgrace, into the unknown.

2

The message came the morning after the girl left them. Mr. Starling, still shaky after last night's experience—more from shock and rage than from the blow to his head, though that had left him with quite a painful lump under his thinning hair—was the only one home to receive it. Mrs. Starling had gone visiting, eager to relate to her friends this latest harrowing episode in the adventures of raising a foster child for the state. The boys had gone to work on the farm; and Megan, who showed promise as a crystal artist, had gone to the workshop to begin a new sculpture.

Mr. Starling felt mildly put out that nobody had stayed home with him to make sure he would be all right; but that was more than balanced by his pleasure at being left entirely to his own devices, even briefly. There had been, in Mrs. Starling's reaction to last night's events, a certain undertone of disapproval for his own weakness that had gone a long way toward spoiling his sense of importance at having been viciously attacked by their ungrateful foster child.

In his solitary morning reflections he realized for the first time that their foster child wasn't exactly a child anymore. The thought was an uneasy one; if she wasn't a child, then perhaps they had brought some of this on themselves by continuing to punish her as a child. The scriptures were quite clear on the point—children were to be treated strictly. "The wanderwood stick makes a good child" was one of his favorite quotes. But neither he nor his wife had taken a stick to one of their own children in years. Of course, their own children were several years older than the fosterling, and none had been as difficult to raise as the fosterling. They were human, and that made quite a difference. She obviously wasn't; she had been found in the Terran settlement on Freehold, but the two settlements there had not been isolated from each other. She might be one of those hulking native People of Paradise; the other settlement was theirs, and their Freehold king had been found dead in the Terran settlement. Others of the giants had been there too, and Ugly might have belonged to any of them. The Rangers had decided she was human, but Emmett Starling disagreed. Still, whether or not she was a giant—was she a child?

The government would go on paying—paying inadequately, Starling thought bitterly—for her keep for three more years, till she was twenty-three, but that was an arbitrarily standardized age at which anyone of any race, sex, and social background might reasonably be considered adult. The message didn't refer to her as a child. It called her an "adult fosterling." It also demanded that the Starlings bring her at once to the nearest government office, and the tone was such that Starling felt distinctly uneasy at his inability to comply. He telephoned his wife straightaway; she often knew what to do in situations that baffled him.

Mrs. Starling was just relating the previous evening's adventures for the fourth time, having found a new audience in the unexpected arrival at her friend's home of another neighbor who hadn't answered her phone that morning. "That child has been such a burden to us," she was saying, unaware that she sounded more satisfied than distressed. "You can't imagine what we've been through with her. And to top it all off, last night she actually attacked us. Can you believe it? I was just telling Amanda, I thought at first the girl had killed Emmett, that's how bad it was. An entirely unprovoked attack, too. It was horrible."

Mrs. Starling was a fine woman in many ways, and a good mother to her own children. But she had never been able to summon any feeling for her foster daughter beyond self-righteous pride (at having given a good home to an abandoned infant) and indignation (at having been selected by the government for the purpose). True, she and her husband had signed up for the foster program in a youthful burst of patriotism when they were first married, but so had most of their friends, and none of *them* had been suddenly burdened with an unwanted orphan twenty years later, just when their own children were old enough to begin to fend for themselves, and their lives were comfortably planned out devoid of further infants.

That the child had proved useful once she was past the most unpleasant stages of infancy was something Mrs. Starling seldom mentioned or even considered. In later childhood the ugly fosterling had fallen ill—some psychosomatic nonsense, the doctors thought, but just as dangerous for all that; the child nearly died, and was frail for over a year. She never really recovered; it was after that illness that she became so unbelievably clumsy that she was almost useless around the house, and couldn't be allowed in the crystal workshop at all. In Mrs. Starling's opinion she had been far more trouble than she was worth, and any assistance she had given to the working of the household was more than offset by her unceasing tendency to break things.

"It's good she's gone, really," she said now. "She never fit in, and I don't reckon she was really happy with us, what with being so strange and sullen the way she was—not quite human, I've always said, and those weird eyes of hers—I really wonder if maybe she's *native*, at least partly." Mrs. Starling shuddered delicately. "Anyhow, after the way she attacked Emmett—well, if she dies in the wilderness, it's too bad for her, of course, but really, I hate to say it, it sounds so callous, but it's just no more than she deserves, and that's the truth. I could have called out the men to hunt her down. Of course I would have if she *had* killed Emmett. But as it is, I reckon this way is better for everybody. I don't reckon she'll be any more threat to the community now. And I'm sure she won't have the nerve to come back, even if she survives in the wilderness, not after the way she acted last night. I got to admit, I feel more relief than anything else, now that she's gone. At least we're finally free of all the trouble she's caused us."

The telephone rang at just that moment.

3

Ugly went carefully, and now the skill acquired during all the times when she had hidden for solitary, forbidden hours from her foster family served her well. Clumsy as she was within the confines of their bright, ordered house, she could move silently through the colonnaded shadows of the forest. At first she worked her way straight through the undergrowth, forcing aside heavy vines and branches still dripping with last night's melting snow. But soon she came upon a narrow, almost invisible trail where the going was easier; and since it led directly away from Godsgrace, she followed it, placing her feet carefully on patches of bare rock or on springy emerald tufts of moss where her soft-soled boots would leave no traces.

Her greatest fear was that the villagers would bring out dogs to track her by scent, so as soon as she came across a shrub laden with pale, sticky blossoms whose bittersweet odor would serve the purpose, she paused long enough to crush handsful of the gummy petals against the soles of her boots, rubbing their bitter sap deep into the aging leather to conceal any odors that might already cling there and guide the dogs to her.

Though she had never before traveled so far into the wilderness—indeed, as far as she knew, no Terran had since the Rangers completed their exploration and declared the planet fit for colonization—the forest through which she traveled all that morning was familiar from her forays nearer home. She recognized kitchen and medicinal herbs and their extravagant blossoms, nibbled on heavy clusters of the same sugary starberries that Mrs. Starling used for jam, saw traces of the same game animals—deer and horned rabbit—with which the Starling boys supplemented the family's diet, and even discovered thick clumps of the rare broadleaf grass from which Megan Starling made the heady cologne with which she liked to splash her hair and body after a bath.

The mist was thinning. Slanting rays of morning sun picked out diamonds in the melting lines of snow along leaves and branches beside the path, but Ugly felt colder now than she had in the rush and bustle of the storm last night. A crimson songbird flashed past her, wings on fire in a splash of sun, and she thought of Megan's tame birds caged on the porch at home.

Not home. Never home anymore. Ugly Starling, murderer, had no home. Well, she had never much cared for the home she had—nor been cared for in it. She smiled bitterly to herself: there would be fewer broken crystals in the Starling home now, but there would also be no one to polish the floor and scrub the walls, hoe the garden, harvest the grain, clean the bird cages, mend the fences, and perform all the other menial tasks to which the Starlings had always set her. Now there were only genuine Starlings left, and they didn't like doing their own dirty work.

"I never made a very convincing Starling anyway." She said it aloud and was surprised at the deep huskiness of her voice. Not a melodic Starling voice, any more than her pale eyes were the melting brown of a Starling's, or her big awkward body capable of the delicate grace of a Starling. She had never been a Starling. They had let her use the name because she had none of her own and because as long as she bore their name they had a legal right to the monthly support check from the government. But now that she was a murderer they would deny her right to the name and give up the checks.

Her other name—Ugly—had been only the older children's cruel mockery, not a real name at all. The adults had registered a real name for her, but she didn't even know what it was. They had just called her *girl*, or *you*, or even Ugly, as the children did. She had come to them nameless, and in effect she had remained nameless, identified only by descriptive terms. It was fitting; she was nobody really, a useless waste of food, just as they had always said. And now a murderer. Ugly indeed.

By noon she had found three different kinds of familiar berries to eat, as well as crisp red wilderness apples with which to fill the empty spaces in her bundle; and had collected her favorite variety of tea leaves, smoky and tart when crushed in hot or cold water. She had no water yet, but was confident she would find a spring from which to fill her lidless water jug, so she made a sheaf of tea leaves tied with tough morning glory vine and put it in her bundle with the apples.

The mist was gone entirely by then. Because it was early in the season, the forest had retained the lush green gleaming beauty of morning right through midday, but when the sun was directly overhead its heavy vertical rays washed out the colors and melted the last remnants of snow so quickly they seemed to turn from ice to steam with no wet intermediate stage at all. The path beneath Ugly's feet dried quickly, mud hardening and grasses wilting in the humid heat. On either side of the path where there were open spaces between trees, the vines and weeds and dusty bracken seemed paler in the sun. The path itself was wider now, and it cut more deeply into the dark loamy soil, so that the grass and flowers at the edges overhung it almost as if it were the bank of a creek.

She hadn't noticed the transition from narrow, barely discernible game trail to well-beaten path. Now that she was aware of it, it worried her. If the hunters found this path, they would surely follow it to find her. Pausing, she looked behind her, half-expecting to see hunt-maddened Godsgrace citizens bounding toward her in the distance, but there was no one. Only dappled shadows and stillness and the hot green scent of wild grasses baking in patches of sun. After a moment she turned and went on.

Not long after that, the path diverged beneath a

spreading wanderwood tree that reached gnarled roots out into the two worn ways. On one side, the path was deeper still, the roots worn shiny and pitted; on the other side, the path was only a narrow trail again, and the wanderwood roots showed no wear at all. Ugly had read somewhere that only humans, of all the animals who walked forest trails, ever stepped on tree roots in their paths. She was sure no Terrans had come this way since the Rangers' initial investigation, if then. They couldn't have walked every path on the planet. If they had walked here, they would have passed only once; not often enough to wear those roots smooth. Were the natives of Paradise human enough to step on roots like Terrans? She knew very little about them. If they had worn those roots smooth, she might, by taking that path, learn rather more about them than she wanted to know.

She chose the narrower path and stepped over the roots. Whether Terrans or natives *had* walked the wider path, Terrans *would* if they followed her this far. Faced with that choice, the hunters would surely take the well-trod way, thinking she would have done the same.

She had not gone far down the new path when she found the shrine. It was set back from the path in a little sunlit meadow clotted with bright yellow and blue flowers that nodded serenely in the intermittent breeze and tangled their stems gracefully up around the stone base of the shrine. She could not have said what made her think the thing was a shrine; it was unlike anything belonging to Godsgrace settlers. They worshipped their harsh god in rectilinear structures with high, narrow windows and hard, polished benches. Their altars were austere to the point of bleakness: no sculptures or paintings, no visual symbols, no softening decorations of any sort. There was nothing about their worship, which was the only form of worship Ugly knew, that was in any way akin to this charming stone structure in the wilderness. Yet she was sure it was a shrine.

The base was a slim, carved pedestal, laden top and bottom with clustered stone leaves and blossoms and coiling vines. On this rested a sleek crystal figure in a niche cluttered so thickly with the debris of winter storms that at first glance the figure was only a shapeless lump; yet it drew her. She went off the path and hesitantly approached the pedestal, her steps crushing meadowsweet and mint so that she walked in an invisible cloud of fragrance. The figure had dragon-fly wings, and huge shadowed eyes that seemed to capture, fragment, and reflect the emerald hues of the forest light.

She put her bundle down in bracken at the base of the pedestal and reached impulsively to clean away dead leaves around the figure; then drew back, remembering the hated clumsiness that had broken so many crystal sculptures in past. The little creature seemed to watch her with its strange water-colored eyes. There must be green stones set in the shadowed sockets. And surely that was a tiny gold chain around the creature's neck?

Forgetting her self-conscious hesitation, Ugly reached impulsively into the niche and carefully drew out a cluster of rain-sodden leaves, sweeping them off the ledge and out onto the ground. Her fingers didn't bump and break the statue. And she felt an unexpected warmth, not physical but emotional, as if the little creature were grateful for her care.

Ridiculous. It was only a carved bit of crystal, nothing more. She reached again into the niche and with cautious fingers drew out more rotting leaves, then swept the ledge around the figure as clean as she could of all remaining dirt and puddled water.

The creature was smiling: an open, friendly smile that curved the unhuman lips and lighted the gemstone eyes. Ugly couldn't see the eye stones themselves, but she could see the emerald light they cast from the hollows above the high, sharp cheekbones. Now that the debris was pulled away, she could see the whole figure, and she went down on her knees to view it more closely. It was almost human, but for its improbable slenderness and the feathered wings that sprouted from its narrow shoulderblades. Those could be merely an artist's imagination. Even the unearthly beauty of the face, human and yet not human, could have sprung from imagination rather than from reality. Ugly didn't know what the native race of Paradise looked like, but surely if they were this beautiful and this unhuman, she would have heard of it. Unfortunately, that didn't prove this wasn't a goddess of theirs. People don't always create their gods exactly in their own image. And this certainly wasn't the god of Godsgrace. Which might mean she was all too near to finding out what the Paradise natives looked like . . .

She told herself firmly that the shrine had been deserted and forgotten, or it would not have been clogged with storm wrack. Then she noticed the offerings at the foot of the pedestal. Bits of fruit, gnawed by rodents, might have been left by the wind in the storm last night; but the china plate on which they lay was not brought there by accident. Nor the bowl of sodden grain beside it. Nor the bundle of scarlet flowers, unlike any that grew in this meadow, and tied with a strand of crimson fiber from the palm nut that grew only in the lowlands near the sea.

She had noticed none of these things when she first knelt by the pedestal, because they had been half-hidden by wildflowers and clinging vines she had since dislodged with her knees. Now she stared in growing alarm: those things were not left by the storm. They were not old; the fruit had not even rotted yet; the grain had not gone sour. They had been left here within the last few days—and not by Terrans.

The bowl was delicately carved with leaves and blossoms around a face that wasn't quite human and wasn't like the creature in the shrine, either. It looked vaguely feline; and its eyes, like the eyes of the sculpted creature in the shrine, glowed where there was little light; but here Ugly could see the gemstones, glistening pale sapphire under the rim of the bowl.

The china plate was painted with winged creatures like birds or butterflies, flitting among scarlet blossoms; the same scarlet blossoms that had been laid at the foot of the pedestal. Ugly looked again, almost reluctantly, at the figure in the niche. The eyes glowed, threatening to drown the sun-sparked serenity of the clearing in their emerald light. Suddenly very much afraid, Ugly wanted to rise and flee, but the little Goddess's compelling gaze held her still.

4

Prince Hawke loved cities, and Far Harbor was the city he loved most, even though it was built and occupied primarily by Terrans. He had visited other planets and had explored their cities. None was as perfect as Far Harbor. It had everything a city should have: an immaculate steel and glass financial district, decorated with miniature gardens and orderly parks; a squalid ethnic district, clotted with unsanitary open-air markets and brothels; the resort area known as Watergate, a landfilled marsh stacked high with condominiums and hotels; a major university that yearly reached sharp-angled, airy arms deeper into the mountainous watershed against which it was set; a Fisherman's Wharf famous for lobster, fog, and sourdough bread; artists' colonies, exiles' colonies, factories, transit depots, military reservations, massive shopping malls—and the long-deserted, recently restored Crystal Palace with its old botanic gardens and the new galactic zoo.

There were mountains, forests, deserts, and ocean beaches all within the city or only minutes from it. There were libraries, museums, art galleries, aquariums, planetariums, theatres, prisons, tenements, and hospitals. There were suburbs and shuttles, orphanages, experimental farms, used-car lots, freeways, churches and temples, swimming pools, bridges, and police stations. There were, in short, all the good and bad qualities of any city, packed into the sprawling boundaries of Far Harbor. Few residents were as aware as Prince Hawke of every district and pocket and hillside of the city, because most residents only lived in one area; Hawke lived in them all.

He was a big man by Terran standards, though

among his own kind he was small. Members of the royal family were always small. Some believed that the onset of the royal gift, so much more disruptive than the common gift and usually occurring before puberty, stunted their growth; but Hawke's gift hadn't appeared until he was years past puberty. In fact he had been so long past puberty that there had been anxious rumors throughout the reservation, and the celebration when he finally fell ill had been the wildest in living memory.

He had nearly died. As soon as his gift was diagnosed they had sent throughout the reservation for the complementary gift that would save him, and found none. He was the first Maker born in generations. There were no Breakers. No one was even sure anymore what were the manifestations of the Breaker gift. The anxious rumors started all over again; without a partner ordained by the Goddess, what good was Hawke? Of what use was his gift, a wild and unpredictable thing at best, without its complement? How could he save his People if he could not save himself?

The healers had done their best for him, and the magicians, and the priests. The oldsters had muttered in council chambers and at cocktail parties: it was only right, they said, that the heir to the throne that had fallen should be born with a gift that could not be mated. The Once and Future King of song and story was only that: song and story. The reality was a twenty-year-old boy who would die of his own gift, or at least lose his reason, and of what use was a king without a kingdom? Better for the boy's own sake, they said, if he died in his youth, ignorant of the terrible irony and cruelty of fate.

The healers and the magicians and the priests had won, but only just. Hawke had survived, but only just. And his reason was intact . . . but only just. That was nearly three years ago, and he had left the reservation as soon as he was strong enough, and had seldom returned to it since. In his youth he had explored the Terran city of Far Harbor and had learned to love it in all its primitive vigor. The oldsters said that since the onset of his gift he had been drowning his sorrows in the steaming sewers of Terran vice and corruption there. Hawke smiled, very slightly, at the poetic turn of their accusation, and neglected to refute it.

On the reservation he was the heir to a throne that had fallen. In Town he was only another "alien" who could, if he bothered, pass for human. Most of the time he didn't bother. He liked the way Terrans automatically avoided him and flinched from accidental physical contact even in the most crowded of places. He liked to be left alone.

He wasn't wholly out of contact with his father the High King, and he knew the search was still going on for his giftmate. But he despaired; by now, every reasonable possibility had been explored. Every one of the People had come forward to register his or her gift if any; even off-planet People had reported back, all negative. Now only unreasonable possibilities remained to be explored. Foster children and orphans of dubious parentage were being tracked down and called in. Only those near or past puberty would have suffered gift-onset yet; and those, if they had been adopted or put in foster homes, were the hardest to track.

The Terran government, unaware of the real object of the search (or disbelieving it), but aware of its extreme importance to the King whose kingdom they had conquered, lent their official support to the search as a gesture of goodwill. Their assistance overcame a lot of red tape in the search for lost children who might be of the People; but even Terrans couldn't track every runaway, every child transported off-planet, or every grown fosterling who had escaped into obscurity on the farms or in the anonymous crowds of Far Harbor.

In the time before Terrans came to Paradise, when in the language of the People it was still called Earth and Far Harbor was still a sprawling garden city called, simply, Town, prophets had foretold the coming of a relentless people who would conquer the entire planet in one brutal maneuver that would leave the High King no choice but to relinquish his throne to save his People. And they had foretold the birth of a Maker who would recover the High King's throne.

But a Maker couldn't recover anything without a Breaker to complete and fulfill his potential. The gifts of the People were akin to what Terrans called ESP, but the People of Paradise did nearly everything in pairs: a gift by itself was of much less value, and manifested differently, than a gift that was mated. A Breaker was one who could break patterns—in physical mass, in energy, in nearly anything. The gift had more than usual usefulness by itself, but became an awesome power when combined with a Maker, who could make new patterns where the old had been destroyed. . . .

At least, so legend had it. Of the two, the Breaker was said to be the more powerful alone. Which meant that his or her gift's onset would have been even more deadly than Hawke's had been. Hawke, with all the court magicians and priests and healers to help him, had nearly died. If there had ever been a Breaker to complement him, he or she must surely have died in Onset.

Hawke's father the King still had high hopes of finding a giftmate for Hawke, but Hawke himself had none. Grim and half-mad in his self-imposed isolation, he ignored his father's messages and forgot how to hope. His father would have been pleased if he had taken a lifemate while he awaited the outcome of the search for his giftmate; it would at least have kept him occupied. Hawke had no wish to share his broken life, and felt no need of occupation beyond his pointless wanderings through the city.

The old churches and temples from before the days of Terrans were among his favorite places in Town; the gods were dead or sleeping, conquered by the Terran gods as the People were conquered by the Terrans' technology. But sometimes in the old places of worship Hawke could imagine that the old gods had not entirely deserted their People. Sometimes he could almost hear them whispering in the winds through old temple doorways, shouting down the mountains to neglected churchyards, or riding their scattered waves out from temple piers and across the emerald sea. . . .

And when, as today, the holy places were deserted and the gods were dumb, that suited Hawke too. If the gods were dead, how much could it matter that Hawke's precious gift was only dust and rubble, the sick joke of a twisted Fate?

He entered the temple of Lanalei quietly, even for him, and stood in the doorway for a long moment before the two acolytes tending the altar noticed him. Lanalei stared blindly down at him, her hollow eyes lifeless as always. Hawke had heard tales of the old days, when her eyes spilled the green light of the sea down over the congregation, but he was not quite sure he believed that, any more than he believed that every rainbow was a jewel cast from her hand. Still, he straightened his shoulders under her blank gaze, and tried absently to straighten the ragged, flapping beggar's robes he wore.

When the acolytes turned and noticed him, Hawke let his hands fall to his sides and glared distractedly at the altar candles. "Only thirteen today?"

The acolytes bobbed and nodded, grinning foolishly. "It's the thirteenth of the month, my lord Prince," one said gently.

"Oh." Hawke blinked at the image of Lanalei beyond the acolytes. "She's dead, you know. Look at her eyes."

The acolytes moved defensively between Lanalei and Hawke. "Yes, my lord Prince," they said obediently; then, under her breath, one said, "She *sleeps*."

Hawke's fierce lavender eyes impaled her with a brief, sullen light. "What's that?"

The acolyte was a very young girl, not more than ten or twelve, with the pale blue eyes of nobility and the deferential pride of a priest. She stood straight in the light of Hawke's eyes, though she knew the frailty of his control and the force of his power should it be unleashed, and without a glance at the giftmate at her side, repeated steadfastly, "I said she sleeps, my lord Prince." Her voice broke on the last syllable, but she didn't blink. Her giftmate put his arm around her and stared at Hawke in silent defiance.

Hawke stared at them for a long moment. The light went out of his eyes. He seemed puzzled, as if suddenly uncertain where he was or what he had been talking about. The acolytes had heard stories of the mad Prince—who hadn't?—so they were ready for almost anything, but even so, they were surprised when he said distantly, "I wish I had an apple to give her."

An *apple*? They were hardly a rare commodity, not difficult to obtain, and not much of a gift for the Goddess. The acolytes glanced at each other before the girl said uncertainly, "I . . . I'm sure she understands, my lord Prince."

Hawke frowned in obvious confusion. "In the forest I gave her pears and grain, in a wonderful bowl. A ceramic bowl. At least, if I didn't, I'm sure I should have. And perhaps flowers." He hesitated. "But I haven't been in the forest, have I?"

It was true: the Prince was mad. The girl said gently, "I don't know, my lord Prince."

Hawke didn't seem to hear her. He turned away abruptly, his tattered robe flapping with the sudden motion, and strode silently down the corridor toward the gardens as if he were quite alone. Well, that was how a Prince was supposed to behave, surely? Acolytes were nobody you had to say goodbye to, or be polite toward. But still . . . He looked so awfully *fierce*, somehow. And lost, too. A sullen young animal, cruelly chained. . . .

They shouldn't think of a Prince like that. It wasn't right, even if the Prince was mad. They glanced guiltily at each other and turned back to their candles, the feather-touch of their gentle healing gift trimming a wick here and adjusting the flow of wax there, learning to synchronize their care by tending these inanimate objects and the bright little tongues of flame over them. They were so quickly immersed in their work that they never saw the dim, brief glow of green in their Goddess's eyes.

5

The meadow glowed with emerald light spilled from the winged creature's eyes, as green and rippled as if it were deep underwater. The wildflowers that had nodded gently in the breeze seemed now to sway instead in green water currents. Ugly felt her hair lift softly away from her shoulders to float in the air around her head, exactly as it might float in deep water. Yet she was not underwater: she could breathe, though the air did seem almost thick, with a heavy scent of moisture that was hot from sun and perfumed by leaves and blossoms crushed under her weight.

Those green eyes seemed to tug at something within her: something deep and hidden that she had never been aware of before. She felt a sudden, almost overpowering longing—for what, she didn't know, except that it was something or someone or someplace that belonged to her, that fit with her, that was *right* for her—unappeased and perhaps unappeasable, though she leaned toward the Goddess in a half-conscious effort to immerse herself fully in the light and the promise of those eyes, as if by surrendering herself completely she might somehow gain that half-recognized something that would fulfill her. . . .

Clumsy as ever, she lost her balance and had to lunge for support against the base of the pedestal. The light winked out the instant her fingers touched the stone. The dappled sun was yellow again, hot on the top of her head. The scent of moisture was only the damp of leaf mold from the storm wrack she had swept out of the niche. Her hair moved only in the wind, not floating, just pulling and shifting as it always did in the smallest breeze because it was too lank and heavy to stay neatly bound in the coil at the back of her head that was such a poor imitation of Megan's elegantly curled hairstyle.

The creature in the niche wasn't smiling. Its eyes were blind hollows with no hint of green, only shadows. An iridescent bee hummed to itself over the abandoned plate of fruit and settled greedily on a golden slice of apricot. Ugly climbed uncertainly to her feet. Tendrils of vine clung feebly to her shoes, and a fat golden spider, disturbed by her movement, scuttled, gleaming, into the protective heart of a waxy ivory blossom. A magpie cursed and whistled overhead.

Nothing had happened. The meadow was as it had been when she first came upon it: just a small, sunny meadow in the wilderness, shimmering in hot afternoon sun. She looked again at the figure in the shrine. It wasn't human. The torso was like a human female, but the legs seemed to be scaled, and ended not in feet but in something more like fins or flippers. The wings, too, were scaled rather than feathered as she had first thought. Not wings, perhaps, but fins. The arms were human enough, and ended in entirely human, five-fingered hands. But the face was alien. Narrow, with high cheekbones and straight, thin lips, it had a nose that was little more than a bony ridge and eye sockets huge out of all proportion to the face. In an odd way it was beautiful, but it was not human.

The idea that this cold little carved crystal face could have smiled in welcome, or watched Ugly with compelling emerald eyes, was laughable. She leaned forward, putting her face almost into the niche with the figure, to peer into the hollow eye sockets. There were no gems within. Just carved hollows designed to catch shadows and give the impression, at a distance, of dark, limpid eyes.

A pink and white cockatoo swooped down from a nearby tree branch, startling Ugly, causing her to back away from the shrine as it settled on the ridgepole there. It sidled toward her, head cocked to watch her with a comical expression of such measuring curiosity

that Ugly, caught by surprise, laughed out loud; and
with the sound of her laughter, the last lingering sense
of something magical having happened here was
dispelled. Of course nothing had happened. She was
just tired and frightened; and the overactive imagination for which the Starlings had so often mocked her
had been working overtime again, turning an abandoned native shrine into a living goddess.

The cockatoo, apparently deciding Ugly had nothing to offer him and that she was not dangerous to
him, hopped off the ridgepole and spread his pink
wings to glide smoothly down to the plate of fruit, to
feed on the offering there. Ugly lifted her bundle and
turned back to the path, but a nagging sense of unease
stopped her. She stood for a moment looking into the
niche at the figure.

Slowly, almost sheepishly, she reached into her
bundle and took out one of the apples she carried.
There was no one here to laugh at her. Still, she
hesitated for a long moment before she stepped forward again and placed her offering gently, almost
reverently, at the foot of the pedestal. "I'm sorry I
haven't anything better." The harsh sound of her own
voice startled her and she blushed, feeling as foolish as
if the Starlings were there to mock her.

She turned away then, too abruptly to see the brief
flash of green that shone from the Goddess's eyes, and
started resolutely along the path again.

Hours later, when the path had dwindled to nothing
so she could not convince herself she was actually
following a path, she paused again, hot and sweaty
and thirsty, in a petal-carpeted clearing under a wide
tree clouded with miniature blossoms. Sitting, she
disturbed the thick carpet of fallen petals and sent
clouds of them up into the still, sweet air. They settled
slowly back down again, clinging like a rainbow of
powder to Ugly's hair and skin wherever they
touched.

For the first time since she left Godsgrace, she was
beginning to really understand what had happened to

her. She would be alone for the rest of her life. Not the kind of alone she had always been before, where there had been people around her but she had felt isolated by their alternating indifference and hostility. From now on she would be really alone. There would be no people. None. She might as well be the only person on the entire planet.

Sudden fear shook her. *What if I break a leg?* Not a great danger here, perhaps, but the wilderness would not all be relatively level forest like this, and she knew she was clumsy; she didn't need the Starlings to remind her of that. In a rocky area like that around the cave where she had spent the night, she had to be extremely careful. Once, years ago, she had climbed a rocky scree in pursuit of a butterfly, and had realized only after she was well off level ground what a risky thing that was for a clumsy person to do.

Of course she had fallen, and while she hadn't actually broken anything, she had sustained a number of severe bruises and one badly sprained ankle. From her cave, on a sprained ankle, it had taken her the rest of the day to work her way through the forest, back to Godsgrace, where her ankle could be tended (and a few additional bruises administered as punishment for missing hours of work). If something like that happened to her now, she had no settlement to creep home to. A sprained ankle she could probably tend by herself; but she might have broken it, and what would happen to her if she broke any bones now?

Breaking things is what I do best.

She tried to laugh at herself; but the fear was still there. Even just getting sick would be a real danger now. There would be no doctors, no nurses, no medicines, no help. She was alone.

A gentle breeze sang through the leaves overhead and whispered in the tall grass at the edge of the clearing. A fresh cascade of sweet rainbow blossoms drifted down around her, dusting her hair and arms with their pastel petals. A narrow golden sunbeam winked through the flowered canopy above to warm the jeweled back of a tiny green lizard basking on a rock. Nobody had ever been in that clearing before Ugly came there.

If people had been there, they would have raked up the beautiful carpet of petals; trimmed the underbrush to rigid Terran designs; planted domestic herbs, maybe, and organized the scattered rocks. And then they would have tossed their food wrappers on the ground as if the world were a garbage can. There were worse fates than being alone.

She had picked up a little knowledge of medicinal herbs from tending Mrs. Starling's garden, useful for minor complaints, and she would just have to be careful not to get seriously hurt or ill. From now on, at least whatever hardships she faced would be impersonal, and there was a certain satisfaction in that. Maybe they would be worse than those she had known in Godsgrace, and maybe they would be made worse still by her general clumsiness, but the wilderness was indiscriminate in its hostility. It would not single her out for special cruelties because it considered her worthless and laughable.

She smiled, aware of a growing sense of freedom. She had always sought solitude; now she was guaranteed it. Rising, she dusted tiny blossoms off her arms and the front of her jumpsuit, then squared her shoulders and set out briskly to forge a path through the wilderness. The basking lizard, startled by her shadow, flashed sudden green across a bare patch of earth and she was reminded for an uncertain second of the hollow-eyed Goddess in the shrine she had passed. But she shrugged the thought away; by tomorrow she would be truly beyond even the fringes of the Terrans' hunting areas, and after that she would just have to go carefully and hope she didn't stumble onto the natives' reservation or into some hidden pocket of "wild" natives. There wasn't much else she could do about that danger.

Meantime, she had already left the shrine well

behind without running into whoever had left offerings for the Goddess. She was safe enough for now. A
yellow-breasted sparrow sailed past her, trailing its
long creamy tail and singing. She followed it through
hot afternoon shadows till it soared abruptly upward
and disappeared in the sun.

6

Emmett Starling read the government message for perhaps the fortieth time, and found no new insight there. Someone important wanted to see Ugly right away. There was absolutely no hint as to why.

Mrs. Starling and the children had all read the message several times by now, too. The children were gathered with Emmett around the kitchen table while Mrs. Starling cooked dinner, and from time to time one of them picked up the message to read it again as Emmett had just done; or offered suggestions while someone else read it.

"I don't think you should have sent out the hunters," Karn said suddenly.

Mrs. Starling glanced at him over a steaming pan of vegetables. "Now, Karn," she said patiently. "They'll bring her back alive, just like the government asked for. We got to turn her over if we can."

"It's not that," said Karn. "I don't mind turning her over. We don't know what they want of her. Besides, I wouldn't care if we did. I mean, it's not as if she was family."

"Then why shouldn't the hunters have gone after her?" asked Megan.

Karn scowled at her. "You're so stupid."

"I am not!"

"Are too."

"Children." Mrs. Starling's voice was sharp. Karn and Megan scowled at each other, but stopped arguing. Mrs. Starling sighed. "I've been thinking, too." She poured water off the vegetables and added fragrant crushed herbs judiciously, a pinch at a time. "I should never have let you children give Ugly that ridiculous nickname. It was fine as a family joke, but it's gotten all out of proportion. What would these government people think if they heard it?" She shook her head over the vegetables and set them aside, then turned to survey the table with her hands on her hips. "I want you all to start calling her by her properly registered name. Is that clear?"

Emmett shifted in his chair. "Well . . . What was it, then, if we're going to use it?"

Mrs. Starling smiled triumphantly. "Suzy. Don't you remember?"

"Oh, sure." Emmett nodded. "Of course."

"But, Karn, why don't you think the hunters should have gone?" asked Megan. "You know, she could be royalty or something. She used to imagine she was. I caught her one time mooning over that silly Far Harbor Zoo token, thinking it was some kind of symbol of her royal family." She smiled in fair imitation of fond indulgence. "Of course I told her what it really was. But what if she *is* royalty? What if they just never found her records before? That would explain why they suddenly want her now. What if that's it? Think of it: our foster sister, the Princess. Mary Warga would be so jealous! Her dumb old cousin-the-court-doctor would be nothing beside my-sister-the-Princess."

Joel guffawed. "Megan, bad enough you made a mess in the crystal works today. Don't start building even worse fantasies in your free time."

"Oh, honey," said Mrs. Starling, "did you have a hard time at work again today?"

Megan pouted prettily. "I don't understand it, Mama, I really don't. The crystal just doesn't work for me anymore. I can't do anything right."

Karn lurched suddenly halfway across the table to look into Megan's eyes, causing her to lean away from him in irritation and alarm. Before she could say anything, he sighed in relief and fell back into his chair. "Just checking," he said officiously. "You're okay."

"Okay! Of course I'm okay!"

"Megan, don't raise your voice like that to your brother," said Mrs. Starling. She had covered the vegetables and was stirring a pan of chopped meat over the stove. "Now, Karn, what was that all about? What did you mean about Megan being okay? And why in the world did you lean all across the table like that to look at her?"

"He's afraid of disease," sneered Joel. "Creeping purple eye disease, right, Karn?"

Megan stared.

"It's okay," Karn said quickly. "Your eyes are still brown . . . so far."

"You're joking . . . aren't you?" Megan touched one eyebrow with a delicate, painted finger. "Ugly had purple eyes."

"Lavender," said Mrs. Starling. "Karn, explain yourself at once."

Karn shrugged. "What if she had some rare alien disease, that's all. Something contagious."

"Who, me?" asked Megan.

"No, stupid," said Karn. "Ugly."

"What makes you think Ugly had a disease?" asked Mrs. Starling.

Karn hesitated. "Well, that would explain this message, wouldn't it?" He picked up the printout and waved it in the air over the table. "All of a sudden they want an ugly little fosterling nobody cared about before. What if it's 'cause they found out she's a carrier of some horrible, contagious disease?"

"What disease?" Mrs. Starling asked sharply.

Karn shrugged. "I don't know. Something that turns your eyes purple and makes you clumsy. Look how clumsy she always was, ever since that time when she was little and she got sick. Are you sure her eyes weren't normal brown before that?"

"Well . . ." Mrs. Starling stirred her meat. "Not *sure*, exactly." She looked worriedly at Karn.

"See?" said Karn. "And look how clumsy Megan's been with the crystal ever since Ugly left."

"But Ugly was sick years ago," said Megan. "I

couldn't be catching it just now. Besides, the doctors said it was her imagination or something, right, Ma?"

"That's right," said Mrs. Starling. "And that was the only time Ugly was ever sick, so it must be all right."

"Maybe, maybe not." Karn looked at Megan speculatively. "Did you recently share food with Ugly; you know, out of the same bowl or anything?"

"Of course not." Megan's eyes widened in sudden terror and her hands flew to her throat. "Oh! A week or two before she left!" She stared at Karn in growing dismay. "I took a glass of ambrosia from her—she was drinking from it, but it was the last glass, and I wanted it—oh! Do you think I caught . . . *it*? A disease? A clumsy disease? Then?"

Karn shrugged. "Maybe so."

"He's teasing you, honey," Emmett said uncertainly.

"But it's true!" Megan stared at her mother, her eyes still wide with shock and fright. "I can't work the crystal decently, not since Ugly left. Everyone said I was the most promising young crystal artist in the whole community, and now I'm as clumsy as Ugly!"

"It's just an emotional reaction, lovey," said Mrs. Starling. "Ugly's leaving was a shock to us all, especially the horrible way she attacked us that night. Like a wild animal, she was. Unprovoked." She suppressed a shudder, then tried to smile at her daughter. "All great artists are emotional, Megan, everybody knows that. When you get over the emotional shock of Ugly's going, you'll be just fine again."

Joel tipped his chair back till it was balanced on just two legs. "Ma, Ugly was a loathsome foster sister, not family. Not even a friend. I don't think you can blame Megan's problems on the shock of losing that."

"But the fight that night," said Mrs. Starling.

"Put your chair down," said Emmett.

Joel put his chair down. "Meggie's been in worse fights than that, Ma. You should see her down to the theatre on Friday nights."

"Joel!" said Megan.

"None of that, young man," said Mrs. Starling.

"What about how she almost killed me that night?" asked Emmett. "That would have been a shock. Maybe that put Meggie off her work, huh, sweetheart?" He smiled pleadingly at Megan, who looked away.

"Papa, don't be dumb," she said.

"Dinner's ready," said Mrs. Starling. "Emmett, help the boys set the table."

7

Ugly had no clear idea how long it had been since she ran away from home: a week, at least, and possibly two. It hadn't occurred to her to keep track of the days until they had already blended into a succession of hopelessly tangled memories that she could not organize into day-sized sections.

The first few nights had been the worst. The days were fine; she was busy traveling during all the hours of light, with no other goal than to put distance between herself and Godsgrace. But there was nothing to do at night but wait for sleep, listen to the unfamiliar sounds of the wilderness, and try not to think; an effort that was almost invariably unsuccessful.

The knowledge that she would be utterly alone for the rest of her life was terrifying. She loved solitude, and had always gone to great lengths to find it. She still enjoyed it now: one of the most pleasant aspects of the wilderness was that she was alone in it. Yet when she lay awake at night, often that blessed sense of solitude transformed itself into a vast, aching hollowness, an unfillable emptiness, a terrible loneliness. At such times, she felt she would willingly trade all the cherished solitude of the days for a companion in the night. Any companion; even a Starling.

That mood seldom lasted, but the underlying fear of spending all her life, years and years of it, wholly alone was seldom quite absent even during the day, when she was otherwise happy. Throughout her life she had been alone; isolated from those around her by invisible barriers she could neither understand nor overcome; yet there had been people around her most of the time. If she could not trust them, confide in them, love or be loved by them, she could anyway see and hear them, feel them, know they existed and that in a purely physical sense she was not alone in the world. Even their ruthless beatings had been a sort of confirmation of Ugly's existence.

Now she sometimes had to suppress a mad impulse to run, to shout, to wave her arms at the sky, or even to turn and go back to Godsgrace just to prove that she was real. Everything now existed for her only in terms of her own senses and intelligence, both of which she had long been taught to distrust. She felt oddly invisible, as if her ability to be seen depended wholly upon the fact of being seen. She knew there were creatures in the forest that saw her, but she didn't know what they saw when they looked at her. To them she could be a shadow, a wraith, a monster, or a god, not human at all, not even real in an everyday sense, just a passing danger.

Yet when she thought of it that way, she knew she must be as real now as she had been in the Starlings' house, where they had not thought of her as human, and had either never known or never cared that she had individual thoughts and feelings probably very similar to their own. When she was with them she had dreamed of days of solitude: now she had the solitude and dreamed of the Starlings' reassuring curses.

In more sane moments, she was pleased and impressed with her survival in the wilderness. The dangers had not been very great. She had not seen even one of the big cats that were, as far as she knew, the most dangerous creatures in the wild. But, knowing her own clumsy incompetence, she had not at first been confident that she could survive even an unthreatening wilderness. Yet she had managed very well.

There were fruits, berries, and roots to eat even this early in the season, and she had found a store of last year's nuts in a hollow tree, presumably hidden there and forgotten by a squirrel last autumn. A carefully trimmed corkweed stem provided a satisfactory stopper for her water bottle, and so far she had been successful in finding springs to refill it before it was empty.

It had not stormed since the night she ran away from Godsgrace, and in that she had been lucky, because she had not often found such shelter as she had that night. One night she had slept in the hollow tree where she found the nuts, but most nights she spent in the open, curled among cradling tree roots or in soft nests of bracken under the starry sky.

The country through which she traveled had changed very slowly over the kilometers, thick rain-forest giving way to the deep colonnaded shadows of a much older, more spacious forest with moss-covered roots and bright lichens spattering the tree trunks, and delicate orchid blossoms cascading from smooth branches twined with emerald vines that grew rapidly in the balmy spring air. The ground was covered with a thick loam of dead leaves, and was much springier than it had been in the rainforest. The tiny, delicate wildflowers that grew everywhere were here more delicate, and smaller, and more sweetly scented. Many of the herbs she found were unfamiliar to Ugly, but there were still many she recognized; enough, easily, to satisfy her needs. The number of edible roots she recognized was increasing in both quantity and variety.

She had not yet found any means of either killing or cooking meat, but so far she didn't miss it a great deal, though she certainly thought of it with some desire when she saw a fat horned rabbit hop across her path, or when a succulent squirrel scolded her from a tree branch. If she was going to live alone in these forests for the rest of her life, she would eventually have to find some way to make fire and perhaps to kill game. The thought filled her with such a sense of her own unfittedness to live that she shoved it aside. She wouldn't need fire this summer. Not unless she did kill something, which she had absolutely no idea how to do.

So far, the two most notable lacks in her life—the

ones that most often troubled her thoughts—were companionship and purpose. Just as she had, with some surprise, come to realize that she had been in an odd way fond of the Starlings despite their cruelties, and would probably have gone back to them if she weren't a murderer sentenced to death, she had also with equal surprise come to realize that she missed the sense of purpose she had found in her work for them. All the menial tasks over which she had slaved for them had been useful. She had been helping the whole family. Now she helped only herself.

Staying alive by her own efforts, finding food and water and shelter at night, was a difficult task, and she was often as weary at the end of the day's travel as she would have been at the end of a day's work for the Starlings. Yet it seemed, in a way, pointless. She moved only because there was no place where she particularly wanted to stay. She ate and drank to satisfy basic bodily needs: to stay alive. She spent each day, essentially, on the effort to remain alive till the next day. If she decided, one day, to stop that effort, who would care? Who would even know? Her life benefited no one outside herself.

After twenty years of living to satisfy the needs of others, she found it difficult to adjust to the concept of satisfying only herself. She did not even know how to value herself. Her whole self-image was based on the Starlings' frequent curses and meager praise that had come her way over the years.

No one had ever suggested a different value system, and she wouldn't have known what to do with one if someone had. For a child, the parents' (or foster parents') voices are the voices of God. Even when the child is grown and wishes to refute those voices' judgments, the early lessons hold. Thus he finds himself saying, "I am not that," when what he wanted to say was, "I am this."

Ugly didn't really know what she was, anyway. Some things that the Starlings had always told her were obviously true: she was ugly and clumsy. Other things they had told her might be true, though she didn't want them to be: that she was useless, for example, and a waste of food, and that she couldn't do anything right. She could not realistically claim to be of any particular value to anyone. It didn't occur to her that being of value to oneself counted for anything. She couldn't think of anything worthwhile that she ever had done right. Come to that, she couldn't think of anything worthwhile that she ever had done at all. Anyway, nothing that someone else—someone equally worthless—couldn't have done as well, or better.

"If only I weren't always going to be alone," she thought, "I wouldn't mind so much." In the early days, she had longed for someone to help her. Now she wished for someone whom she could help. Suppose, for instance, Megan had decided to run away from home, and had brought Ugly along to do the work. Ugly smiled at the thought; beautiful, fragile Megan would be so helpless in the forest, there would be plenty of work for Ugly.

She would be foraging for two instead of for one, and if Megan didn't get frightened and make Ugly show her the way home (she certainly wouldn't be able to find it herself) before the first night, Ugly would have had to find shelter for them both and make a soft bed for Megan. She would have had to prepare their food as attractively as possible; Megan wouldn't eat roots straight out of the ground. She would have had to wash Megan's clothes as well as her own. Megan probably wouldn't even have recognized soapweed in the wild.

In fact, without someone to take care of her, Megan probably could not survive in the wilderness. Awareness of that did not, however, bolster Ugly's ego. Like many people with damaged self-esteem, she judged all things with a self-defeatist logic that defied all logic: if she could do something, then it wasn't worth doing; and if someone whom she admired could not do something, then it wasn't worth doing. Most of her talents, therefore, lay in areas she considered worthless.

Lost in thought, Ugly didn't notice the gradual thinning of the forest till she stepped out from under the last, stunted, twisted trees onto the sere grass and white sand of the wide desert that bordered it. Sudden heat stunned her. For a moment the glare of sun blinded her. When she could see again, eyes narrowed and one hand lifted to shade her face, she peered dazedly out at acres of sand. In the distance, across the sunburned kilometers, the shimmering green ridges of the Mysterious Mountains thrust seemingly straight up out of the flat white plain, splashed with shadows and sun, misty under the cloud-scattered sky. She blinked. They looked like an unevenly crenulated green wall across the world. She had heard of the Mysterious Mountains, and had even seen a picture of them once, but that had not prepared her for their startling beauty. Elves might live there, or dragons, or at the very least fierce witches with wild eyes, who had lightning at their command. If anything could live on those steep slopes, it surely would be something magical and mysterious. Something beautiful, perhaps, but dangerous, too: something unhuman.

While she watched, a rainbow sprang to life beneath a low, tattered cloud over a mountain valley, arcing up from the valley floor to the fluted wall of the mountains, vivid primary colors delicately blending into one another with shattering brilliance, like crystals in the sun. For no clear reason, Ugly suddenly longed to be under that rainbow, on the steep emerald slopes of the mountains at the edge of the world.

They weren't really at the edge of the world, of course. Far Harbor was beyond them, on the sloping plain between the mountains and the sea. Town, the natives called it. She had seen pictures of that, too. If she could cross the desert, and find her way through the mountains, she would see it in life. She would see Town. People. Millions of people. Acres and acres of houses, buildings, streets, and people.

She closed her eyes hard, trying to hold back sudden hot tears that burned her eyes and threatened to spill down her cheeks. To see people again . . . maybe even to speak to someone, or to be spoken to . . . The thought was intoxicating. But she was a murderer. If she were recognized, she would be sent back to Godsgrace to be killed. Rightly so; murderers ought not to go unpunished; but she didn't want to die.

Neither had Emmett Starling. Yet she had killed him, and because of that, she was contemplating spending the rest of her life alone. She was shaken with a wave of self-loathing so powerful it left her dizzy. If only she hadn't fought back! The Starlings were good people. They meant well. If only she hadn't fought them, if she hadn't pushed Mr. Starling, or at least if only she had better control of her awful, unhuman strength. . . .

If only. One thing she had well and truly learned in her life was the uselessness of the phrase "if only." She *had* fought back. She had pushed Mr. Starling, and it had killed him. "If only" could not change that. She would have to live with it—or perhaps, if she went into Far Harbor, she would have to die of it. She could not change it.

Sighing, she opened her eyes to stare again at the distant mountain ridges, jewel green and mysterious. Very well, she would live with what she had done . . . and perhaps die of what she had done. She would not live alone. She would go into Town, if she could, to see the people. She *needed* to see people.

She eyed the desert vastness and hefted her water bottle. It was nearly empty. To cross those sun-baked kilometers, she would need plenty of water. She glanced once more at the distant, green, vertical ridges shimmering beyond the desert heat, and turned back into the scrubby edge of the forest.

It took her most of the afternoon to collect all the fruits, berries, and greens she thought she would need for that day and the next, and in all that time, she found no spring from which to fill her water bottle, though she wandered deep into the forest in search of one. What led her to it at last were the pitiful mewing cries of a creature in trouble.

It sounded small and very frightened. Whatever it was, it was desperate, and she could not ignore it. On the chance that she could help in some way, she followed the sounds, moving cautiously through slanting pillars of afternoon sun between moss-softened tree trunks, till she came upon a deep, still, forest pool bordered with cascading marsh orchids and cool dark blades of watergrass.

The frightened creature she had heard was a kitten that had somehow got itself trapped above the pool, dangling by its front paws from a branch bent almost to the dark, cold, mirror-flat surface of the water.

8

Prince Hawke's father the High King Arkos was convinced that his son's giftmate still lived. He had no reason for his belief beyond simple faith in the old gods, but his faith was absolute. The prophets had sung of the King That Was and Will Be, and Arkos believed that what they had sung would come to pass. It always had. It always would.

Arkos was aware that Hawke no longer believed in the prophecies. His son had been too much among Terrans; his allegiance to the old gods had failed him. In Arkos's opinion that explained all Hawke's problems. Perhaps because his own gift was a modest one that had not troubled him since his giftmate died many years before, Arkos could not imagine a gift so powerful that the need to mate it, if not met, could drive one mad. And as for the idea of rejecting all hope, because to live without hope was easier than to see one's hope crushed—a concept Hawke had more than once tried to explain—Arkos, who very fortunately for him had never in his life needed anything he could not have, refused to listen to such nonsense.

Therefore, when the High King's chief advisor Mahlo brought news of five more possibilities for Hawke's giftmate, Arkos sent his Messengers into Town to bring the Prince back to the reservation, to the country palace that had been the seat of government since the Terran takeover two generations ago. The Messengers had no trouble tracking Hawke. Unlike them, he was small enough to pass for Terran, but he seldom bothered. Tracking him was a simple matter of asking after a small madman of the People: even those who failed to recognize the Prince usually marked his comings and goings in Town. The Messengers' gift manifested as telepathy that was most effective between the two of them but worked also, to a minor extent, with others, so they did not always even have to ask.

They were not surprised to find him in a bar in a Terran slum. The People reacted badly to alcohol and were forbidden it by Terran law, but the law was seldom enforced, and Prince Hawke was known to have a perverse fondness for the drug. A death wish, the healers said, and shook their heads over him in well-mannered regret. The King's Messengers, an earthier breed, concealed their irritation with him and did not even privately call him an idiot, though it was what they thought. They called him "my lord Prince" with straight faces and angry eyes; and they seldom told the High King where they had found his son unless they could not avoid it.

This time they knew they had the right bar before they entered it; the sound of the fight was audible in the street. The two big, grim-faced Messengers glanced at each other, a wordless communication of weary contempt, and ducked their heads to step through the low Terran doorway, past the swinging doors, into the dreary noise of the bar.

Inside, the lighting was dim, the decorations dusty. The air smelled of stale beer and urine. The bar was named The Western, as proclaimed by flickering neon in the window, and much to the King's Messengers' mystification its walls were hung with a confusing array of plastic Terran animals' heads; bits of leather and metal; saddles quite unsuited for any Paradise animal; antique projectile weapons; peculiar, wide-brimmed hats; a wooden, spoked wheel; and vast, dingy canvases depicting a tan and sandy country dotted here and there with improbable tablelands and rocky mesas.

The bar itself was just inside and to the left of the door, its high gleaming surface polished to a fine sheen, liquor in every color of the rainbow stacked on low shelves behind it. Above the shelves on the wall was hung a long, garishly colored hologram of a Terran woman, nude except for sheer black stockings and another of the broad-brimmed hats. She winked and shifted her legs in limpid seductiveness as one's viewpoint changed. Her eyes were flat, muddy brown.

Most of the barstools were empty. The few patrons who were not in the back of the room with the Prince were seated at round tables that filled the front half of the room, their bottles and glasses sweating damp rings onto the tables' surfaces. When the King's Messengers entered, a few of them glanced up indifferently, and only one or two looked troubled. Even the bartender, lazily polishing glasses behind the bar, looked away from them without interest, back to the cluster of men around Prince Hawke in the back.

One of the Messengers paused at the bar, towering dangerously over the bartender. He glanced up at the Messenger, shrugged, and gestured with his grimy towel toward Prince Hawke. "He started it."

"Terran alcohol is forbidden to the People by your own laws," said the Messenger.

The bartender shrugged again, untroubled. "I thought he was human. He looks human enough, except for the weird robes and those damn eyes. The light's dim in here, what can I say?"

In the back of the room, Prince Hawke was drunkenly holding his own, but only just, against four Terran combatants, while a dozen or more onlookers cheered the Terrans on, ready to take their places if they fell. "How many has he damaged?" the Messenger asked.

The bartender's eyes flickered toward the back. "Three so far. They'll live. They got his knife off him first thing, or I'd've had to call the cops."

The Messenger glanced at the fight. "*They* have knives."

The bartender smiled lazily. "That's different."

The second Messenger pulled the first away from the bar with a grimace of impatience. The bartender had known he would; the Messengers' objections were just a formality. The giants didn't like their idiot Prince any more than he did. (When one of the Messengers glared at him for that thought, he wondered only absently what provoked the glare; he would not have believed it if he had been told they were telepaths. He wasn't much concerned about them. He was safe enough as long as their silly Prince came to no real harm.)

The Messengers moved slowly to the back of the bar, judging the fight, ready to take advantage of the first opening. If the Prince had been in any real danger, they would have cut through the Terran crowd to his side without hesitation or mercy; but he was not. One of the peculiarities of Terrans was that they regarded combat almost as a game, with rigid rules of conduct that gave their opponent every advantage. Of course the opponent was expected to fight by the same rules, but even Prince Hawke wasn't that much of an idiot. He fought to win.

Originally, Terrans had used the same set of combat rules fighting the People that they used fighting each other. The People, naturally, thought them mad, and won every battle: they were bigger, stronger, and quicker than Terrans; and although slow to resort to violence, they were quite ruthless once provoked. The concept of rules in battle was beyond them. As a result, a number of startled Terrans died or were irreparably damaged, till they realized they needed a new set of rules.

Now they fought at least four to one against People, with hand weapons for themselves only. If their opponent had a weapon he could not be made to relinquish, they fought eight or more to one if they fought at all. In place of any weapon, their opponent was permitted—since he would use them anyway—all the "low blows" and "dirty" fight techniques the Terrans themselves would not use. They had even devised a complex system of rules about the "dirty" techniques, including prompt replacement of some victims but not of others; a system they seemed to

understand almost by racial instinct, though it mysti-
fied the People.

While the Messengers watched, Hawke neatly
dodged one knife thrust and hit its owner solidly on
the side of the neck with the edge of his hand,
rendering him unconscious. The Terrans did not
replace him; that must have been an acceptable blow.
Hawke blocked another knife with his free arm and
kicked that Terran in the groin, which must not have
been acceptable, since the Terrans promptly replaced
him. Hawke turned in a swift move that should have
been as graceful as a dancer's and wasn't, because he
was drunk, and grasped the third Terran firmly by the
armpits, ignoring his slashing knife, and threw him
against the fourth Terran so they both fell in a tangle
of arms and legs and knives. Then Hawke stumbled,
and the replacement Terran was on him before he
could regain his balance.

Even drunk as he was, Hawke was a good fighter.
Off balance, he simply relaxed and let the Terran's
momentum carry them both to the floor and then over
in a roll, during which he was able to get his feet on the
Terran's belly and push. The Terran went flying.
Oddly, the other two, who had by now sorted them-
selves out and got to their feet, politely waited for
Hawke to rise.

In his place, the King's Messengers would have
taken full advantage of the breathing space to get their
bearings and assess the damage, but Hawke didn't
bother. He scrambled dizzily to his feet and headed
belligerently for the nearest Terran, who didn't happen to be one of the remaining three he was supposed
to be fighting. None of the Terrans had noticed the
Messengers yet. If they had, they might have stopped
the fight. Instead, they laughed at Hawke as they
caught him and turned him back toward the chosen
combatants.

He should have been able to knock aside the ones
who grasped him to turn him, but he was too stupidly
drunk and unsteady. He let them turn him and stood,

wavering drunkenly and bleeding from half a dozen knife slashes, while the Terrans descended on him.

They didn't use their knives. Either it was one of their bewildering rules not to use knives against combatants too dazed to defend themselves, or they simply didn't want to kill Hawke. They put their knives away and attacked him with their bare fists.

It took all three of them to get him down. The King's Messengers didn't interfere till he fell. They could hardly in good conscience delay any longer. "That's enough," said one, while they pushed through the Terrans to the Prince's side.

The Terrans backed off in some haste. The King's Messengers loomed over them, huge and powerful and dangerous. It took four Terrans to have a fair chance against Prince Hawke: it would have taken six or eight against a King's Messenger. Most of those who had been involved in the fight against Hawke moved quickly and quietly away from the Messengers to settle at nearby tables as though nothing had happened. There were four in various stages of pain or unconsciousness who did not move from the floor around Hawke. The Messengers ignored them.

One Messenger, the taller one, lifted Hawke to his feet as easily as if he were a child. "My lord Prince," he said, while the other dusted Hawke's clothing and briefly examined his wounds to see that they were not potentially fatal. "Your father the High King commands your presence at the country palace."

Hawke, swaying on his feet, nonetheless pushed the Messengers' helpful hands away testily. "I can stand by myself, damn you."

The Messengers stood one on either side of him, ready to catch him if he fell. Their telepathy did not work with him, which was perhaps just as well, since if it had worked at all, it might have worked both ways. Their faces were politely expressionless masks out of which the eyes burned with the dull fires of loathing. "Yes, my lord Prince," they said together. "You will come?" asked one.

"Have I a choice?" asked Hawke.

"No, my lord Prince."

"Then I'll come." He looked around uneasily. "What happened here?"

"A fight, my lord Prince." They guided him gently toward the swinging doors.

"Did I win?" He looked like a small boy, rumpled and torn and dusty, his hair awry, his expression mildly worried.

"No, my lord Prince."

"Oh." Crestfallen, he dusted his hands on the front of his beggar's robes and fell into step with them.

"Just a minute!" said the bartender.

The three of them paused just inside the door, looking back at him.

"There's damages." He waved an arm toward the back of the bar. "Broken chairs, glasses. . . ."

Hawke started toward him, violence in his eyes. One Messenger caught him by the nape of the neck while the other stared down at the bartender. "My lord Prince is of the People. It is against your own law to serve him alcohol."

The bartender shrugged. "He's small. How was I to know?"

"Royalty is always small. He is dressed as the People dress, as you can see."

"So are half the students up at the college."

"He has the eyes of royalty, and his skin is pale."

"There are Terrans with blue eyes. Plenty of 'em. And pale Terrans, too." The bartender lifted his chin belligerently. "He coulda been a student."

"His eyes are not blue."

Hawke, kept from physically attacking, was glaring at the bartender with a dangerous light of rage glowing in his eyes. Probably he was too drunk to do much damage, but one never knew. The Messenger who held him noticed the faltering light and shook him gently. "My lord Prince, please control your anger," he said. "Do not waste your powers on such as this."

The bartender, hearing this, stared from Hawke to

the Messengers and back again. "Powers? What's this? I ain't seen no powers. You think the drunk can do magic? How come he let those barflies beat 'im, if he can do magic?"

"Not magic," said a Messenger.

"I've heard about you giants' magic. What can he do?" The bartender rubbed the bar with his grimy rag, watching Hawke curiously. "Can't he do it when he's drunk, or what?"

"It is not magic," repeated the Messenger. "It is . . . a gift he has. Be glad he did not use it." They started Hawke toward the door again.

"Hey! What about my damages?"

One of the Messengers tossed the bartender a coin as they stepped through the doors. The sound of laughter followed them. The Messengers glanced at each other over Hawke's oblivious head. To the Terrans, their Prince was a joke. It was hardly surprising, but it was depressing. Silently they hustled him toward the aircar that would take them back to the reservation.

"Where are we going?" asked Prince Hawke. He looked dizzily from one to the other of them. "Where have we been?"

9

The kitten stopped struggling as soon as it saw Ugly. It gazed at her steadily with eyes as vividly lavender as her own. She could not tell whether sight of her frightened it or gave it hope; the unblinking gaze revealed nothing.

Cats on Paradise were not the little toy-sized darlings of houses and alleys on Earth. They were shaped more like Terran house cats than like any Terran variety of wild cat, but the adults usually weighed fifteen or twenty kilos. This one was about the size of a large Terran house cat, but it still had the triangular tail and oversized ears of a very young kitten. When it opened its mouth to mew once, piteously, at Ugly, she could see that it still had its needle-sharp milk teeth. Its fur was beautiful creamy white, an unlikely color for a forest creature in summer.

The branch to which it clung was bent nearly double under its weight, dangling its back legs perilously near the still surface of the water. Like a warped mirror, the pond surface reflected the gleaming white fur and the green leaves above it, flecked with sparkles of light in the moment when Ugly arrived, before the clouds that had been piling up over the forest all day suddenly obscured the sun.

"How did you get there?" asked Ugly. "You must be almost as clumsy as I."

The kitten looked at her. The sun disappeared behind clouds and a weird amber gloom descended over the forest. The slanting pillars of light that had fanned down between the leaves were gone. The water in the pond became a blank, black sheet of glass with only a pale smudge on its surface just under the kitten.

The pastel colors of the marsh orchids seemed to dim while Ugly watched, and the watergrass began to curl its spiked leaves for the night. A sparrow swooped down low over the surface of the water, looking for insects, its long tail trailing gracefully.

The kitten blinked. Ugly found a dead branch to test the depth of the water. It was too deep to wade, and she didn't know how to swim. She circled the little pond slowly, eyeing the kitten. It watched her, tail twitching. In the weird, muted light of the impending storm its eyes seemed almost to glow.

"Can you swim?" she asked. "That would be simplest." She paused, hands on her hips, judging distances. "But I suppose not, or you would have by now." She thrust her pole into the water in a new place, and found it still too deep. "Well, hang on. We'll get you out of this somehow."

She considered trying to snag the kitten's branch with her pole, to swing it away from the water; but even if the kitten didn't lose its grip in the process, its branch wouldn't reach to shore.

It wouldn't do any good for Ugly to climb the same tree, either; she couldn't reach the kitten that way. None of the branches near it would support her weight. Nor were the branches of any of the nearby trees sturdier or better placed.

The part of the pool under the kitten was no more than three meters wide. Probably if the kitten did fall in the water, even if it couldn't swim a stroke, she could fish it out before it drowned. But clearly it wouldn't want to resort to such drastic measures. There must be a better way. She wandered away from the pool, looking for inspiration.

This far into the forest there was very little underbrush, and not many of the trees had branches low enough for Ugly to reach. The ground was covered with fallen leaves that smelled damply of mold where her feet disturbed them. The kitten's head moved as it watched her. Its arms must be getting tired. She must do something quickly, but what?

Feeling increasingly frantic, Ugly stared helplessly at her surroundings in the gloomy light. A cockatoo chattered busily somewhere out of sight. A brown lizard scuttled past Ugly's feet and disappeared into a patch of clustered yellow daisies that grew at the end of a rotted log. The kitten made a tiny, involuntary sound as its claws slipped, then held again. A frog plopped into the water, leaving widening rings on the surface that stirred the stiffly furled watergrass and made the orchids nod solemnly. A twig bobbed away from the edge of the water, disturbed by the miniature waves, and floated serenely out toward the middle of the pool, turning as it went.

"How stupid I am," said Ugly. "Wood floats!" She rushed to the log in its nest of daisies and leaned her weight against it. The bark crumbled under her hands, disclosing communities of grubs that scurried anxiously away from her fingers, and the surface beneath the bark felt spongy, but the core of the log was solid. It moved reluctantly under her weight, rolling one slow turn toward the water, leaving behind it a long indentation in the soil. Round white heads of toadstools unfolded slowly, relieved of the burden that had protected them from the light.

It took Ugly several minutes to push, drag, and roll the log to the edge of the water. Twice it got hung up on obstacles—once on a group of saplings and once on an outcropping of rock—from which she disentangled it mostly with sheer brute force and determination. The Starlings would have been shocked that she could move such a heavy object at all, but they weren't there to express disapproval, and she didn't think of them. It annoyed her that she couldn't move the log more easily. It was the first time she had ever done anything "unhuman" without shame.

The kitten couldn't possibly hold on much longer. She moved one end of the log out into the water till it was under him. Waterbugs skittered on long legs from light to shadow. An iridescent dragonfly hovered on invisible wings over a drooping lavender orchid. The kitten stared at Ugly with expressionless eyes. The weird, muted light of the coming storm gave an odd underwater look to the little clearing around the pond. Ugly thought fleetingly of the Crystal Goddess and breathed a confused prayer for luck.

What she proposed to do was hardly a sensible plan for a person as clumsy as she believed herself to be. Fortunately that thought didn't occur to her, or she might not have tried it, and would certainly have failed if she did. She wasn't thinking of herself, and there was no one there to remind her of her failings. The log, with two meters of its length projecting out into the water beneath the kitten, still had a full meter or more of its length on shore, securely sunk into the oozy marsh-mud out of which the pastel orchids lifted their laden stems. Ugly pulled off her boots, tossed them onto firmer ground, and stepped carefully onto the landward end of the log.

Mud squelched under her weight. The log sank downward, black mud seeping up its sides, and stopped. Ugly took a cautious step toward the kitten, toes clinging to the log's rough, crumbly bark. She half-expected it to roll or slide off the mud and into the water, but it remained steady. The kitten blinked.

"If you let go now, you'd land on the log," said Ugly. "You wouldn't drown." She took another step toward him. The log sank another few centimeters, but it still didn't roll. "Don't be afraid," she said softly. "I won't hurt you. You're safe now. The log will catch you if you can't hold on, and I'm coming to get you. You'll be all right."

Incredibly, the kitten began to purr.

"I thought cats only did that when they're happy," said Ugly. "Do you do it when you're frightened, too? It's all right, small one. You'll be all right."

She was moving sideways on the log, her feet underwater now, arms outstretched for balance. As she neared the kitten, left side first, she lowered her left arm so her shoulder would reach him first. He was higher above the water than she had at first thought;

his back feet hung less than a meter from the surface, but he was long and thin, and she had only to duck her shoulder a little to get it under his belly and carefully lift his weight off the bent branch that supported him.

To her surprise, he accepted her proximity calmly, and made no effort to escape her encircling arm. Even when he transferred his grip from the branch to her shoulders, he did it carefully, his claws delicately catching her clothes without pricking through enough to scratch her. He held on with his arms around her neck and his face pressed trustingly against her ear, his breath tickling the small hairs on her cheek, while she adjusted her balance to accommodate his weight and moved cautiously back up the log toward dry ground.

It was a surprisingly pleasant experience to be so near a living creature, to feel its soft arms around her neck and its damp nose against her jaw. His fur was deep and soft and warm against her skin. He still purred, and she could feel the vibration of it throughout his small body, as if he had a little motor inside. Without any awareness of what she was doing, she began to gently stroke his back with her free hand while she edged carefully along the log, past slippery watergrass thickets, to safety.

He didn't move in her hold till they were safely off the log on dry land. Then he squirmed just once, very briefly, and lay still again under her hands. It was almost as clear a communication as words; he wanted down, but wouldn't jump for fear of hurting her. She bent quickly, and regretfully set him on his feet among the dead leaves and bracken shoots at the pond's edge.

Without a glance at her or even a second's hesitation, he bounded away into the forest and in seconds was out of sight among its gloomy pre-storm shadows. Ugly straightened slowly, staring after him with an unexpected sense of loss. She could still feel the impression of his arms around her neck. She rubbed her cheek where his breath had tickled it. For those few moments while she held him, she had not been wholly alone in the universe. She had thought she was used to being alone, but now she knew she wasn't.

"You knew he would run away," she thought. "He's wild." It didn't help. Desolation settled over her like a palpable weight. Her shoulders sagged with the burden of it. The strange amber light under the clouds had transformed the forest from a vibrant, living place to a landscape of isolation in which nothing stirred, not even a breath of wind. The waterbugs on the surface of the pond were still, barely visible in the shadows. No birds sang. There might be nothing left alive on Paradise but Ugly.

She sat down suddenly on the end of the log and put her elbows on her knees and her chin in her hands. The mud under the log made a tiny sucking sound as her weight shifted the log; and the rich, tangy scent of damp earth made her think of the Starlings' garden after a rain. Who would tend their garden now that Ugly was gone? None of the Starlings understood green growing things. Even Mrs. Starling's herbs would die with no one to tend them. Mrs. Starling wouldn't know how much water they wanted, or how much sun, or when to nip off buds to keep them from going to seed. . . .

Probably they would already have hired someone to take Ugly's place. They would have done that straightaway; none of them could do her work, and Emmett Starling wouldn't be there to complain of the expense. . . .

Don't think of that. She bent slowly to retrieve her boots and rinsed her feet in the pool before pulling them on again. The effort to achieve that without getting muddier than she already was took her mind off the Starlings, anyway. Afterward she rinsed her water bottle, filled it, corked it, and hung it by its twist of morning glory vine to her belt, then collected her little bundle of belongings and glanced at the sky. The patches she could see between tangled tree branches were charcoal gray with heavy clouds. The storm wouldn't wait much longer. It was late in the day anyway. She would find shelter for the night, and tackle the desert tomorrow when the storm had passed.

There was no shelter near the pool. She started off toward the desert again, looking for a wanderwood tree; their crowded roots sometimes formed cavelike areas where she might be at least partially out of the rain. Where would a cat go to get out of the rain?

"Not my problem. Besides, he was only a kitten. He'll find his mother, and she'll shelter him." She frowned at the sky, trying not to think what it would be like to have someone to whom one could go for love and shelter. The clouds were lowering, trailing their gray skirts across the crowns of the trees overhead. The muted amber light was rapidly dimming to a blue-gray gloom through which it was difficult to see far ahead, but she thought she saw the broad trunk of a wanderwood a little to the right of her path. She turned toward it.

A flicker of motion in the nearer trees caught her attention briefly, but when she stared, there was nothing there. The first misty drops of rain filtered down through the leaves to dampen her face. She hurried toward the wanderwood, hoping for a good root system. Nothing was moving in the forest but her. Even the birds were still. Something was watching her.

She whirled to stare at a clump of tall grass half-obscured by the gathering darkness. Surely that had been a flash of white, a movement, the whisper of some creature paralleling her path?

Nothing moved. Puzzled, she hurried on again. Probably only a horned rabbit or a squirrel frightened out of hiding by the sound of her passing. The rain was heavier now. She lifted a hand to shield her face and exhaled sharply in relief: the wanderwood was just before her, and it was an old one with gnarled roots tangled up into mounds and twisted hillocks, shingled with fallen leaves and branches. One of them would surely provide her shelter from the storm.

10

The hunters returned to Godsgrace late on the fifth day after their departure, hot and dirty and tired and empty-handed. Of the seven who had set out after the Starlings' fosterling, only one returned without injury, and he was ill with fever contracted after falling into the river. Two of the others had sprained ankles. One of these also had a black eye where a branch, slipping from someone else's grasp, had slapped him in the face. One had a sprained wrist and one had a whole collection of bruises, scrapes, and scratches; those two experienced forest trackers had fallen down the side of a ravine. The last two had a broken finger and a badly bruised shoulder, respectively, from similar mishaps during their trek.

"And after the first day," one of them said, "we never saw sure sign of her again."

Another one, younger and more bitterly resentful of their failure, said fiercely, "She's a witch." He looked earnestly at the Starlings, in whose gleaming yellow kitchen the seven battered and bloody men were making their report. "You're better off, honest to Joe you are."

"Language," their leader said almost absently. "Mard's overexcited," he told the Starlings apologetically. "He and young Porter here have never been on a track before; they didn't know what it would be like. They blamed our troubles on the girl."

Porter, standing on one foot beside Mard, with an improvised cane to help him keep his weight off his sprained ankle, straightened as best he could and glared, boylike, through a shock of dark unruly hair at the group's leader. "Sir." His voice cracked. Blushing, he cleared his throat. "Mr. Jonson, sir. I know you don't want to believe us, but look at it. Mard and me're the only new ones you took. The rest of you've been on a lotta tracks, and when did you ever come back *all* injured or sick before? It's gotta be a spell of some kind. 'Beware the witch of the full moon,' that's what the scriptures say—"

"Doesn't mean witches," Jonson said patiently. "Full moon doesn't have anything to do with the foster Starling, and the scriptures don't mean witches anyway. Means don't get silly. Full moon makes a lot of men silly. 'Specially young 'uns." He glanced at Megan, who looked anxious to speak. "Girls, too." He shook his head paternally. "Don't mean women witches like in the old tales. Means moonlight can witch ya. That's all."

Megan couldn't contain herself any longer. "If she isn't a witch, she's a monster. It's not just you she's put her filthy spells on. Look at us! Ma's bread won't rise more'n half the time anymore. Pa's computer's down more'n it's up since she left. The farm's goin' bad, an' Joel smashed his thumb with a hammer just yesterday trying to mend a fence. And—" Her voice rose in a nasal whine. "And I was gonna be a great crystal artist, and now it all shatters, I can't even make a simple bowl, I can't do anything right, *just like her*!" Her eyes flashed with hatred and tears of rage. "She put a spell on us, maybe on all of Godsgrace, you don't know, if she isn't a witch she's some kind of alien monster, or else why is all this happening? She's *ruined* us!"

Mrs. Starling moved to put an arm around her daughter. "Honey—"

Megan squirmed out of her hold, glaring. "You don't care. You don't *care*! I can't cut crystal anymore and all you care about is if the new girl scrubs the floor right, you don't care about me, you don't *care*!"

"Meggie, I do care." She tried to put her arm around Megan again, but Megan whirled away to face the hunters, who were looking on in various stages of embarrassment and sympathy.

Eyes flashing, hair streaming, graceful hands raised in a gesture that might have been defense or entreaty, Megan looked perhaps not unlike a witch herself, but a very beautiful witch. "You're all experienced trackers," she said. "And you went out after a *girl*, and look how you came home!"

A few of the hunters shifted uneasily. At least two stared awestruck at Megan, captivated by her beauty and excitement. Porter and Mard looked at each other, then back at Megan. Porter decided he was in love. Mard was made of sterner stuff—or was more frightened of the fosterling they had tried to track. He tore his gaze from Megan and said defiantly, "What about that heathen shrine we found? Everything was okay till we got there. What if she left some kind of spell there? That thing had some kind of magic." He glanced around at the other hunters. "You all saw how it glowed." He sounded defensive. "And we couldn't break it."

Jonson shook his head impatiently. "The thing didn't glow. That was a trick of the light. And you can't break good quality white crystal with your bare hands, everybody knows that. Not unless it's flawed, or carved to a flaw."

Porter, distracted at last from Megan, made an incautious gesture with his arms, forgetting his cane, and nearly fell. "But—" He regained his balance and gestured widely again, this time with only one arm. "It *was* carved to a flaw! It *had* to be!" He looked imploringly at the Starlings. "It was delicate. You can't carve white crystal so fine, not without it'll shatter, I swear you can't. It was practically whittled to nothing, honest to Joe it was, and we still couldn't break it!"

"Language," Jonson said sharply.

Porter had the good grace to look embarrassed. "Sorry, ladies." He hesitated, then added in a sullen undertone, "But it was."

Jonson nodded reluctantly. "It was a beautiful piece, very finely carved." He frowned at Porter and Mard. "But *not* to a flaw."

"You say that because we couldn't break it," said Mard.

"I say it because it's true, young man. Don't you two be getting too big for your headbands just because you've been on one hunt. And a failed one, at that. You know better than to be arguing with your leader and taking Joe's name in vain—"

Another hunter, previously silent, cleared his throat. "Point is we didn't catch the girl," he said softly. His face was old, weatherbeaten, and deeply lined, though his hair was still dark and his body hardened by years of farmwork and hunts. He was the one with the sprained wrist, and he cradled it gently in the other hand while he spoke. His eyes were dark and patient, like a dog's. "We tracked her as far as that heathen image they're talkin' about," he told the Starlings, "and that on the first day. The rest of the time we been out, we couldn't find hide nor hair of her, and that's a fact."

Mard tried to say something, but the older man just spoke louder to drown him out. "Now, we ain't gonna find her here, and we ain't gonna figure out why we spent the rest of our time out there blundering around like a bunch of pupscouts. We might just as well go home. If this all has to be talked out, we can do that better after we've had a good rest and a cleanup and some hot food to eat."

Nobody spoke for a moment. Mard and Megan were staring at the man with the sprained wrist. Porter was watching Megan again. The Starling boys, like the rest of the hunters, stared at the floor or walls or ceiling, anywhere but at each other, their expressions thoughtful or worried according to their characters. Mr. and Mrs. Starling looked at Mr. Jonson, their expressions openly dismayed. After a long moment Jonson said reluctantly, "Jamad's right. We might as well go on home. I'm sorry, folks, but you're just going to have to tell those government people that ungrateful fosterling plumb run away and can't be found."

11

Sunlight filtered down through the trees to splash like a patchwork of molten gold on the forest floor. Between the trees, morning mist rose in a blue haze that veiled distances and lent a fairytale beauty to the scene. Birds sang in the branches and flitted like bright shadows across open spaces. Butterflies danced like glittering scraps of confetti on the still air. Moisture from last night's rain still dripped from the leaves overhead. Wildflowers seemed to have sprung up everywhere, their fragile blossoms glistening with raindrops, their pale new leaves as lucent green as precious gems. Ugly Starling, curled in her nest under the wanderwood roots, opened her eyes to stare for a long, uncomprehending moment at a hot little patch of gold on the damp leaves near her nose.

The root cave had not been as snug as it might have been; her clothing was damp and she could feel a pool of water under her hips. Still she didn't move; in spite of the water, she was warm and comfortable, still half-asleep, mesmerized by the bright coin of sunlight on the leaves by her face. As she stared at it, she became aware of a weight on her ankles, not very great and not uncomfortable, but mildly puzzling to her in her sleep-drugged state. She considered it for several moments before she became curious enough to lift her head to look.

It was the kitten. They stared at each other, Ugly surprised and the kitten suspicious, for several seconds before the kitten realized Ugly was awake. Then he was off her ankles and out of the cave in one swift motion, a flash of white in the sunlight and then gone.

"Wait!" Ugly tried to sit up, and banged her head on a root overhead. "Kitten! Cat, wait!" But he was gone. Her ankles, relieved of his furry presence, felt cold. The cave seemed suddenly small, and she was sitting in a pool of cold, muddy water. She crawled out into the sunshine and looked dazedly around, but there was no sign of the kitten. For a moment sadness constricted her throat, but somewhere overhead a lark burst into glorious song and she smiled at herself, half-ashamed of her moment of self-pity. She was no more alone than she had expected to be. It was a glorious morning. And she had a plan; something purposeful to do.

Gathering her belongings, she returned to the forest pool where she had met the cat, stripped off her clothing, and found a grassy bank from which she could wash both her clothes and herself without getting muddier than she already was. The sun was hot on her back as she knelt naked by the water, rinsing her tattered jumpsuit. When she spread it on a bush to begin drying in the warm morning air, a dragonfly hovered over it and a broad-winged yellow and blue butterfly flitted awkwardly to a landing on one sleeve.

Her hair was tangled and matted. It took three sudsings with soapweed to get out the worst of the dirt, and even then it didn't feel quite clean, but she was tired by then of leaning precariously over the pool with her hair in the water, so after the third rinse she stopped. Combing her hair with her fingers was difficult and not terribly effective, but she managed to get the major tangles out of it. Most of the pins that had held it were gone. Those remaining were too few to hold its weight, so she put them in her bundle and left her hair to stream golden brown around her shoulders and down her back. Megan would ridicule her if she could see it, but Megan wasn't there. Ugly was quite well aware that she must look uglier than ever with her too-straight, too-pale hair loose, and her big-boned, awkward body pale and naked in the sun, but she liked the feel of the breeze on her skin and the softness of her hair flowing around her as she moved. It was another blessing of solitude; it no longer mattered how ugly she was.

She sat in the grass among butterflies and wildflowers and breakfasted on tart early blueberries, sugary redberries, juicy spring apples, and smoky tea steeped in cold water in her stained plastic cup. Afterward, feeling clean and contented, she gathered her belongings and reluctantly put on her damp jumpsuit; in the desert she would need its protection from the sun.

Again, as she had last night, she felt an odd sense of being watched, but there was no one in sight and the forest around her seemed serene and in every way normal. She told herself she was being silly; who could be watching her? The feeling persisted. She thought briefly, hopefully, of the kitten, but there was no reason to think he would stay near her. Even though he had sheltered with her from the storm last night, by now he must have gone off into the forest to find his mother. Ugly had just been in the forest too long; the closed spaces were beginning to play on her imagination. The desert, although it was a daunting prospect in some ways—hot and dry and very wide, it might turn out to be more difficult to cross than she expected —would at least be open. One could see for kilometers in every direction across that glaring white wasteland.

It did occur to her as she approached the desert again, this time very aware of the abrupt dwindling of the forest around her, that it might be wiser to undertake the journey in the cooler hours of darkness. But the mountains looked only a day's walk away, and if she found she couldn't handle even one full day in the glaring desert sun, she would surely be able to find some shelter until evening. The thought of waiting all day at the edge of the forest and then setting out across unfamiliar territory in the dark was unappealing in the extreme. She stepped resolutely out from among the last scrubby bushes onto the bare, glittering sand, and resisted the impulse to glance back at the cool, shadowed forest. She was determined to reach the mountains, if only because they provided a temporary goal in a life now otherwise directionless.

The desert sand was deep in places, and difficult to walk in. Her jumpsuit dried completely in the first twenty minutes, and half an hour later was wet again, this time with sweat. She realized straightaway that she would have to ration her water; she probably had ample for the journey if she used it sensibly, but the impulse to gulp at it every few minutes in an effort to alleviate the heat was strong. She hadn't realized the sun would be so hot. Godsgrace, sheltered by forested bluffs and cooled by winds that swept through vast, shady forest and across the snow-fed expanse of the river before it reached the settlement, was always slow to warm in the summer, and never got as hot as this.

When she had been walking steadily for an hour or so and still had not got over the feeling of being watched, she turned suddenly to look back at the forest. It was farther away than she had expected, and looked cool and inviting from where she stood. The green line of trees shimmered as if she were viewing it through water. If there were anyone back there watching her, she wouldn't be able to see him from so far away.

A movement to her right caught her attention. She looked that way, and saw only sand, with an occasional small rock or scrubby desert weed to relieve the flat emptiness. Far in the distance, the land seemed to rise a little, and the green of forest or fields outlined the perimeter of the desert. The movement had been much nearer than that, but nothing moved now. Shrugging, she turned to go on, and saw out of the corner of her eye the unexpected shifting of a rock or a patch of shadow.

She hesitated, staring. It was a shadow, not a rock. A shadow, and no form to cast it. Just the smallest of shadows, oval, with a triangular projection at one end almost like an ear. Sunlight glistened on sand. Ugly glanced at the sky, expecting a bird or a tiny motionless cloud, but the deep blue expanse stretched from horizon to horizon empty of anything but sun. She looked at the shadow again. If it were cast by a rock, she should be able to see the rock against the sand just there. . . .

And there, just where the rock should have been, a pair of pale lavender eyes regarded her mildly, seemingly out of the sand itself. After the first shock, she realized that the sand there didn't glitter as it did elsewhere. An exactly cat-shaped patch of it didn't glitter at all. "You!" She stared at him with conflicting dismay and delight. She had wanted to see him again, but how could he survive the desert? "You shouldn't have come out here, cat. Didn't you find your mother? You should stay with her, in the forest."

The lavender eyes blinked once, slowly.

"Go back," said Ugly. She made sweeping gestures with her arms as if to brush him away. "Go to your mother. Go on. This isn't any place for a cat." Her eyes were adjusting to the sight of him, white and soft against the sparkling sand. His tail twitched. It was his only response to her gestures.

She didn't really want him to go back. She was afraid for him, but she also wanted his company. Lifting her gaze from him to the sun-sparked sand behind him, she wondered whether it was already too late for him to make his way back alone. "I won't go back with you." Turning her head, she looked at the kilometers still to go between her and the mountains. "It's not my job to take care of foolish kittens." But it *was* her job if he followed her. "Please go back."

He didn't go back. Even when she, despairing, decided she must lead him back to safety, he refused to follow. He was completely lost to sight when she gave up and turned toward the mountains again. She retraced her steps and found him waiting where she had left him. Yet when she started on from there, he promptly rose to follow her toward the mountains.

The next time she drank from her water bottle, she found a flat rock with a shallow bowl-shaped depression in it and poured water for him. He wouldn't come near her to drink it, but when she backed away from it, he moved eagerly forward to stand over the bowl with his eyes half-closed, his pink tongue carefully lapping up the water before it could evaporate in the sun.

When she stopped for lunch, the cat stopped too, still at a careful distance from her, and watched her with hungry eyes. Even if he would have come near enough for her to offer to share her food, he wouldn't have wanted it; she had only the same kinds of fruit she had eaten for breakfast, plus some nuts and herbs she had been saving; none of it anything a cat would eat. She gave him water again in the rock bowl that she had brought along from the first time, and he accepted it, but still only at a cautious distance.

She found herself talking to him as if he could understand, telling him why she was there and where she was going, her voice the only sound in the wide white silence. He listened with every appearance of interest, round lavender eyes solemn, tail twitching sometimes when emotion roughened her voice. They were alone together in a shimmering wasteland, the only living creatures in a landscape that stretched flat and barren from the horizon behind them to the mountains far ahead.

When she started walking again after lunch, he stayed nearer her than before, still keeping well out of reach, but now always in sight. Afraid he would leave her if she stopped talking, she chatted aimlessly well into the hot afternoon, till her mouth and throat were too dry to continue without water. By then she had begun to realize how badly she had underestimated the size of the desert. More than half her supply of water was gone, and the desert still stretched endlessly before them. The mountains still loomed, a green and peaceful wall across the world, seemingly no nearer than they had been that morning. Ugly knew that had to be an optical illusion. She knew, too, from maps she had seen in past, that they couldn't be farther than one more day's travel. That was still one day more

than she had planned. It might be one day more than
the cat could manage. She had reduced her own ration
of water as the day wore on, but she dared not reduce
his by much. She might not be giving him enough, as it
was. He drank every drop he was offered, and still
between times his pink tongue lolled dry from his
open mouth and he watched her mournfully, so eager
for water that twice now, when she put down the rock
bowl for him, he had come almost within reach while
she filled it.

When the sun finally slid behind the Mysterious
Mountains on its way down into the western sea
beyond Far Harbor, Ugly made a nest for herself in
the sand beside a tumble of broken gray boulders and
settled for sleep. The cat watched her a moment, then
turned suddenly and bounded off into the sand and
soon out of sight.

Startled and anxious, Ugly sat up and hugged her
knees, watching the last place she had seen him. Had
he left her at last? Where could he go? Should she have
given him yet more water? There wasn't enough; she
had to save some for tomorrow. But he didn't drink
much at a time, and it would have been worth at least
half of tomorrow's ration to her if he had stayed.

The desert, which had been only wide and bleak
and silent, was suddenly an eternity of emptiness. She
felt fragile inside, as if her bones were hollow. Once
she opened her mouth to call to him, but the sound
caught in her throat. She didn't know a name for him.
And she couldn't bear to hear her small voice swallowed by the vast, indifferent emptiness of the desert.
Her throat ached with unshed tears. Her face and the
skin of her arms felt hot and tight with sunburn and
the sudden weakness of being unexpectedly alone. She
closed her eyes hard against the deepening shadows
and thought of nothing.

He was gone nearly an hour. When he returned,
there was blood on his face, and dark stains on his
paws, which he began to wash away as soon as he saw
her; somewhere in that sere landscape he had found

game, though of what sort Ugly couldn't imagine. It didn't seem possible that anything actually lived on the burning sand.

She hadn't cried when she thought he had left her, but hot tears spilled down her cheeks when she saw him return. She wiped them away with the back of one hand and blinked to clear her vision, to be sure she really saw him in the gathering dark. "I was afraid you weren't coming back." It didn't matter, now, that her voice sounded small and flat in the wide silence. His tail flicked once and was still. She stared at him for a long time before she finally lay down again to sleep. When she did, he moved nearer her—nearer than he had ever willingly come before—and sat down, facing away from her, seemingly indifferent to her existence. But he kept one ear cocked in her direction till she finally closed her burning eyes and fell asleep.

12

On the way back to the reservation, the King's Messengers had done what they could to clean up the Prince and get him fit for an audience with the King, but he was still a mess when they entered the reservation palace. They walked the long echoing halls and climbed the wide curving staircases together, a Messenger on either side of Hawke, quick to steady him when his steps faltered. None of them spoke. The Messengers, their faces expressionless, looked straight ahead, down the torchlit corridors or up the worn stairs before them, their eyes flat and blank and empty. Hawke glanced at them occasionally, but mostly his gaze wandered vacantly over the corridors through which they passed, his face as expressive as a child's; he smiled in idiot pleasure at bright lights and friendly people, looked anxious when confronted with the stern faces of the palace guards, and stared in round-eyed wonder at a passing priest in his glittering vestments.

At the doors to the King's audience chamber, the unlikely trio paused for a moment. Hawke seemed fascinated with the golden daggers crossed over a crystal flame on the wide double doors, symbol of the High King's power. The two Messengers looked him over again and brushed ineffectually at spots of dust and blood on his battered beggar's robes, but it was a hopeless gesture. His hair hung in red-gold strings across his bruised and bloodied face; his homespun sleeves, once white, were red and gray with blood and dirt, and torn at shoulders and elbows; his heavy, knee-length tunic was slashed in several places and irrevocably stained; even his knee-high soft leather boots were splotched and torn and would have looked more at home in a rag bag than on his feet.

The palace guards opened the double doors and Hawke and his escort were ushered through into the presence of the High King. The room was brightly lighted with hundreds of candles. The walls were hung with thickly woven tapestries patterned with scenes of life as it had been for the People when the government was seated in Town and there were no Terrans on Paradise. The King and his chief advisor Mahlo were seated companionably at the far end of the room, under a blazing light fixture whose candles dripped icicles of wax down the wall behind them.

They looked up as Hawke and his companions entered the room. Mahlo was a mild, middle-aged man with weak eyes and a ready smile, which he started to display at sight of Hawke, and quickly curtailed when he saw the condition the Prince was in. He seemed to withdraw from the Prince without making any more physical movement than a fastidious twitching of his robes and a glance at Arkos the High King.

The King was past middle age, but looked younger than Mahlo. His eyes were sharp, and he seldom smiled. The hard granite planes of his face looked as though he might never have smiled. He was a fierce man, as tough and relentless as a king must be, as capable of compassion as a king can be, and as vulnerable as any father is. The vulnerability seldom showed. He was High King first; he had to be; and the High King produces offspring only in order to provide the kingdom with an heir to the throne.

Hawke didn't look, just now, like a very promising heir to the High King's throne. Arkos looked past him at the kneeling Messengers, his gaze both fierce and weary. "Another Terran bar?" he asked.

Before the Messengers could respond, Hawke exclaimed drunkenly and wandered unsteadily away from them to begin a stern lecture in the Terran tongue, badly slurred, to a marble sculpture set on a pedestal near the door. The Messengers, startled, glanced at him and looked back at the King, their expressions identically wary. "Yes, my lord King," said one.

The High King watched Hawke, unblinking, his expression unreadable. "Take him to the healers," he said. "Bring him back when he is fit for audience. Quickly. Take him away." He made a dismissive gesture with one hand and turned back to Mahlo without hesitation or apology. "You were saying, Mahlo?"

Mahlo's bright, foolish eyes watched the Messengers lead Hawke from the room. "Yes, my lord King. I was just listing our last hopes for giftmate for your son and heir, my lord King. As you know, we have sent out for all possible children, even those who may be Terran, having exhausted all more realistic avenues of search—"

"Yes, yes," said Arkos. "More ambrosia?" He poured it. "There are no known People who could bear the gift. The old records were searched, and any children who were found in the earthquake rubble on Freehold are being sought. All who were not identified were brought to foster homes on Paradise soon after the earthquake. I know all that, and that the foster families, even the Terrans, have been contacted. But as far as I know, the fosterlings have all turned out to be Terran."

"There are four who may not be Terran, and one who is certainly not."

The High King's gaze sharpened. "Five in all? What do you know about them?"

"I know the foster mother of one. I have met him, though now he cannot be found. I know he is of the People. His mother never reported him because—"

"And the other four?"

"Three are runaways. They are being tracked: Davis, Kabar, and Starling. The Davis and Kabar children both had unhealthy childhoods, but the Starling one is reported to have been quite healthy. She is probably Terran. I doubt—"

"You said four."

Mahlo shrugged, his amiable smile lending a cheerful innocence to his countenance. "There is one whose family has as yet made no report. That's four who may not be Terran. The one in Town, whose foster mother I know, is certainly not Terran. Petal is the boy's name. My lord King, he is a very good possibility, I promise you. His mother didn't report him because she is estranged from the People, but—"

"I had hoped Hawke's giftmate would also be his lifemate." The King frowned into his ambrosia. "It does simplify things." His own giftmate had also been his lifemate and his Queen. Their gift had been negligible: languages, the weakest of the royal or noble gifts. But their life together had been a time of such joy. . . .

"My lord King, if his giftmate can be found at all," said Mahlo.

"Yes, yes." Arkos swirled the golden ambrosia in his crystal goblet and watched the way it caught the light. Queen Lian's hair had been just that color, strawberry gold with highlights pale as the sun. He sighed and looked away from the glass. "Tell me more about this Petal."

"Nobility, my lord King, I'm sure of it," said Mahlo, not quite eagerly. "Blue eyes, small stature—I'm surprised he wasn't mistaken for Terran when they found him, but of course he was in the rubble of the King's palace, and dressed in garments of the People. He was fostered to Lady Sara, you've heard of her?"

Arkos concealed his distaste, but only just. Mahlo had known him long and well enough to guess at it, anyway. "A drunk," he said, and then smiled faintly, ruefully. "Like my son."

"My lord King, Prince Hawke isn't a drunk. He's only . . ."

The High King glanced at him quizzically. "What, Mahlo? He's only what?"

Mahlo squirmed uneasily. "My lord—"

"My son is not mad," Arkos said firmly, but without real conviction. "He is not mad. And . . . his giftmate will be found."

Mahlo seized on that. "Of course, my lord King. That's what I was just saying. Lady Sara is a drunk, and she lives among Terrans because of it, but my lord King, she is of the People. She has not forgotten our ways. And she believes her son Petal to be my lord Hawke's giftmate."

Arkos was staring into his ambrosia again, and said almost indolently, "Why?"

Mahlo hesitated. "I—because he is clearly noble, my lord King. And because he was ill." The question, put so innocently and so abruptly, had caught him off guard. "In childhood, my lord King. . . . Petal is grown now, of course, but in childhood—at puberty or perhaps just past—he suffered a terrible illness. The healers could not identify his gift. My lord—"

"Perhaps he has none. Perhaps he is Terran, after all. It is possible."

"No, my lord King. Oh, I'm sure not."

"We will see," said the High King. "But continue the search for the other four. Even that Starling one. I want them all investigated."

"Yes, my lord King." Mahlo rose, aware he had been dismissed, and put down his ambrosia to bow his way out of the audience chamber. If he was displeased with the outcome of the interview, he was much too well controlled to let it show.

The High King Arkos did not even watch him go. He was thinking of Lian again, remembering the fey beauty of her smile, how she used to laugh and dance away from him and end always, inevitably, in his arms. . . .

He shook his head, and the vision faded, and he was alone again with a thousand candles and the memory of a dream. No sense asking himself what Lian would have thought of their bright-haired boy-child now. She was not here now.

For just a moment, in the flickering brilliance of the candlelight, he thought he saw the ghost of her smile, and he sighed again for the sorrow of it, that she who had been the golden center of his sunlit universe could not have lived to light her son's path, too.

13

When Ugly woke in the morning, the kitten was bonelessly draped across her ankles again. This time when he saw that she was awake he didn't flee; he merely rose and moved with regal dignity to what he must have considered a safe distance, then sat and began to wash his face.

The sun, barely over the eastern horizon, was already oppressively hot. It lighted the vertical ridges of the Mysterious Mountains in the west, and cast deep shadows between them so that more than ever they looked like an unevenly columned wall of cool emerald against the hard blue morning sky. Ugly could not tell how far away the mountains were now, but they loomed so high above the desert that she thought they must be very near, perhaps only a few hours' walk, certainly not more than another day. She didn't have enough water for another full day.

The kitten watched her pour out a meager ration for him in the rock bowl, and lapped it up as fastidiously as he had done the day before. Then, while Ugly breakfasted on fruits and nuts from her improvised pack, he started across the sand away from her. Remembering her needless fear of the night before, she told herself he was going hunting, but that didn't keep her from staring anxiously after him, long after he was out of sight.

When she packed up her belongings again to move on, he had not yet returned. She hesitated over his water bowl, then packed it. He would come back. She lingered, needlessly repacking her belongings twice. The sun climbed relentlessly in the sky. She eyed the water bottle, far more than half-empty now, and knew she could not afford to wait any longer. Still she waited fifteen more minutes before she started reluctantly across the sand toward the mountains.

Before she had gone far, he was there beside her, just out of reach, pacing with an easy stride like a big cat, lavender eyes watching her. "I thought you'd left me," she said. His tail twitched. "I'm glad you didn't. I'd miss you."

He seemed refreshed, probably from having again found some sort of game. Under the hot desert sun, that didn't last. When they rested at midday he was clearly flagging, and threw himself down on the sand with a heavy sigh. Ugly poured water for both of them and made tea for herself. The cat drank thirstily, then dug briefly in the sand to uncover a cooler layer on which to lie.

Ugly was hot and thirsty and sunburned, and the fruits she had saved for lunch did little to assuage her thirst. She sipped her tea as sparingly as she could, and dreamed of the wide river by Godsgrace. There wasn't even the smallest breeze to cool the sweat that soaked her jumpsuit. At least she *could* sweat. She looked sympathetically at the panting cat with his heavy fur coat. He blinked at her.

"Lucky you're white," she said. "You'd be worse off if your coat were dark." But he hadn't had enough water, and this was proving to be a very long trek for a cat. Ugly had read about cats once, when she was trying to talk the Starlings into letting her have one for a pet. Cats hadn't much stamina: their strength was meant to be used in short, powerful bursts of activity, not on endless, arduous marches like this one. She stared across the white sand at the still-distant mountains, and decided to cut her own water ration still further, to leave more for him.

By midafternoon it was clear that even that wasn't enough: he was miserable. He had begun crying piteously as they walked, and occasionally threw himself down in any small patch of shade he could find. He would watch her walk on, till she was nearly out of sight, then rise and lope after her, only to repeat the process when he caught up. She gave him water as often as she dared, and no longer had to back away from it; he drank as soon as she had finished pouring.

Nowhere could she find a patch of shade large enough to shelter them until nightfall. The desert stretched flat and empty all the way to the mountains, with only small rocks and a few weedy shrubs, nothing to provide water or shelter. The kitten was losing his fear of her, or was too uncomfortable to care; he walked next to her when he wasn't lying down or chasing after her, and sometimes he bumped against her legs and mewed for water.

She had been talking to him as they went, but with her own water ration so limited, her mouth dried, her lips cracked, speaking became far too much effort. She was dizzy and increasingly weak, with a headache that nearly blinded her and a constant high, piercing tone in her ears. It was all she could do to keep plodding on and on toward the heat-blurred mountains before them.

More than once she fell, and had to rest a moment and sip more precious water before climbing awkwardly to her feet again and stumbling on. The vision of the mountains, cool like emeralds, shrouded in misty rainbows, shaded by clouds, had become dreamlike and improbable: she no longer even knew whether they were near or far. She only knew that she and the cat must keep walking toward them, or die.

14

Healers tended Hawke's cuts and bruises and gave him a herbal decoction to counteract the effects of alcohol. A giftmated pair of them hovered over him with a crystal to focus their powers, reached delicate mental probes deep into the damaged cells of his body where the wounds were most severe, and gently pushed the natural healing processes, speeding and guiding them, cleaning away incipient infections and encouraging new, healthy cells to growth. When they were satisfied, servants bathed him and dressed him in new garments scented with princely perfumes. New boots were provided, soft and supple and freshly brushed. His hair was washed and dried and brushed till static electricity made it stand out from his head in a red-gold halo, framing the lean shadowed planes of his face with a soft, ambiguous light. His pale lavender eyes belied the angelic halo: they were savage, dangerous, wild. He accepted the ministrations of servants and healers with docile indifference, but the pale eyes looked out from under hooded lids with the wary ferocity of a caged beast.

When he was clean and patched and presentable, the Messengers took him back to the audience chamber and deposited him in the care of the palace guardsmen at the door. He sat, apparently relaxed, on one of the hard wooden benches provided, and stared at the wavering shadows cast by torches on the opposite wall.

His wounds hurt him. He felt stiff, encrusted with bandages and salves. The only visible injury now was a discolored swelling under his left eye, but there were bruises and cuts and abrasions in plenty, concealed by his clothes. A bad knife slash on his left upper arm, only partially healed, made him hold that arm stiffly away from his body, the scarred hand resting palm-upward in his lap. A deep puncture wound just under his ribs, although it had been almost completely healed to prevent infection, still ached dully, and painfully resisted his efforts to relax.

There were a good dozen more knife wounds, all minor enough that the healers had used conventional medicine rather than waste healing energy, plus any number of bruises and scrapes to which they had paid very little attention at all. He felt as though he had been run over by a whole fleet of groundcars, and he resolved once again—as he had done countless times in past—not to drink Terran alcohol ever again. It was a death wish that drove him to it, and in his rational moments he was ashamed of that. But the impulse that sent him into Terran bars was not conscious enough to be forestalled by shame. He never knew he meant to drink until afterward; never knew he would go to a bar till he was in one; never knew he would pick a fight till he had done: so the pattern was repeated, and all the resolve in the world wouldn't help.

What might help would be for his father to just face facts and stop always harping about Hawke's giftmate. Hawke had no giftmate. It was a grim joke of the gods that had provided the People with a Maker on which to fix their hopes, and no Breaker to make him whole.

His mind skittered nervously away from that thought: he wanted to believe in a Breaker; wanted it so badly that the mere unwary thought was like a physical pain, a knife viciously twisted in his mind, scrambling his brain. He dared not hope. A person could die of hope. He was adjusted well enough to the lack of a giftmate. He had survived Onset. Now most of the time his need, if left alone, was like an abscessed tooth aching dully at the edge of consciousness, which would react with agonizing pain if he touched it with even the gentlest edge of a questing tongue of hope.

If his father would leave him alone, he would never touch that need again. He shifted uneasily on the hard bench, feeling the anger rise like a cleansing flame, cauterizing need. It was stupid and cruel of his father to keep trying to get Hawke to join the hunting parties. Arkos wanted Hawke, if not in the field searching with the front lines, then at least in offices searching by telephone and computer. Couldn't he see that the search was a form of slow torture for Hawke? Didn't he know what it was like to dare to hope, and to see his hopes crushed time and again? Couldn't he guess what a fierce and delicate adjustment Hawke had made to life without hope?

Or did Arkos simply not care? He wouldn't listen when Hawke tried to explain. Yet Arkos had had a giftmate once. Hawke didn't remember his mother Queen Lian, but he knew that when she died Arkos must have known the wrenching despair and emptiness that Hawke endured now. Had he made some mad adjustment, as Hawke was trying to do, and denied the pain so completely that he dared not believe in it, even when he saw the same pain in his own son, lest he himself suffer it again?

If that was it, the King was an even more despicable coward than Hawke. In any case, he was vicious, heartless. Rage glowed dully in Hawke's eyes as he thought of it. He had expressed his pain, and his father had told him it did not matter. The same response he had given to nearly every hurt in Hawke's growing-up years: a Prince did not feel pain. A Prince must carry on. He could not live for himself, but only for his People. It was true of all the little things, but to this one thing it could not apply. Without a giftmate, Hawke was not really Prince. He was not whole. He was hardly even human. He was just half a thing, like a broken goblet, drained of everything that mattered, useless, all but dead.

Maybe that was it: maybe Arkos hoped Hawke would die. Maybe he couldn't countenance the existence of the empty husk his son had become at Onset.

Maybe he feared to see his People ruled by a man without purpose or dreams, and he forced the search on Hawke in an effort to kill him wholly, to sweep him aside, to make room for some less brutally gifted successor from among distant relatives. . . .

Hawke scowled at the far wall so fiercely that the torches sputtered and died. The palace guardsmen at the door glanced at him and then at each other, their faces startled and pale; they could relight the torches easily enough, but what else might the mad Prince extinguish in his rage? Hawke didn't notice; the door to the audience chamber opened and Bush, the King's workmate and personal servant, came out. "My lord Prince," he said, bowing, "my lord the High King commands your presence now."

Hawke rose silently, his face impassive now, and moved stiffly toward the door. Bush held it for him and glanced past him at the dead torches. "Get those things lighted," he told the guards.

"Yes, lord," said a guard. Since their gift was fire they had only to glance at the torches, now that the Prince was gone, and *will* them to light, and they did. They could have brightened the corridor without torches, had there been need; the gift of fire was a very useful one.

Hawke stepped into the High King's presence, bowed deeply with one arm pressed hard against his aching side, and straightened without quite looking at the King.

"Are you angry, Hawke?" the King asked in evident surprise.

"Yes, my lord King." Hawke's voice, as rigidly controlled as his eyes, revealed nothing.

"With me?" asked Arkos.

"Yes, my lord King." Hawke had moved forward till he was before the King. There he stopped, waiting, his head bowed and his eyes hooded.

"Why?" asked the King. "What have I done?"

"You have tried to kill me, my lord King."

A flicker of pain showed in the King's eyes before he

sighed and gestured toward the chair next to his own.
"Be seated. Will you have ambrosia? Or tea?"

"Neither." Hawke sat, still without looking at his
father.

"Come, come, don't be foolish," said Arkos.
"Whatever you believe I have done, you won't change
it by drinking or not drinking, and you have been
recently healed. I well recall the thirst that leaves.
Tea?"

Hawke nodded sullenly. "Tea, then."

The High King nodded at Bush, who silently
poured tea for them both and backed away discreetly.
"Now, Hawke, what's all this about me trying to kill
you?" asked the King. "I've just been talking by phone
with some Terrans, and before that with Lord Mahlo,
when you first came in—I realize you may not remember that, but he was here—about you, Hawke,
and your giftmate. There are five more possibilities—"

"*Damn* you!"

At Hawke's explosion, Bush leapt forward, sword in
hand, but Hawke didn't move and the High King
waved his workmate away. "Leave us," he said softly.
"It will be all right; leave us. I command you."

Bush bowed deeply, sheathed his sword, and backed
away with a worried look at Hawke and a pleading
look at the High King, who perhaps didn't realize his
danger because he would not recognize that his son
was mad.

"Leave us!" Arkos glared until Bush was gone, then
turned to the Prince, his eyes as dangerous as Hawke's
ever were. "You forget to whom you speak," he said
coldly.

"I speak to my father," said Hawke, sullen like a
small boy caught at mischief.

"You speak to the High King," said Arkos. "You are
not so mad as all that. You know full well that however
much you may wish your father damned, you may not
speak it for fear of damning the High King—and
yourself. My son, what is it?"

"I am damned already."

Arkos sipped his tea. "And your People? Are they damned, as well?" When Hawke did not respond, he said gently, "My son, is it so much to ask that you should take an interest in the search for your own giftmate? It would please the People: it would give them hope."

"Do not speak to me of hope." Hawke's voice was flat with rage and despair.

"You forget yourself. Again."

"My lord King," Hawke said very carefully, "I forget nothing. It is you who forget—if you ever knew—" He broke off, sighed, picked up his tea and drank it down greedily, then stared into the empty cup. "For one minute, Father, forget you are King. Forget your duty to the People. Forget my duty to the People. Think only of me as a person. As one of those People. As your son." He looked up suddenly, his eyes pale and savage. "Can you do that? Can you?"

Arkos met his son's gaze soberly. "I can, yes. Briefly. What would you have me think of this person who is my son?"

"Think what you ask of him." Hawke's voice remained steady, expressionless. His lean face revealed nothing; it was a sculpture, ethereally beautiful, in marble; cold, serene, and damned. "I can't hope again, Father. I can't." Only the lavender eyes were alive, like hot coals in the cold stone of his face.

"Then don't," said Arkos, his own face a study in granite, his eyes as savage as Hawke's. "Even if I would command your thoughts, I could not. Only your actions. Think what you like—hope or don't hope—but *do* what you must: join the search." He forced a lighter tone, but his eyes belied it. "I'm not asking you to go out in the field, you know. Only show an interest. Help with the telephones, the computers—"

"Terran technology." Hawke made a sour face. "Isn't that why you want to find a Breaker for me? So that together we can confront the Terrans, and rid the People of them once and for all? It seems contradictory to use what you want rid of."

"Not really." Arkos didn't quite smile. "I forget sometimes how idealistic youth can be. But one does, you know, occasionally fight fire with fire."

"Then we will become the fire."

"An interesting use of the analogy, if a trifle romantic. But the real point is that it's not Terran technology we must escape; only Terran rule. We can live with their technology."

"Can we? As a people, can we?" For the first time since he had entered the room, Hawke looked like his old self, eager and involved and, above all, sane. "If we embrace Terran ways, won't we lose our own? Already we use Terran telephones instead of crystal whistlers, Terran computers instead of counters and storytalkers, Terran gods instead of our own. If our gods are forgotten and our gifts aren't used, won't they fade? Won't all gifts become like mine, something that crops up once in a century, so rare it can't even be mated? Won't we, if we lose that, lose who we are? Without our gifts, we might as well be Terran."

"I think we are more than our gifts," said Arkos, "but never mind. I think we can retain our gifts, even in the company of Terrans and their gods, if—" But the intelligence had gone from Hawke's face as suddenly as it had come. He wasn't listening anymore. His eyes were vacant, his jaw slack, his posture suddenly clumsy.

"Ah, Mahlo," he said, his voice high and clear like a child's. "I see you've brought your crystal harp. Do play us a song!"

"Hawke?" Arkos heard the tremor in his own voice and cleared his throat. "Hawke, stop it!"

Hawke's gaze strayed to the King's face. His eyes widened. He giggled drunkenly. "My lord King, you've been listening to dreams again. He will sing us the Death Song." He waved an arm randomly. "All this is only a game, you know that, don't you?" He frowned. "Or do you? Your advisors have their secrets."

Bush had come back into the room, and he approached them deferentially, bowing to the King. "My lord King—"

"But no one sings crystal like Lord Mahlo," said Hawke. Leaping suddenly to his feet, he danced around Bush, flapping his arms. "Tell the King! Tell the King!"

"What is it?" asked Arkos, trying to ignore his son.

Bush glanced sideways at Hawke, shifted nervously, and said, "My lord King—"

"He is a fool," Hawke said quietly to Bush. "Pay no attention to what he says; he schemes." He leaned toward Bush as if to whisper in his ear, but spoke aloud. "Ask Mahlo: what breaks can be broken. What makes can be made to break. And what rules can be ruled!"

"My lord King." Bush raised his voice, looking steadfastly at Arkos. "Lord Mahlo is here to see you, as you requested."

Arkos looked at his son for a long, puzzled moment before he said at last, in a flat voice, "Send him in."

Hawke laughed. It was a high-pitched, painful sound that interrupted the nursery rhyme he had begun to sing. The lyrics seemed to amuse him. He sat abruptly on the floor, crooning to himself and swaying dizzily, his pale eyes shadowed.

Arkos looked at Bush. "And send someone to—" He hesitated, closed his eyes, opened them, and said steadily, "To see to it that my son is fed and put to bed."

"Yes, my lord King." Bush bowed and backed away, his face absolutely expressionless, without a glance at the spectacle Prince Hawke was making of himself.

15

The sun had slid mercifully behind the Mysterious Mountains when Ugly and the kitten finally reached the edge of the desert, but the baked ground retained the day's heat and radiated it back up, so there was very little relief even with the sun hidden. Worse, the tantalizingly green line of trees that for the last two hours of their hike had seemed so promising a goal did not, as Ugly had hoped it would, conceal a stream. It was only a dry stream bed, as dead and dusty as the forbidding landscape over which they had traveled for the last two days. The leaves were green under a thick layer of dust, proving that their roots deep underground must be reaching water, but there was none on the surface, and clearly had not been for some time.

The mountains were steep and abrupt; no foothills, just sudden fluted ridges, mountain-high cliffs, and one deep misted valley out of which that dry creek curved with such empty promise. Through that valley, Ugly and the kitten might find a pass to the other side of the mountains, but only if they had water. The last of their supply was gone hours ago, and now both of them were exhausted and dehydrated to the point of collapse. Without water they would die right here.

The kitten threw himself down on the cooler sand under the trees, looked up mournfully at Ugly, then closed his eyes and rested his head on his paws. Ugly wanted to join him. She dropped her bundle and it was all she could do not to follow it to the ground. If she had been alone, she might have done just that, allowing herself the luxury of the merciful unconsciousness that would precede death. Here was just one more proof that she couldn't do anything right. Foolishly proud of herself for surviving in the forest, she had not been content with mere survival. Instead, she had imagined herself competent, and had risked her own life and the kitten's on a pointless desert crossing for which, predictably, she had not been properly prepared.

Now, wavering unsteadily over the fallen kitten, she could not quite remember why it had seemed so important to come this way. Darkness tugged at her mind and starred the edges of her vision. It would be such a relief to give in to it, to relax with the kitten on the dusty ground, to welcome the last long sleep.

Then there would be no one to care for the kitten. Sighing, Ugly turned wearily toward the mountains and stumbled away from him, heading upstream in the dry creek bed, hoping for some sign of water. The trees along the banks leaned inward, making a dusty tunnel in which the air was just a little cooler than that outside, where the sun had been beating on the soil all day. Wiping her forehead with the back of her hand, Ugly peered dizzily up the shadowy stream bed. It seemed to her that the trees thickened ahead, though there seemed still to be no underbrush or weeds as there would be in the presence of water. Still, more trees meant there might be water nearby. She trudged forward, leaning from time to time on boulders or against the steep creek banks for support.

The nature of the trees was changing, too. The same kind that had looked wizened and weedy where she had left the kitten were fuller here, and taller, the space under them more effectively sheltered from the heat. An occasional cluster of gnats hung silent in the still, dry air, barely disturbed by Ugly's passing. New trees appeared, some of them common varieties Ugly had known all her life, some strange to her, with thick branches and papery bark that smelled vaguely of cinnamon; or oddly flat, twisted branches with spongy bark that smelled of turpentine. In the growing gloom beneath their thickening canopy she thought she saw, not too far ahead, a sudden cluster of undergrowth in the middle of the stream bed, such as might grow around a pool of water left from the winter, when this baked-dry bed must have held a cool, rushing stream.

She had already increased her stumbling pace toward the possible water when she realized she had not brought the empty water bottle with her. If she found water, she would have no way to carry it back to the kitten. Minutes might matter: if he still lived when she returned, could he survive the long wait while she made this trip again with the bottle?

She didn't even know yet whether there would be water here. First things first. But as she moved toward the cluster of undergrowth she was filled with a deep, despairing remorse: *I can't do anything right.* To come after water for the kitten, and forget to bring anything to carry it in, was typical for her. She was as incompetent and as stupid as the Starlings had always said she was.

If there were water here—and as she neared the clump of weeds she was sure she could smell water, under the cloying foul odor of something rotting— maybe there would also be something here in which to carry it. Or, failing that, maybe the kitten would let Ugly carry him to the water.

In the deep gloom it was hard to see, but she thought the cluster of weeds and shrubs ahead, which she had hoped were growing around a pool, grew instead around one tall, straight tree in the center of the stream bed. That didn't make sense. It must be an optical illusion. Surely such a tall tree couldn't have grown up in the stream bed without being washed away by winter floods; and, if it had, why would bushes and weeds grow up around it as they would around a pool of water?

That was what it was, though: a tall tree, its trunk wrapped in heavy-fruited vine and surrounded by underbrush. No pool. Not even moisture under the shrubs. Just dry, sandy soil, heavily shaded, deep with fallen leaves and rank, rotted flowers from the fruited vine, but no moisture at all. Even the rotted flowers, though they smelled horribly of moist decay, proved on close examination to be desiccated and sere, all moisture sucked out of them by the dry desert air.

Ugly fell to her knees under the bushes and scrabbled hopelessly at the soil with her bare fingers, digging for the water that had to be there. It wasn't there. Whatever made it possible for those weeds and bushes to grow at the base of that improbably tall tree, it wasn't a surface pool of water.

Ugly sat back on her heels and stared at the tree in despair. The vines that grew in strangling profusion about its trunk didn't grow from the soil at the base like the other weeds, but seemed to spring from the trunk itself. Perhaps they were actually a part of the tree.

She watched dizzily as an insect blundered up against the tree trunk and away again, perhaps drawn by the foul reek of the fallen flowers. Suddenly, several flowers on the vine near where the insect had flown opened wide, and a new stink drifted in an almost tangible cloud out across the little cluster of greenery. In seconds the insect had blundered drunkenly back up from the fallen flowers, buzzed the fresher ones for a moment, and trustingly landed on the thick, waxy petals of one. It closed with an audible snap, the insect trapped within. The tree was carnivorous.

That explained the foul stink of the blossoms. And the moisture from the insects, added to what a deep taproot could draw from beneath the desert soil, might be enough to sustain even such a large tree through the long, dry summer. But what could sustain the underbrush around it? Surely whatever moisture there might be in the vine's heavy, grapefruit-sized fruit wouldn't be enough to encourage such growth even if the fruit fell steadily all summer.

Still, that might be part of the answer. There might be enough juice in those fruits—if they were edible at all—to sustain Ugly till she could find a source of water to bring back for the kitten. She climbed to her feet and had to rest for a moment, fighting a swirling darkness, before she could approach the tree and pull down one of the heavy, hard-skinned fruits.

It sloshed when she shook it, like a partially filled water bottle. Her heartbeat quickened. She told herself sternly that the liquid inside might be undrinkable, even poisonous, but that didn't slow her anxious efforts to pry off the skin.

It was so hard, she could barely dent it with her fingers. Increasingly frantic, she snatched up a sharp rock, placed the fruit carefully on the hard-baked ground, and struck it with the rock. The top caved in, and clear, cool liquid splashed out onto her hands and arms and the dusty ground. The sweet, sharp odor of it mixed with dust was unmistakable. She didn't hesitate, or taste it cautiously; she lifted the fruit to her lips and drank the juice down.

The liquid was water, pure and sweet and clean. If she had not spilled so much while getting the fruit open, she probably would have made herself sick from guzzling it without restraint. As it was, she had time between gulping what was left in that one and plucking and opening another to realize she should quench her thirst slowly. Instead of drinking the second one, she poured it over her head and shoulders and laughed with delight at the cool wetness of it against her parched and sunburned skin.

Without any further delay, she tore down half a dozen of the fruits from the tree, bringing with them enough vine to braid together and carry them by, and started back toward the place where she had left the kitten and her belongings. On the way back, she noticed her surroundings much more than she had on the way up the creek bed.

The sand here was darker than that in the desert, but it glittered in bright patches as if sprinkled with crystal dust. Many of the trees were of a kind wholly unfamiliar to her, not like anything that grew in Godsgrace or in the forest around it. The desert must form an effective barrier to plant migration that, coupled with differences in the soil and amount of rainfall, created a radically different ecosystem here even though the altitude and climate must otherwise be much the same as in Godsgrace.

That meant there would be fewer edible plants she would recognize—possibly fewer edible plants at all. The thought nearly sent her into another fit of anxious depression, till she realized that the ecosystem would inevitably have changed anyway, when she climbed higher into the mountains, and that if she no longer recognized plants from the lower elevations, she would surely be able to find new edible ones as she went along. What she couldn't identify from past reading, she could sample carefully, slowly building a new diet from whatever she found.

The kitten was waiting where Ugly had left him, head lolling sideways, eyes closed, fur alarmingly dull and lifeless. For a frightened moment she thought he was dead, till she saw his ribcage rise and fall in a weary sigh. Then she ran to him, knelt beside him, and got her broken knife from her bundle to open one of the waterfruits. "I found water for you, cat," she said. "I'm sorry it took so long, but I found it; just a minute and you'll have it."

He opened his eyes to study her without interest. Even his eyes looked glazed and lifeless. Just the very tip of his tail flicked once or twice as he watched her.

Opening the waterfruit was easier and neater with the knife. She cut two holes in one, got out the kitten's bowl, and carefully poured water into it. At the scent of it he purred and his tail flicked again, but he didn't lift his head to drink.

"You can do it," she said. "Come on, try, cat. Come on, it's water. It's good. Please drink it."

He levered his head up slowly, and nearly dropped his chin in the water when his strength gave out. Head wavering with weakness, he managed to drink a little before he collapsed again, purring.

She poured more water and tentatively began to stroke him. The purr increased. After a moment he lifted his head, more steadily this time, and lapped at the water again.

When they both felt recovered enough to move on, there was at least an hour and a half of daylight remaining. Ugly thought of camping where they were, but she was anxious to move on into the mountains, so she decided to go on at least a little way. The kitten, apparently none the worse for their ordeal in the desert, trotted cheerfully along beside her. They were both weakened, but recovering quickly, and glad to be on their way.

Once past the waterfruit tree, where Ugly paused to collect several more fruits to bring with them, they found the going increasingly steep as the ground sloped up toward the mountains. Within a kilometer they found a trickle of moisture in the stream bed, which widened as they climbed till it became a rushing torrent too deep to ford. Fortunately there was fairly level ground most of the way beside it, though now and then they had to scramble across tumbled boulders beneath the steep canyon wall, and once Ugly had to carry the kitten across a particularly difficult stretch. He accepted the indignity with surprising good grace, and didn't even leap to freedom the moment it was safe to do so, but waited till Ugly put him down.

In spite of her earlier fears, Ugly found plenty of familiar fruits and berries along the way, and ate as she walked, stuffing mountain apples and some blueberries in her bundle for later. Evening was drawing in on them and she had begun to think of finding a place to camp, but was reluctant to stop where they were, because their path had climbed steep canyon walls high above the stream bed, and offered only precarious space for sleeping. Then they rounded a curve in the canyon, and a little valley unfolded before them, serene and silent in the glooming light.

At the far end of it a waterfall plunged six hundred meters to the valley floor, enshrouding that whole end of it in a mist as blue as smoke. This was a secret little world of trees and meadow through which the stream meandered between wide, grassy banks. On all sides, the mountains rose like mossy walls to shelter the valley from the outside world. Ugly paused, staring: in that barren, rocky landscape, this was like a scrap of heaven fallen unexpectedly to earth.

Without a sound, the kitten streaked past her along the path toward the valley floor some three meters below them. Ugly, still staring, moved more slowly, feeling her way so she wouldn't have to take her gaze from the valley. Perhaps if she had been watching the path, she never would have noticed the cave. As it was, she nearly missed it; she reached with one groping hand toward what, in the corner of her eye, looked like a patch of black rocks, and met only empty space. With a quick glance for another handhold, she moved on past it three full paces before she realized what she had seen, and turned back.

It was too dark by then to investigate within; by daylight there would be enough light to see how deep it was and whether it was already occupied. But even in the pale light of dusk it was easy to see that if the cave were deep enough, and as dry as it smelled, and unoccupied, one could hardly ask for a better dwelling place. It was only about three meters off the valley floor, perhaps less. It was well sheltered from wind, and easy to defend from predators. From its mouth, one should have a good view not only of the valley ahead, but also of the desert they had crossed, and of the forested plain beyond that, perhaps all the way to Godsgrace if the air were clear.

For the first time in her life, Ugly had a sense of coming home. She moved quickly on down to the valley floor, heart singing, resolved to investigate the cave the next morning. But even if it didn't prove suitable, this valley was *home*. She couldn't have said why, and she certainly hadn't expected it, but it was true: she had come home.

16

Juan Hashimoto was one of very few Terrans who understood the real importance of the search for Prince Hawke's giftmate. He had made a study of the ways of the People, at first out of idle curiosity and later out of deep interest and sympathy; perhaps because his own ancestry included people of another dispossessed race, the American Indians of Terra, he found himself drawn to the People and concerned about their dispossessed status on Paradise.

It was and had always been the Terran way to expand Terran territory by any means they could, conquering new lands and subjugating the peoples there, first on Earth itself, later in the solar system, and finally throughout the galaxy. Terran need for space and resources expanded relentlessly so that it always exceeded the supply; as a species, Terrans had always lived beyond their means.

As individuals, however, they were capable of great compassion for the people and places so irrevocably overrun, altered, and often destroyed by Terran expansion. Hashimoto was such an individual. He was also, unfortunately but perhaps inevitably, a romantic idealist. It never occurred to him that there might be political factions among the People with which he would disagree, or even that there might be individuals of that or of any other oppressed race who were less than noble.

He understood that the People would reclaim their planet from Terran rule if they could, a possibility most Terrans would have regarded as both treacherous and traitorous, but which Hashimoto regarded as natural and acceptable. He understood that the rebellion, should it come, would almost certainly involve bloodshed on both sides, and probably full-scale war; but the distress he felt at that thought was not over potential Terran losses, but over the very real possibility that the People, comparatively few in number to begin with, would be wiped out as a whole.

Since he had begun his study of their ways, Hashimoto had come to identify more closely with the People than he did with many Terrans. He had volunteered to help with the search for Hawke's giftmate because he believed that with a Maker-Breaker pair to lead them, the People had at least a fighting chance against the relentless Terran invasion, and he wanted to help them get that chance.

When it was suggested that he accompany the native Tran and his giftmate Hesta to the Starling residence to inquire about the missing foster Starling, Hashimoto had jumped at the chance. He had studied the five remaining possibilities and, despite Mahlo's stated opinion to the contrary, believed that the Starling child was the most likely. And while Tran and Hesta spoke and understood the Terran trade language quite well, their appearance alone might unnerve the Starlings; Tran was a huge, hulking brute, with masses of brown curls down his back and totally expressionless pale green eyes that seemed to penetrate one's soul—and find it wanting. Hesta was only slightly smaller, and looked so much fiercer that, at Hashimoto's suggestion, she agreed to wait in the aircar during the interview.

Hashimoto looked quite small, almost frail beside Tran and Hesta, although among Terrans he was above medium height. He was a very thin, erect man with warm brown eyes, neat silver-gray hair, and a pleasant air of dignity; a gentle patriarch with a disarming smile.

His pleasant appearance was extremely helpful in his interview with the Starlings, who stared in nervous awe at Tran and displayed obvious discomfort over questions about their foster daughter's childhood.

Hashimoto knew that their religion required very strict discipline for children, and he tried to reassure them, but it wasn't much use. What he wanted to know was whether the fosterling had suffered Onset illness. What he learned was that she had been treated much more harshly than the Starlings' religion required or than their biological children had been; and that now, forced to re-examine their conduct, the Starlings were not entirely comfortable with what they had done.

"A beating in time saves the child that's mine," Mrs. Starling quoted, trying to sound pious. "She was never well behaved, and the scriptures tell us again and again that the only salvation for an ill-behaved child is physical punishment for every wrongdoing."

"Ma and Pa beat us, too," said Joel. "It's not like they singled her out for it."

"Though she did need it more," said Megan. "She was always an uppity thing. The child learns humility at the hands of its family, that's what the scriptures say."

"The wanderwood stick makes a good child," said Mr. Starling. "Joe said that, Chapter Ten, paragraph three. And he said thou shalt not suffer the little child . . . what was that quote, Ma?"

"It doesn't matter," said Hashimoto. "I'm sure you did your best with the girl. What was her name again?"

"Sandy," Megan said firmly, at the same time as her mother said, "Suzy." They looked at each other, and Mrs. Starling sighed, looked at Hashimoto, and spread her hands. "We had nicknames for the child. We didn't often use her registered name."

Hashimoto nodded. "Okay, we'll use her nickname if it's more convenient for you. What is it?"

"Oh, um," said Megan.

"I want to know why you're asking us all these questions," said Mrs. Starling. "We raised Ug—um, Suzy just the way we did our own children . . . well, maybe a little more harshly, but that was only because

. . . Look, I don't know what your interest is in the girl, but I have to tell you that she's just not clever, not at all. She's a sullen, clumsy thing, not attractive in any way, not obedient, not anything you'd want in a child, just . . . well, unsatisfactory. She always has been."

"What I wanted to know about, Mrs. Starling, was childhood illnesses. That's why I was asking what her health was like years ago. Now, you said she was ill one time?"

Mrs. Starling sniffed. "So she *said*. The doctors couldn't find anything wrong with her, of course. I bet she just didn't want to do her share of the work around here. She was always trying to shirk her duties."

"It was after that time she was sick that she got so clumsy, though," said Megan. She looked earnestly at Hashimoto. "Honestly, we couldn't let her *touch* the crystal, it just seemed to shatter in her ugly big hands. She never knew her own strength."

"Indeed." Hashimoto, rigidly trained by years in politics, sounded only casually interested. His pulse, however, was racing. "Tell me, by any chance have you noticed a tendency, well, I don't know quite how to put this, but . . . since Suzy left, have you had particularly bad luck in small matters?"

Mr. Starling stiffened. "We don't believe in luck. According to Joe—"

"Oh, Pa, don't be stuffy," said Megan. "You know what he means, and it's what I said, isn't it?" She looked at Hashimoto. "Isn't it?"

"Isn't what?" he asked innocently. "I'm afraid I don't know what you're talking about."

Megan flounced importantly. "I knew it! Either she put a curse on us, or we've caught some sort of terrible clumsy disease from her. Which is it, Mr. Hashimoto? That's why you're here, isn't it? Because it's a disease? Will we die?"

"Megan," said Mrs. Starling.

"There's no such thing as curses," said Mr. Starling.

"I can't cut crystal anymore," Megan announced. "I was the most promising sculptor in the community, and now it just breaks. Is there a cure? What do we have to do? Ma and Pa've got it, too, and prob'ly the boys. There is a cure, isn't there?"

"Time," Hashimoto said absently. "You'll improve with time. It's not actually a disease, you know."

"Then what is it?" demanded Megan.

"If I'm right—" Hashimoto glanced at Tran and was startled at the big native's expression; caught off guard, Tran looked positively enraged. But this was wonderful news! He should be elated. From all Hashimoto could piece together about the Breaker gift, it would almost certainly have made things around the Breaker work smoothly and well, though she herself might have appeared extremely clumsy. Then, when she left, taking with her the Breaker aura that had eased the way for the Starlings, they would naturally perceive the many little problems of ordinary daily life, which they had for so long escaped, to be really very bad luck. . . .

"Tell me," said Hashimoto, forgetting Tran in his excitement, "do you have a hologram of, um, Suzy? Or even a photograph?"

"Why?" Mrs. Starling asked suspiciously.

"Or," said Hashimoto, "maybe you could just describe the girl for me?"

"Ugly," said Megan. "And big."

"Not so big," said Joel.

"Just strong . . . and clumsy," said Karn. "That's why she seemed big."

"She had big hands, anyway," said Megan.

"Nasty straight pale hair," said Mrs. Starling.

Megan shuddered prettily. "And her eyes are positively lavender, can you imagine?"

The amethyst eyes of royalty! There was no question in Hashimoto's mind: this child was Prince Hawke's giftmate. He looked again at Tran. The big native returned his look this time with his customary bland, expressionless gaze. Puzzled, Hashimoto looked away. "It's very important that we find this girl. If she should return here—"

"She won't," Mr. Starling said certainly. "She tried to kill me, remember. We told you that."

"If she should return here," Hashimoto said firmly, "please get in touch with me at once." He gave them his card, exchanged parting pleasantries with them, and followed Tran back to the aircar to return to Town. They had promised to send a hologram of the child, but he didn't need to see that to be convinced. He was anxious to discuss it with Tran, to see why the native had seemed so displeased to hear the evidence that Hashimoto had found so exciting, but he waited till they were in the air to ask his questions. Tran and Hesta's gift amounted to telekinesis, which was a common gift among the People, and they used it as much as they used the aircar's engines to get them aloft and set their course. Hashimoto was aware of that, and did not interrupt their concentration.

Once they were in the air, Tran assured Hashimoto that they would discuss the Starlings when they got back to Town. He seemed distracted. Hashimoto decided that Tran wanted time to absorb what had happened and to discuss with Hesta what it would mean to the People. Perhaps he had misread Tran's expression. Perhaps Tran was as excited as Hashimoto was. He certainly ought to be. They hadn't found the girl, of course, but they knew now that she was the one they wanted. Tran *must* be as excited as Hashimoto was.

Hashimoto died believing that.

17

When Ugly woke the next morning, the rising sun had cast one broad beam of gold through the pass into her hidden valley, lighting it with a fragile amber glow like a faded watercolor. She lay in a sheltered nook of rocks below the cave, from which she could see across the green valley floor to the waterfall that cascaded down the back wall of the valley, building a fairyland of rainbows over a misted pool at its foot. A scarlet cockatoo flew past her, carrying a twig in its beak. Its bright wings flashed like metal in the sun.

From where she lay, she could see a pear tree in blossom—not much use now, but later in the summer it would be another source of food—and several mountain apple trees, some in blossom and some heavy with winter fruit. There were cattails beside the stream, which would provide edible roots and delicious tender new "ears" to roast if she found a way to make fire, and whose leaves could be woven into baskets and matting. There were clusters of mountain lettuce, small fields of edible dandestar flowers, and on the rocks beside which she had slept there were vines laden with tiny golden rockberries. Her mouth watered at the mere thought of their tart, sugary juice. They were a job to collect because they were so small, but well worth it. Their juice was one of the main ingredients of ambrosia.

In the early morning stillness she could hear a meadowlark singing in the distance and the gentle, papery chime of morning breeze through a windchime bush somewhere nearby. She lay still for a moment, listening to the splash and gurgle of the stream and the quiet coo and calling of doves in the meadow.

The cat was nowhere to be seen. Ugly sat up, feeling

deserted, and chided herself for becoming too dependent on the presence of a cat that had no reason in the world to stay with her. All the same, she hoped he was only on one of his foraging trips, and would return when he had fed. Never having had a friend before, she was unfamiliar with the emotions involved in friendship and wasn't quite sure she liked all of them, but she certainly liked the cat and wasn't ready to lose him.

Glancing up at the rock wall above her, she saw that sunlight was spilling into the cave she had seen last night. Impatient to know whether it would make a suitable home, she rose and ran up the narrow rocky path that led past its mouth. It didn't occur to her that only a few weeks ago she would have considered that precarious path totally impassable for a person as clumsy as she. As her confidence in herself increased with no Starlings to mock her, she was becoming increasingly graceful, capable of a great many simple feats like climbing that path; feats that would have been beyond her abilities when she lived with the Starlings, and that still might be if she remembered their taunts.

The cave was perfect. The mouth was small enough to defend if need be, but large enough to let in plenty of light and air. The roof was higher inside, so she could comfortably stand upright. The floor was covered with clean, soft, dry sand. There was even a shelf along one wall, uneven and covered with rockdust and rubble, but wide enough to make into a snug bed in one corner, and narrower elsewhere for storage.

Near the entrance there was a fissure in the roof that might act as a chimney if she built her fireplace beneath it. If she didn't want a fire for food this summer, she would certainly need one for heat next winter. She had no real idea how she would start a fire; but she thought wryly that if she began now, she might manage to get one going before the first snowfall.

Returning to the valley floor, she gathered up her belongings and brought them back to the cave, along with a leafy branch with which to sweep her shelf. When it was clean and everything put away, she made a ring of stones for her fireplace and carefully laid a few dry sticks and tinder in it, ready for fire-making attempts. Then she went back outside and gathered up dry wood, which she stored in the cave along the back wall.

Several pieces of flint she had found on the valley floor went on the shelf with her other belongings, but she made no attempt yet to start a fire. Instead, she made more trips into the valley to collect fruit, berries, and roots to store in the cave for future meals, and cattail leaves from which she made a cushioning mat for her bed. Then, feeling very much the master of her small household, she stood proudly on the little ledge in front of the cave, surveying her domain.

The sun was higher now, filling the valley with amber morning light. The foot of the waterfall was hidden in mist and rainbows. The stream was a silver ribbon curving among green, flower-dusted meadows. The cat was struggling up the path toward Ugly, dragging a dead horned rabbit that was bigger than he was.

"How in the world did you kill something that big?" she asked.

He lugged it on up the path, dropped it at her feet, looked up at her with expressionless amethyst eyes, blinked, and began to clean his paws.

While she was cleaning the rabbit with her broken knife, and worrying about whether she would be able to light a fire with flint and tinder, the cat investigated their new home. Ugly had spread the cattail mat and a nest of soft fronds from a fern tree on the wide part of the shelf. The cat hopped onto the shelf when he had investigated the rest of the cave, sniffed all Ugly's possessions, tiptoed around on the fern fronds looking extremely suspicious of them, then settled in the center of them to perform his toilet.

"Does this mean you approve?" asked Ugly.

He paused in his cleaning, one hind leg stuck

straight up in the air, to look at her. The pink tip of his tongue projected, forgotten, between his teeth.

"You know, I meant that to be *my* bed," said Ugly. He resumed his toilet.

She wrapped the rabbit's entrails in a broad leaf for later burial, put the skin aside to be further cleaned, and sat back on her heels to look at the cat. "Frank? Leon? Abernathy? Jones?" The cat didn't respond. "Do you have a name?" He didn't even look at her. "Never mind, neither have I. I'm called what I am. I guess that's what I should call you." She thought about it. "Pretty? Soft? Swift? Graceful?" She shook her head. "Maybe not what you look like. What else are you? Friend?" He looked up. "Is that your name? Friend?" He blinked, shifted, and began to wash the other hind leg. "Okay, Friend. Now, how am I going to start a fire?" He purred.

She put a little pile of dried leaves in the fireplace, looked at them, crumpled them up, and piled them again. Then she got two pieces of flint and spent the next fifteen minutes diligently striking them against each other over the leaves. Sparks flew everywhere except onto the leaves. Twice in that time, very nice big sparks landed on the leaves and she leaned forward to encourage them into flame. The first time, the spark was gone before she could draw breath. The second time, it glowed encouragingly, brightened when she breathed on it, and then went out.

At last, hot and sweaty and discouraged, she threw the flint at the back of the cave and was rewarded with a lovely, useless shower of sparks. "I can't do it," she said. "I can't do anything right."

Friend, who had been watching her with narrowed eyes, purred loudly.

"Oh, you think so, do you?" she asked belligerently. "Well, I don't. In fact, I know I can't. You saw what happened."

He continued purring.

"I don't know *how*!"

He began to clean his tail, still purring.

Okay. What did one do when flint failed? Flies were settling on the uncooked rabbit. She brushed them away and covered the meat with a leaf, wiped her forehead with the back of her hand, and frowned at the fireplace. What now?

She had heard of starting fires by rubbing two sticks together. It sounded preposterous, but she was ready to try anything: the mere thought of tender roast rabbit made her almost sick with hunger. She needed protein, and she loved rabbit meat. But not raw.

With a wry grimace, she pulled two sticks out of the fireplace and, holding them one in each hand, began to rub them vigorously together. Naturally enough, the only heat she generated that way was her own body heat. Sweating with exertion, near tears with rage and frustration, bitterly determined, she kept at it long after it was clear that nothing was going to come of it.

"Why did you bring me meat, anyway?" she gasped finally. "You *knew* I'd want it, and I can't have it because I can't start a fire. It's hopeless. Oh, *damn* it!" She hurled the sticks back into the fireplace and glared at them in total, helpless rage.

They burst into flame.

18

Tran was late for his appointment with the High King, and made little effort to improve his bruised and battered appearance before entering the audience chamber. He was bleeding from a small cut over one eyebrow, his clothes were torn and stained, and his face was smudged with grease or soot. King Arkos had been prepared to deliver him a stern lecture on the evils of tardiness, but at sight of him settled instead for lifted eyebrows and an expectant silence.

"Your pardon, my lord King," said Tran, kneeling. "Perhaps I should have cleaned up, but I was already late. . . ." He waited for the King to ask him what had happened, but Arkos didn't oblige. After a long moment, Tran said hesitantly, "It was an aircar crash, my lord King. The controls jammed. Hesta and I did our best to compensate, but . . . Juan Hashimoto was with us. In his fear, he knocked the crystal from Hesta's hands and we lost control. He didn't survive; Terrans are so frail."

Arkos turned away. "A shame. He was a good man, for a Terran."

Tran, still dutifully kneeling, nodded heavily. "Yes, my lord King."

"And Hesta? She is well?"

"A broken ankle, my lord King. I sent her to the healers." That part had not been planned; for a moment, they really *had* lost control. But neither was seriously hurt, and their injuries lent verisimilitude to the tale. Tran waited patiently at the High King's feet.

Arkos glanced at him and made an impatient gesture. "Rise, rise, for the gods' sake, old friend. I am glad you and Hesta were not more hurt."

"Thank you, my lord King." Tran rose, swayed, and had to put one hand on a pillar for support.

"You are injured?"

"A small bump on the head only. My lord King, it is such a shame; the trip was a waste of time. That Hashimoto should die in the course of such a useless journey . . ." He shook his head mournfully.

Arkos gestured for Bush's attention. "You would like tea?" he asked Tran, and without awaiting Tran's answer told Bush to bring it. "The journey wasn't wasted, Tran. Not even if all it established was that the child is not my son's giftmate. You saw her?"

"No, my lord King. We spoke with the family." He shook his head again, winced, and gently touched the bleeding cut over his eyebrow.

"You should have that seen to," said the King.

"Yes, my lord King. The child—a grown woman now, of course—was never ill. Only the usual childhood maladies. And her description—well, I suppose it's possible, my lord King." He sounded dubious. "They did say they would send a hologram, so you can judge for yourself."

"Tell me about the family."

Tran grimaced. "Terrans, who can understand them? They beat their children. With weapons, they beat them. They have a saying: The wanderwood stick makes a good child. By this they mean that it is wise to beat one's child with sticks. Their own children! It makes no sense."

The King shrugged. "I have heard of this. Perhaps for Terran children it is wise, who can say? They are not of the People. Ah, our tea. Come, sit with me, Tran. Tell me, aside from this beating, did these Starlings seem fond of their foster daughter?"

"Oh, yes, my lord King, quite fond." Tran waited till the King was seated, then sat on the edge of the chair next to him and accepted a cup of tea from Bush.

The King studied his own tea, watching the steam

rise. "There was no indication that they found her alien or even odd in any way?"

"No, my lord King." Tran sipped his tea and looked politely, innocently, into the King's searching eyes. His own eyes revealed only regret, nothing more.

Arkos frowned. "And no illness."

"No, my lord King."

Arkos sighed and leaned back in his chair, balancing his tea on its arm. "What did Hashimoto make of them? He was Terran: perhaps he saw or understood something you could not?"

"Nothing that he mentioned to me, my lord King. He told me she seemed an unlikely candidate."

"Damn."

"Yes, my lord King."

19

"Maybe there was a spark left from when I was trying the flint. Maybe it just finally caught from that. That must be it, right, Friend?" Ugly glanced briefly from the flames to the cat lying unperturbed on the bed, then back again. She was sitting against the wall, as far from the fireplace as she could get, though she had no memory of having moved there from sitting beside the fire when she had been trying to light it.

The few sticks she had laid out were crackling merrily with bright, dancing flames, the smoke moving upward and out through the fissure overhead just as she had hoped it would. Obviously no frail leftover spark had lighted that. If there had been a spark smoldering, she would have seen or smelled the smoke. And it would have grown slowly to flames, not burst suddenly out like that, all over.

Ugly rose slowly, watching the fire, dusting her hands and knees absently as she crossed the cave. The fire looked ordinary in every way, and was already diminishing from lack of fuel. She got more wood from her stack at the back of the cave, and added some good-sized pieces to the fire. They caught readily; before long it would be just right for roasting horned rabbit.

First things first. Later she would determine how the fire started. Now she would use it. She went outside and found a long, straight, green stick to skewer the rabbit, and after a moment's thought found six more fairly straight, sturdy branches all roughly the same length, from which to make two tripods to support the skewer. She used morning glory vines to tie them together near one end, set the bundles upright on opposite sides of the fire, and used rocks to brace their bases. The sand that covered the stone floor helped keep the rocks from slipping. When the tripods seemed stable, she skewered the rabbit, laid the skewer carefully across the tops of the tripods, and sat back to observe her handiwork. The flames sizzled as juices began to drip down onto the fire.

"That should work," she said, and sighed. There was nothing more to do but feed the fire and occasionally turn the skewer. She couldn't avoid thinking about it any longer. Something had started that fire, and it hadn't been a leftover flint spark or any heat she had generated by rubbing two sticks together. She knew what it had been, and the knowledge frightened her. She had started the fire. By looking at the wood, she had caused it to burst into flame. She knew it. She had *felt* herself do it.

"Okay, then, you should be able to do it again, right?" Her voice was belligerent. "If you're so sure you did it, go ahead. Do it again."

She got fresh wood, put it on the sandy floor well away from the fire, and glared at it. Nothing happened. She tried to remember exactly how she had felt before, and to duplicate it. Nothing happened. Frustrated, she got up to turn the rabbit, then returned to her efforts. She managed eventually to duplicate the frustrated rage she had felt before, but she could not duplicate the miracle.

Friend hopped down from the bed to sit beside her when the rabbit was nearly done. "Maybe it's just that I don't need another fire now," she told him wearily. "Or maybe I didn't really start the first one. I don't know. I thought I sort of felt it jump out of me. . . ." She hesitated, glanced at him, and shrugged. "It sounds silly when I say it out loud. But if I didn't start it, what did?"

Friend stood up, stretched, and leaned against her, purring.

"I think the rabbit's done." She tossed her firewood back onto the stack at the back of the cave. "How d'you feel about roast rabbit?"

He followed her to the fire and looked expectant.

"I guess you think you'll like it." She took it off the fire and laid it on a flat rock she had carefully scrubbed with leaves for the purpose. Dividing the meat neatly into two equal parts, she put his in her wooden bowl and gave it to him. "Be careful; it's hot."

He blinked at her and settled down at the bowl, eating daintily.

She ate hers right from the rock, and was so hungry for meat that she was halfway through it before she remembered the salty leaves of bitterweed she had meant to use to flavor it.

After lunch, she cleaned their dishes in the stream and buried the remains of the rabbit. She kept the skin, which she hoped to cure, and the horn, which seemed too potentially useful to discard, although she hadn't yet thought of anything to do with it. She wrapped the horn in the skin and put them aside for later consideration. Using the stick with which she had skewered the rabbit, she raked the coals of the fire into a neat pile that she hoped would keep burning for a while, then went outside to investigate her valley.

Friend went with her as she walked the lush green meadows, occasionally gathering herbs, but mostly just staring at the wonderful, untouched beauty of the place. The valley walls were as steep and as vividly green with moss and lichen as the rest of the Mysterious Mountains. The stream was cold, and so clear she could see the colored pebbles that lined its bed. The sun had risen too high to make rainbows anymore at the foot of the waterfall; now the water plunged like a narrow, glittering ribbon straight from the top of the cliff to the enshrouding mist over the still pool beneath it. Ugly and Friend moved toward it across a meadow littered with daisies.

The stream curved neatly down the center of the valley to rush down small rapids in the pass just past Ugly's cave and from there on out toward the desert. It was easily fordable, being wide and shallow, but it seemed nonetheless to divide the landscape into distinct halves. On Ugly's side there were more meadows and open ground, with evidence that deer or other grazing animals had recently spent some time there. The other side was rockier, with taller shrubbery that became actual forest as it neared the valley wall. There were more birds in evidence on that side, and less sign of deer.

Friend ran ahead of Ugly, bounding gracefully across the meadow, and pounced playfully at a clump of tall grass, sending a whole family of yellow doves up in a startled thunder of wings toward the sky. He sat on his haunches and watched them with satisfaction till Ugly caught up with him, then leapt up and bounded forward again to chase a big orange butterfly across a carpet of crimson firegrass. A solitary gull hovered overhead and cried out once, like a rusty gate swinging in the wind, then banked its wings and soared effortlessly across the valley toward the trees on the other side.

The sense of solitude, which in the forest had seemed oppressive, here seemed oddly exhilarating. Without conscious decision, Ugly had ceased to think about the trip through the mountains to Far Harbor, and was instead planning an indefinite stay in the valley. She was collecting housewares like a nesting bird: two bits of driftwood from which she thought she could carve a fork and a spoon, flannelweed leaves to use for napkins, watergrass to dry and save for soup stock or pillow stuffing, and an assortment of medicinal herbs to hang up to dry. She noted patches of berries to be raided in future, collected a few winter pears to eat now, and generally kept an eye out for anything that might prove useful or edible now or later.

The ground became rockier as she neared the waterfall. There were more rockberries here, and some of the tapa bushes whose broad leaves she knew could be soaked and beaten till the pulp wore away and only the soft, strong, fibrous core was left, like a leaf-shaped piece of cloth. She would come back for those; her jumpsuit was wearing out already from rough usage, and while she hadn't much need for clothing in the summer, she would certainly need it next winter. It wasn't too soon now to start preparing the fabric.

First, though, she wanted to investigate the waterfall. She scrambled over the rocks with Friend bounding along beside her till they stood in the cool mist on the last broad boulder with the waterfall like a sheet of dancing silver above them and its wide, clear pool sparkling like gemstones at their feet. It was magnificent. From this near, the rush of the waterfall was the basic sound of the universe, like a heavy rain beating on the pool and the mountainside. It fell so far and in such a thin stream that by the time it reached the pool, it had been turned to mist and rainbows by rocks and wind on the way down. The water in the pool was so clear that Ugly could see the stony bottom to about halfway out; after that, the bottom dropped steeply, and the surface was so churned by falling water that she couldn't tell how deep it became.

On impulse, she pulled off her jumpsuit and stepped carefully into the water, clinging to the rocky edge for safety. The water wasn't as cold as she had expected. It felt clean and soft and exhilarating after the long walk they had taken in the hot spring sun. She found a secure handhold near the surface and let her feet float out from under her. The water closed over her shoulders and lapped at her chin. It smelled of damp rocks, mud, and sunlight.

Friend stalked down to the water's edge to stare at her in disapproval. Wind blew the mist of the waterfall to one side, where it cast a brilliant little rainbow at the cliff face before the wind veered and the mist settled back over the pool. Ugly got her feet on the bottom again and climbed up out of the water, onto a flat rock warmed by the sun. Friend padded cautiously to her side, sniffed distastefully at her damp hair, and uttered a brief, distressed meow before he began the weary effort to lick her dry.

She giggled and squirmed away from him, leaving him looking at her in pained surprise. "Your tongue is like sandpaper," she said. "I *need* my skin."

He blinked and retreated a few steps to avoid splatters when she shook her hair. Then he meowed again and turned away to chase a dragonfly. Ugly watched him with affection. He might not be quite as good company as people, but neither would he laugh at her, or condemn her for murder. With him for company, she felt completely at home in her magic little valley, which held everything she really needed for survival. They both needed a rest after their journey across the desert, anyway. Maybe later she would think again about Far Harbor, but for now she was content.

She stretched out on the rock, basking in the misted sun, and began to think about making some rudimentary furniture for her cave. It was nice that the bed was already there, but she could surely make a better mattress than cattail mat and fern tree fronds, and perhaps even make a table and chair so she wouldn't have to sit on the sand to eat her meals. . . .

20

"You're sure?" asked Mahlo.

Tran shrugged heavily. "As sure as I can be, without seeing her. They even called her an alien. What are you going to do?"

"Sh-h-h!" Mahlo glanced around apprehensively. "I thought I heard someone." They were in a deserted corridor in a wing of the palace given over mostly to servants' quarters and rooms for unimportant guests. At this hour of the day it was seldom frequented; the servants were at their work in the better wings of the palace; and the guests, mostly merchants and entertainers, were plying their trades in various parts of the palace, grounds, and surrounding village.

For a long moment the two men stood still, their eyes searching the shadowy corridor, their ears straining for a sound. Then it came again: a scuffling sound as of someone, improbably, dancing, just around a corner and out of sight. After a moment a thin, high voice began to hum tunelessly, and Tran relaxed. "It's only the Prince."

As if on cue, Prince Hawke emerged from a side corridor, moving backward in one of the slow, graceful folk dances of the People. Swooping and dipping as elegantly as a professional dancer, he executed the passage known as the Courting Swan from a long, intricate dance about the plight of birds before the gods had granted them wings. In the course of the dance, Hawke turned toward Tran and Mahlo without any indication that he saw them, and continued dancing till his attention was distracted by a dark portrait on the wall. He paused before it, his head cocked. "Do you think it will rain?" he asked suddenly.

Tran and Mahlo stared, transfixed.

"Oh, no, I think snow is most unlikely this time of year," said Hawke. "But must we always talk about the weather? Don't you have any other interests?"

"He doesn't even know we're here," said Mahlo, but he studied Hawke closely as he said it.

"I did *not* bring it up," Hawke said petulantly. "You did. You always do."

"What will we do?" asked Tran.

"About the Breaker? Eliminate the possibility." Mahlo was still watching Hawke.

"What I don't understand," said Hawke, "is why I always find you standing around in the dark." He closed his eyes. "It's not fun in the dark."

"How?" asked Tran. "They can't even find her. She's lost in the forest."

"When I was in the forest I gave her fruit," said Hawke.

"He *is* listening," said Mahlo, moving away.

Hawke opened his eyes. "It wasn't dark in the forest."

"He can't understand; he's mad." But Tran, following Mahlo, nonetheless lowered his voice.

"Perhaps," said Mahlo.

Hawke wandered aimlessly after them, grinning. "I like the forest," he said cheerfully.

"He's mad," repeated Tran. "Listen, that Breaker will never be found. We're safe enough."

"We lied. If it were ever found out that we lied to the King, we'd be dead," said Mahlo.

"Nine dead men make a fairy ring," said Hawke. He was dancing again.

"How could anyone find out?" asked Tran.

"We can't afford any chance of it," said Mahlo. "Or that the child will survive. A Breaker . . ." He stared at Hawke, who smiled and nodded at another portrait nearer the two men. "If the Maker and the Breaker did get together, they could overcome the Terrans. Then where would we be? We *need* the Terrans, their technology, their tools—" Mahlo's amiable smile seemed somehow overlaid with evil. "And their rule. When they take over the reservation—"

"I know," said Tran. "I was at the planning session, remember? And I'd like to be governor of a whole sector just as much as you would."

"Good afternoon," said Hawke.

Both men started nervously and stared at him, but he was addressing the wall, so Tran went on, "But I tell you, the Breaker is safe enough. She's probably dead by now."

Mahlo frowned at Hawke. "Lower your voice, Tran. You're not in power yet." His own voice was heavy with disapproval.

"Oh, I know," said Tran. "You're not doing it for the power: your reasons are all noble and pure. For the greater good of the People, right? Poor backward People need fine, modern Terran technology and clever Terran rulers. . . ."

"Shut up!" snapped Mahlo.

"Shut up!" said Hawke. Mahlo and Tran both looked at him. He did a graceful pirouette and bowed to the portrait on the wall. "Shut up, shut up," he chanted happily.

"We're not here to discuss politics," hissed Mahlo. "We're here to decide what to do about that damn Breaker."

"That damn Breaker is an ignorant peasant," said Tran. "And the Maker is mad. Where's the threat, even if the Breaker survives?"

"The Breaker must die," said Mahlo.

"Shut up," said Hawke.

"How can we find a runaway in the eastern wilderness?" asked Tran.

Hawke began to stalk up and down the corridor, his back straight, his hands clasped behind him, muttering to himself in a continuous, singsong undertone.

"We needn't search the whole wilderness; only the forest," said Mahlo. "You said that was where she went. She'll still be there. The forest is bounded on two sides by impassable mountains, on the third side by a great desert, and on the fourth by the sea."

"The mountains aren't entirely impassable," said Tran.

"The Breaker was raised by Terrans." Mahlo raised his voice over Tran's interruption. "If a Terran survived that forest, he wouldn't leave it. They call it 'remaining with the known evil,' or something of that sort. Once they have coped with a thing, they don't leave it."

Tran stared. "You say that of the race that conquered the galaxy?"

Mahlo shrugged, dismissing Tran's incredulity. "An accident of their technology. Which," he added forcefully, "is why *we* must have their technology. If such a timid and peculiar race could use it to conquer the galaxy, think what we could do with it!"

Hawke's stalk up and down the corridor had gradually become clumsy and his mutter merely a repetitive keening sound. The pitiful mad Prince was such a common sight and topic of gossip about the palace that both men had nearly forgotten he was there in the corridor with them; he was a mindless fixture, like the portraits on the walls.

Tran shook his head. "Maybe the Terrans aren't as timid as you think."

Mahlo drew breath to argue, thought better of it, and merely scowled. "Never mind that. The Breaker will be timid enough to stay in the forest, that's the important point. And the forest is not too large to search. Send out all the aircars you can. Put gifted hunters in as many of them as you can. Run a standard search pattern, and make sure your instructions are understood; we don't want them bringing that damn Breaker in alive."

"I'll say it's an escaped criminal, shall I?"

"A traitor," said Mahlo, grinning suddenly. "That should make the hunters bloodthirsty enough." His gaze fell on Hawke and he started visibly. "Damn, I'd forgotten he was here."

"He won't have understood," said Tran.

"I'm not so sure he's as mad as he acts," said Mahlo.

Hawke lurched against a wall and began to sing in a high, clear voice. While Tran watched nervously, Mahlo approached Hawke and thrust a hand against his chest, pinning him to the wall. "You!" said Mahlo. "What are you doing here?"

Hawke blinked, stared, and cringed away from Mahlo. "I don't like the dark," he said in a small voice. "I like singing."

Mahlo pushed at him, bouncing his head against the wall. "Answer me! What is your business here?"

Hawke leaned against the wall, his arms and legs oddly limp and rubbery. "Won't I get my dessert after all?"

Tran moved forward uncomfortably. "Mahlo—"

"Ah, Mahlo," said Hawke, "I see you've brought your crystal harp. Do play us a song."

"You've been spying on us," said Mahlo, pushing at Hawke with angry little jabs that made his loose arms flap like a rag doll's, and bounced his head hard against the stone wall behind him.

Hawke giggled, seemingly unaware of the solid stone hitting his head. "No one sings crystal like Mahlo," he said. "Tell the King! Tell the King!"

Mahlo gave him an especially hard shove and released him. "Tell the King *what*, little man?"

Hawke bounced off the wall and slowly let his knees collapse, sinking to a sitting position against the wall, grinning idiotically at Mahlo's legs. "Tell the King, here's Mahlo," he said. "My lord King, I've found your crystal harpist—"

"I don't whistle the crystal anymore!" Mahlo's voice was taut with rage and pain. His gift was crystal singing. Together, he and his giftmate had whistled the crystal for years, bringing communication to areas

where the Terrans' technology had not yet reached. Neither telephones nor radios worked with only a sender; there must also be a receiver. In remote areas it took time for the Terrans to bring in their technology, but there had always been crystal whistlers.

They sang, or "whistled," into their crystals, and the frequencies excited the crystal molecules. Even the Terran scientists could explain no further than that, but the vibrations were carried somehow—by mental power or as something akin to radio waves, no one knew—across vast distances, sometimes augmented by "carrier crystals" along the way, till they reached the intended receiver, a crystal whistler who could "hear" the song in his crystal and translate the message for its intended recipient.

In a variation of that, meant purely for entertainment, the singers also fashioned crystal harps and sang for pleasure. Mahlo and his mate had indeed been among the best and most brilliant pleasure-singers, creating powerful melodies that stirred one's blood; or poignant ones that tore one's heart; or strange, eerie little pieces so full of emotion that one did not know whether to laugh or cry or shiver in fear, though most listeners did all three. . . .

Since his giftmate died, Mahlo had never sung again. There was, indeed, only one song he could sing alone: the Death Song. Perhaps originally evolved as a means whereby a crystal whistler could join his gift-mate in death, and certainly often enough used for that purpose, the Death Song had, over generations of evolution, become far more than merely a method of suicide. One of a mere handful of gift abilities that could be exercised by a singleton, it was by far the most powerful and potentially deadly, and not just for the singer alone. But Mahlo would not sing his Death Song, not yet, not even to kill the King, unless there were no other way, because it would kill him as well, and he was not ready to die. Not unless the dream that was bigger than life demanded it of him as the only way to Terran rule.

"A man is nothing without his giftmate." Hawke's voice was suddenly clear and rational, but his eyes were unreadable. "Nothing. Tell *that* to the King."

"Treason," whispered Tran. "The King's gift-mate . . ."

"And Mahlo's," said Hawke. His eyes closed. "And mine." A single tear escaped the corner of one eye to run down his cheek; then, while Mahlo and Tran stared at each other, wondering how rational Hawke really was, he began to giggle again and then to sing.

Tran shrugged. "If he did understand, who would believe him?"

Mahlo shook his head. "We're taking too many chances as it is. . . ."

"What would you do then, kill him?" asked Tran.

"Nine dead men make a fairy ring," sang Hawke. While Mahlo and Tran watched, he climbed to his feet and stood wavering, apparently oblivious to their presence again. "Now, which way was I going?" He peered owlishly down the corridor. "That portrait said the north wing, and this one said—what *did* this one say?" He looked up at the portrait and said pleasantly, "Excuse me. Was I looking for someone?"

"No need," said Mahlo. "You're right. He doesn't understand. He's quite mad." For a moment he stared at the Prince, his expression almost pitying.

Tran swallowed hard. "You wouldn't have killed him?"

Mahlo looked amused. "And you're the one who wants to be governor? Come along, we must get to work." They went out of the corridor, leaving the mad Prince babbling in the shadows.

When they were gone, Hawke touched the back of his head gently, where Mahlo had banged it against the wall, and stared pensively at the door through which they had departed. He wasn't babbling any-more.

21

Ugly might not have noticed the aircars flying a crisscross search pattern over the forest beyond the desert if Friend hadn't called them to her attention with his fascinated complaints. When she woke in the cave that morning, he was sitting on the ledge in the sunlight staring out of the valley, back toward the desert, meowing plaintively. From time to time he rose and paced a few steps, stiff-legged with irritation; then he sat again, staring and complaining.

Alarmed, Ugly jumped out of bed and hurried to the cave entrance to stand beside him, looking where he was looking. It took her a moment to realize what he saw; the aircars were so far away that even the nearest ones were barely more than dark spots against the bright morning sky, and the sound of their engines reached across the distance only because there were so many of them all flying at once, creating a high, thin buzzing sound like swarming insects.

The moment Ugly realized what they were, she backed away in sudden, blind terror till she came up against the rock wall of the cliff beside the cave mouth, then whirled and ducked inside. Aircars flying a search pattern like that could mean only one thing: hunters! More hunters than Godsgrace could have provided. They must have called out the hunters from surrounding villages. So many hunters, all looking for her. All ready to kill her, if they could catch her. . . .

She had sometimes imagined, in her happier fantasies, that Emmett Starling had only been stunned by his fall when she pushed him, not killed. That would have explained why the hunters had never come after her as she had expected. She had pretended it was unlikely that she could have outrun or evaded them, and so the fact that they never caught her meant they weren't chasing her.

It had been a daydream. A childish fantasy. The hunters had been behind her the whole time, slow and methodical and relentless, and they were behind her still. They were coming after her. They would not give up the search for a murderer. They would find her. They would kill her.

She huddled against the far back wall of the cave, trembling with fear and horror, staring with wide, anguished eyes at the bright cave mouth and beyond it at a patch of pure, brilliant blue in which, at any moment, a nearer aircar might appear with bristling guns, ready to blast the cave to rubble just on the chance that Emmett Starling's murderer was inside. . . .

She must send Friend away. They would kill him, too, if they found him with her. "Friend!" she called. "Friend, run away! Go! Quick, before they find us!"

Friend stalked regally into the cave to look at her, his amethyst eyes glinting with reflected sunlight, his tail straight up in the air. She noticed, irrelevantly, that he had already lost the baby shape he had when she found him. He was by no means full grown, but he was much heavier and his ears and tail no longer had the triangular look of kittenhood. She thought with absurd regret that if only human children grew as rapidly as kittens did, she might have left the Starlings years ago, or even never have been placed with them, and so never have brought them harm. . . .

"Friend, listen to me! Those are hunters out there, looking for me. You mustn't be with me when they find me, or they'll kill you, too."

Friend moved sedately forward and began to strop himself, purring, against her legs. The only way to get rid of him would be to chase him away with threats and violence, and she couldn't bring herself to do it. The hunters weren't very near yet. Perhaps they never would search this far from the forest.

With a start, she realized it might be true: the search

pattern was concentrated over the forest and moving seaward. They really might not look this far away; they might suppose she couldn't or wouldn't have crossed the desert. Cheered by the thought, she crept shakily back to the cave mouth to look at them again. They had moved no nearer. Not one had flown past the forest to look at the desert. They must think she wouldn't have tried to cross. She cowered in the shadows, watching them with growing hope.

There was no real need to hide, of course; they couldn't see an individual at such a distance even if they looked toward the mountains, which it now seemed unlikely they would do. But she didn't want to take the smallest chance of being seen. She spent most of the day crouched by the mouth of the cave, watching the searchers, slipping out only when she absolutely had to, and returning in haste. She could have gone deeper into the valley and been safe from any chance sighting, but she felt an irrational terror in the open, even when the aircars were out of sight. She felt vulnerable, exposed under the empty sky, and she imagined she heard nearer aircars where there were none at all.

When she did creep outside, she was as awkward and clumsy as ever she had been in the Starlings' home. Once she nearly fell off the path: she saved herself with a desperate effort, but sustained severe bruises in the process. That deepened her self-loathing: the Starlings had been right. She was a clumsy oaf, a waste of food, a monster, a murderer.

Visions of Emmett Starling lying dead on that gleaming yellow kitchen floor left her shivering in despair and regret. She had killed a man. One moment he had been living, breathing, full of plans and hopes and emotions, and the next he was cooling meat on a kitchen floor. She had done that to him. She had stolen his most precious, irreplaceable asset: his life. In one second's careless rage she had destroyed him and, with him, herself.

The Starlings believed in an afterlife, and Ugly had been raised in their beliefs, but the thought brought no comfort. She had always had difficulty imagining either Heaven or Hell, and to imagine Emmett Starling in either place was even more difficult. Emmett Starling in Heaven, with great white wings and a harp in his hands and a fatuous smile on his face? She couldn't make the vision real. He would have looked less out of place in the Hell that had been described to her as an icy gray wasteland so vast that the inmates would never even see each other. She could almost imagine him plodding wearily across an endless, featureless plain, his face set in its habitual lines of discontent, his eyes narrowed in remembered hatred for Ugly, who had put him there. . . .

She shook her head hard and the vision faded. Wherever Emmett Starling was now, she could not help him: could not give back what she had taken from him. "Maybe I should let them catch me," she said suddenly. "I'm no use to anyone, not even to me. I'm a murderer. I deserve to die."

At the sound of her voice, Friend came back into the cave from his vantage point on the ledge outside, and leaned against her, purring, looking up into her face expectantly until she began to stroke his fur. Then he leaned harder, and purred louder.

The feel of his body, warm against her legs and sleek under her hand, comforted her. Here was a living creature who cared about her, despite what she had done. Maybe he didn't, strictly speaking, *need* her, but he depended upon her for friendship. If the hunters killed her, he would be alone. He would manage, but he would be less happy. Even though he was only a cat, his happiness did matter.

If the Starlings' god wanted her life to punish her for what she had done, he would take it and that would be as it should be; but there was no need for her to think of courting death. If he wanted her dead, she could not avoid it. If he did not, then she had a right to whatever life she could make for herself in the wilderness. Perhaps not just a right, but a responsibility to live.

She had already encroached on the god's province by killing Emmett Starling: it would be just as much of an encroachment to seek her own death when she could avoid it. Death was the province of the god. Life was the responsibility of the living.

Having thus reasoned through despair to a new, frail purpose, she felt a sudden fierce determination to live. The fear that had held her shivering in the shadows throughout the long day left her at last, and she was so weak in its aftermath that she curled up where she was on the sand, with Friend at her side, and fell asleep watching the search pattern of aircars in the summer sky over the distant forest.

22

The People did everything in pairs. Just as no gift was complete without a giftmate, so no life was complete without a lifemate. No one of the People was or wanted to be self-sufficient. Whether this was due to genetics, to social training, or to both, was something only a Terran would ask. To the People it was as natural as eating and sleeping—activities which, like most others, were usually performed in groups of two or more.

Even the High King, whose Queen had been both his giftmate and his lifemate, was never wholly alone. He, like most others of the People, had many mates: workmates, playmates, soulmates, sexmates. They had helped him endure his bereavement when his Queen died: they shared his life and kept him company and always would. The entire society was a complexly *mated* structure of interwoven couples, so that no one was ever left to his own devices for long.

No one, that was, except Prince Hawke, who had no mates at all. He stood alone in the deserted corridor after Mahlo and Tran had gone, and felt the awful weight of his solitude, and wondered with desolate weariness why, in a society so perfectly and completely coupled, he had not since Onset been able to form even one close friendship.

The magicians had told him it was because of the nature of his gift and of his madness, and that once his gift was mated he would be able to lead a normal life. Those were just words. Empty, meaningless words, like the empty, meaningless life of a mad Prince alone in a world of couples.

He turned on his heel and strode purposefully down

the corridor, headed nowhere. "Singleton." He said it aloud and listened to the obscene echoes chase him along the bare stone floor: *singleton, singleton, singleton.* . . . Blind with rage and pain and grief, he walked straight into a wall so hard it knocked him silly.

The impact painfully jarred his half-healed knife wounds and started a new bruise on his forehead. He stood for a moment facing the wall, then raised his hands and put them against it on a level with his head. The stone felt damp and cold against his palms. Turning his head, he leaned his cheek against the stone. The grainy texture felt like coarse ice against his face, and smelled of dampness. He closed his eyes, unaware that his hands were slowly curling into fists. Tran and Mahlo had been talking treason. To whom could he take information like that?

He had heard them speak of a Breaker, but that was not what he remembered: not all of his madness was feigned. His precarious emotional balance depended so heavily on the avoidance of false hope that he unconsciously filtered all such references from his memory and understanding. He would not hope for a giftmate; he could not survive that hope. What he understood and remembered from Tran and Mahlo's conversation was that they were members of the pro-Terran faction that everyone knew existed among the People. The pro-Terrans wanted to overthrow the monarchy and embrace Terran ways. That two of such a faction should also be the High King's trusted friends, one of them his chief advisor, was an impossible situation.

Hawke opened his eyes and blinked against the flickering glare of a nearby torch set in the wall. He turned slowly, still leaning against the stone, and let himself slide to the floor with his back to the wall, indifferent to what such behavior would do to the fine fabric of his tunic and shirtsleeves. To whom could he take the information that Mahlo and Tran were traitors? Not to the High King, not without proof. Even if

Hawke weren't known to be mad, his word alone would not be enough against a man like Mahlo.

Alone. Hawke's word *alone.* His face twisted. He closed his eyes again, hard, and rubbed them with his fists like a child. If he were normal, he would have playmates, soulmates, friends; and even if none of them were telepaths, who through him could have heard that conversation between Tran and Mahlo, their belief in Hawke would have lent weight to his story if he brought it to the King. At the very least, they would have been people with whom he could have talked over the situation. They could have helped him to decide what to do.

He opened his eyes, let his hands drop to his lap, and stared unseeing at the opposite wall. He could go to a priest. One could talk over one's problems with a priest. Even a prince . . . even a *singleton* could bring his problems to a priest.

Not this problem. Not without proof. A priest, like the High King, would believe gentle, trusted Mahlo over the ill-behaved, mad Prince; and rightly so. Besides, how could he know the priest he chose wouldn't be pro-Terran, too? If Mahlo and Tran were, anybody might be. Anybody at all. And who knew what they might be plotting against the King?

He rolled his head against the stone at his back. The Terrans' gods threatened the old gods as insidiously as Terran technology threatened the old ways, but that didn't necessarily mean that no priests were pro-Terran. If Mahlo was, *any*body might be.

He was thinking in circles, and he knew it. He could not solve this problem alone; and without proof, he could not share it with anyone, even if he knew whom to trust. The only solution was to get proof. Enough proof that he could bring it to his father the King.

His sanity was too precarious for that to be a very promising course of action, and he knew it, but he could think of nothing else to do.

"Here, now, my lord Prince!"

Startled, he forced his eyes into focus. There was a

tall old woman standing before him, hands on hips, hair awry, dark eyes flashing. She wore the gray and scarlet of the housekeeping servants, but she scowled at him like a nanny. "Oh," he said stupidly, feeling very young and foolish under her gaze.

"Here, now, why are you sitting on the floor like that, you silly boy?"

"Oh, am I?" He looked around in surprise. "I don't know."

"Well, get up," she said impatiently. "Come on, you're too old to be acting like that, and you know it."

He climbed obediently to his feet and had to stifle a groan at the stiffness of his wounds.

"Didn't they even heal you?" She put out a hand to steady him. "Well, it serves you right, going into Town and getting into fights with Terrans."

When her hand touched his elbow, he looked at her in dull surprise. "You're real," he said.

"Of course I'm real. Don't try that silly mad-Prince business on an old woman like me, young Hawke. I don't believe it." She cackled cheerfully at his look. "Here, straighten your tunic. Look at what you've done to your nice silk shirtsleeves! Really, my lord Prince! What were you doing, sitting on the floor in this old corridor?"

For a mad instant he considered telling her the truth. To share his knowledge of Mahlo's treason with anyone, even an old servant woman, would be a relief. Just in time, he controlled the impulse. "There was no chair," he said dully, and wondered absently whether a person could die of sheer loneliness.

"Well, get along with you; this is the servants' quarters, don't you know that? Princes don't belong in here. Get back where you belong, there's a good boy." She put her hands on her hips again, glaring at him. "And for the gods' sake, *act* like a prince, can't you?" She shook her head, sending loose curls of ratty gray hair flying around her face. "I don't know what this world is coming to, I really don't." She compressed her lips, executed a sketchy curtsy, said, "By

your leave, my lord Prince," and walked away before
he could respond.

He was already out of the servants' corridor, mind-
lessly obeying her orders, before the humor of the
encounter struck him and he began to laugh. Two
maidservants going off duty stared in consternation
and edged nervously around him toward the door.
Their wide-eyed glances only made him laugh harder.

23

The search over the forest lasted for three days before the last of the aircars finally skimmed away toward the ocean. All the time the search cars were there, Ugly stayed in the cave as much as possible, and she deliberately put out her fire and left it out, lest it betray her. She wasn't confident she could start a new one when she wanted it, but the danger of getting caught was greater than her need for fire.

On the fourth morning, when she awoke to find the searchers gone at last, the first thing she did was to construct a shield for the cave entrance so that her fire, should she get it lighted again, would not be visible to the searchers if they came back. She made it out of overlapping layers of fern fronds tied with morning glory vines: the ferns would keep their shape and color as they dried, and they blended well with the color of the weeds and bushes that grew on the rocky slope around her cave.

That done, she just stood outside for a while, enjoying a sense of relieved well-being so powerful that she felt almost light-headed, as if escape from detection were a mind-altering drug. Friend was gone by then, presumably on a hunting expedition. During the days of Ugly's self-imprisonment, Friend had gone hunting each morning, but had brought nothing home to her. Perhaps he knew she was afraid to light a fire while the search cars were in sight. It was difficult to guess just how much he did understand. He often behaved as though he understood what was going on just as well as Ugly did, or better.

She no longer feared he would leave her and not come back. In the past three days it had become clear to her that their friendship meant as much to him as it

did to her. She had found a home in the valley and a
friend in the cat, and the hunters had not found her.
The sun was shining, a mountain orchid spread
magenta and lavender blossoms across a slate-gray
rock beside the mouth of her cave, and in the distance
the waterfall was throwing rainbows at the sky. Smiling with pure happiness, Ugly set out to explore her
valley.

By noon she had wandered clear across the valley
floor and up a ravine that cut through the moss-green
valley wall to one side of the waterfall. She had started
up the ravine with the vague thought that if she ever
decided to look for a pass through the mountains to
Far Harbor, this would be a good place to start. But
she wasn't looking for a pass today, so she was easily
sidetracked, first by a massive cascade of plump
scarlet starberries that covered one wall of the ravine
for a hundred meters, and then by a clotted mass of
creamy, sweet-scented narcissus that filled the air with
their heady perfume.

She was collecting a bouquet of narcissus blossoms
when a snow-white egret flew past her, its graceful
wings spread full out to catch the wind. She looked up
just in time to see the white splash of sun on those
wide-spread wings as it banked for a turn and went
out of sight, a bright flash against shadows and then
gone. She could not have said why she followed it. She
just did. Clutching her fragrant bouquet in one berry-
stained hand, she rose and went after the egret as if
someone or something had called her.

Perhaps someone—or something—*had* called her:
following the egret, she turned a corner in the ravine
and stepped into a blinding rainbow of light. For a
long moment she was so stunned by the brilliance of
the colors dancing around her like jewels in the air
that she couldn't move or think; she could only stand,
blinking, staring in awe.

When her vision cleared, she realized she was
standing at the mouth of a gully whose walls and floor
were completely covered with the brilliant crystal that

Terrans mined, and out of which they created the delicate works of art that had so frequently broken in Ugly's awkward grasp. Unthinking, still caught up in the wonder of her find, Ugly clasped her hands behind her back in an automatic, childlike gesture, as if they might otherwise reach out and destroy this beauty of their own volition. Her bouquet fell to the ground, forgotten. The crystal gully was so astonishing, so beautiful, so precious that Ugly dared not even approach it. Without taking her eyes from the fire and ice of its prism colors, she sank to a seat on a nearby rock.

At first she could clearly see all the crystals, grown several meters deep in the gully like the inside of a giant geode, their faceted sides gleaming in the light: but the brilliance dizzied her and the colors were like explosions behind her eyes. For a moment the world seemed to shimmer, like a landscape seen through heat haze, and the crystals seemed to melt and flow into one another in a blinding display of color on color; crimson and yellow, magenta and blue, deep green and vivid orange, all spinning and exploding like shards of the sun itself cast down upon the earth. . . .

The scene steadied and the crystals sprang apart again, separate and splendid in the light. The colors still shifted and swayed, not dizzily now, but gently, as they might underwater. Ghost forms materialized in the rainbowed haze of light, wavering and shimmering and coalescing: a palace made of crystal like cut diamonds, surrounded by crystal hills and forests of light. Winged creatures swam in the currents of color, their eyes glistening like gemstones, their faces cold and serene and strange.

Ugly blinked hard and stared. It was an underwater court, a prismed castle, a miniature city of crystal, wherein resided the Crystal Goddess whom Ugly had seen before in the forest shrine on the first day of her exile from Godsgrace. The winged creatures were of the Goddess's race. They moved about the miniature crystal palace and grounds on their daily business, apparently unaware of Ugly's presence as watcher. There were humans there too, larger than the winged creatures, but as at home in the palace and grounds as those were. And there were cats.

Everything was in miniature, as if seen at a great distance, and yet as clear as if it were as near as the gully itself. Ugly could see individual shingles on the rooftops of cottages near the crystal palace, and the ornate flower carvings on the columns of the palace. She could see the furniture inside the palace, and the dishes on a table, and the food in the dishes. At the same time, she had a panoramic, gods'-eye view of the palace as a whole, and of the village around it.

The people in the palace and village were almost all in pairs, as were the winged creatures and even the cats. Ugly felt an inexplicable pang of loneliness, though moments before, she had been satisfied with her solitude. It seemed that in the crystal world, no one except the Goddess herself did anything alone. In an odd way, Ugly felt left out, deserted, as if she belonged in that world, with someone from that world.

She watched the people there for a long time before she realized what all those couples were doing: moving things, building structures and works of art, gardening, housekeeping, all merely by looking at the objects they were dealing with. Almost no work was done in the ordinary way, by hand.

There was an old man with a woman at his side and a pair of cats at their feet; the four of them looked at raw crystals and the crystals slowly took on new, intricate, and beautiful shapes, not as though it were being carved, but as though it grew to their command. There was a young couple moving into a new home, bringing in furniture and arranging it by walking beside it and looking at it. There were two men preparing a meal . . . or watching a meal prepare itself. . . .

As Ugly watched, the scene began to shift and

change again, colors flowing into colors, swirling and coalescing into new forms, till the palace seemed to be no longer underwater: now it was perched on a sunlit hill, surrounded by forests that looked less like seaweed, more like the forest in which Ugly had first seen the Goddess. The couples who had swum in light now walked in sparkling gardens, but most of them performed the same tasks above water that they had done underwater. There was one major change: there were fires.

A gardener piled leaves and stared at them till they burned. A young woman looked at a cookstove till cheerful red flames appeared in the aperture of one of its burners. A pair of old men looked at the logs in a fireplace till they burst into flame.

They were doing what Ugly had done! All the work they were doing must be done the same way . . . but *how*? How could one move a piece of furniture or set a log on fire merely by looking at it? Ugly had done it, but *how*?

Prism colors fused and swirled. A flash of green became a brilliant sheet of emerald that drowned the scene and the world and threatened to drown Ugly. She gasped and lifted a hand uselessly to fend away the shimmering wall of color, and it retreated, muted without fading, and became mist. The Goddess smiled at her from the emerald depths, her eyes flashing green fire.

As before, Ugly was drawn to the Goddess almost against her will. She felt suddenly the awful, awesome desolation of her loneliness, and reached blindly toward the Goddess as toward a living creature for comfort, for safety, for warmth. Her hand met a prismed wall of light that it could not penetrate.

The Goddess swam toward her till her crystal hand touched the wall opposite Ugly's hand, and she smiled. "Not yet, child," she said gently. "I cannot reach you yet; you are too Terran, still. Friend will teach you, and this will lead you." She pressed something against the wall, and Ugly felt it against her hand. She automatically clutched it, staring into the Goddess's green, glowing eyes.

"You must find your giftmate," said the Goddess. Her voice was clear and sweet, like an audible manifestation of prismed crystal light. "Follow the crystal: you must find your giftmate. *You must find him!*"

On the last word she was gone, and the gully was just a crystal-lined gully again, transformed between one breath and the next from that green-tinged glorious fantasy to prosaic, shadowed reality. The sun had moved across the sky till the high walls of the gully cut its light from the crystal and broke the vision. Ugly was abruptly, shatteringly alone.

She had been sitting. She remembered sitting down when she first found the gully. Now she was standing at the mouth of the gully, her toes just touching the first glittering crystals, one hand upraised, fist clenched, pressing against . . . nothing. Nothing at all. There was no wall of light, no Goddess, nothing but an ordinary gully in an ordinary mountain ravine. Admittedly the gully contained a rich lode of crystal, but the rest was—had been—fantasy. Blinking back sudden tears, swallowing against a painful lump in her throat, Ugly lowered her upraised hand.

There was something in it. She opened her fingers to look, and a last ray of the receding sun struck crystal, flashing one brilliant sheet of green light across the gully from the shard of crystal in her hand.

24

The new temple of Lanalei, built on the reservation since the coming of the Terrans, was structurally less impressive than the older temples in Town; but it was just as holy, its keepers just as earnest, and its walls and altar decorated perhaps even more beautifully than those in Town, with crystal and stone sculptures and mosaics depicting the history of the People and the Goddess. The air was thick with the scent of sea-roses and the blue, sweet smoke of incense. Hawke did not know why he was there.

He was in one of his difficult moods, confused and consequently arrogant: he spoke to no one, and his expression was so forbidding that no one spoke to him. In his more rational moments he did not mind being called the mad Prince, and in fact he encouraged the belief that he was almost helplessly mad; but at times like this, when he lost control and the confusion of his madness overtook him, he could not bear the thought of doing unintentionally what he so often did intentionally to outwit his enemies: playing the fool.

He could not stand to think that someone might realize he did not know what he was doing and could not rationally control his actions. That was fine for play-acting, but the reality was too frightening. He fought it in every way he could—despairingly, because he knew that he would fail. If he did not know what he was doing or what he had done, how could he give the appearance of anything but a madman?

Now he stood, bewildered and angry with his bewilderment, in the temple of Lanalei, and wondered why he had come there. He recalled no inten-

tion to stop in a temple, and could not think why he
would have done it.

If it had been an ordinary building, he might simply
have cursed and left it. He had nowhere else in
particular to go, and could not remember where he
had been, but he would have gone out to walk in the
wind till his head cleared, if he had found himself
anywhere else. But his presence here might just possibly be the will of the Goddess instead of another
manifestation of his madness. He was never sure he
believed that this Goddess or indeed any of the old
gods still lived, but neither was he certain that they
did not. They had once been powerful. Perhaps they
were powerful still.

He moved toward the altar, ignoring a staring
acolyte who perhaps had heard tales of the mad
Prince but had never encountered him before. There
was a bowl of incense sticks at the foot of the altar,
and a bowl of sand in which to place the lighted sticks.
The crystal image of the Goddess looked serenely over
the heads of worshippers, toward the crystal seascape
on the far wall. Bowing gracefully to her indifferent
form, Hawke threw his cloak back and lighted a stick
of incense, placed it in the bowl of sand, and mur-
mured the standard prayer: "Help me to be worthy."
One never said worthy of what.

Stepping back from the altar, he saw a tawny young
cat come out from behind the altar cloth to descend
the stairs and seat itself beside him. He ignored it. A
gust of wind blew open the temple doors and rushed
down the aisle, singing through the windchimes overhead like a thousand tiny bells.

Even if Lanalei had called him here, he had done
his duty with incense and prayer, and there seemed to
be no further reason to stay. He bowed again and
turned, cape swirling, into the wind that still rushed
down the aisle and shook the crystal windchimes. A
sudden, powerful gust caught at his cloak and crashed
through the windchimes so vigorously that one crystal

broke and a single finger-sized shard fell gleaming to the floor between Hawke and the tawny cat beside him.

Without thinking, Hawke retrieved the crystal shard and put it in his pocket. The weight of it was oddly comforting. "Go away," he told the cat. Placidly unheeding, it followed him out of the temple.

25

When Ugly returned to the cave with her shard of crystal in her hand, she found Friend waiting for her beside the body of a large squirrel brought back from his morning hunt. He watched her clean it, and accepted the job of burying the entrails while she laid a fire.

She proceeded as if she had every confidence that her fire-starting trick would work again, but she was almost as startled when it did as she had been the first time it happened. It seemed easier this time. The shard of crystal, which she had laid on a rock by the fireplace while she made her preparations, seemed to focus her concentration.

When the squirrel was skewered and roasting along with some round, starchy cattail roots she had gathered on her way back from the crystal gully, Ugly sat beside the fire and picked up the shard of crystal the Goddess had given her. She stared at it for a long time, watching the play of firelight off its facets. Friend sprawled in the sand beside her, washing up from his morning's labors.

If fire-starting was easier with the crystal, what about the other things the people in her vision had done? Could she do those things, too? Surely not. And yet. . . .

She looked up from the crystal to the firewood stacked at the back of the cave. She would need to bring more of it to the fire before the food was cooked. Perhaps that nice, round, straight log. . . .

She nearly dropped the crystal in shock when the log lifted gently off the pile in response to her thought. She gasped in surprise, and the log fell back onto the pile with a clatter that dislodged two smaller sticks.

She stared at the crystal, her eyes wide and glinting in the light. Friend rolled over and put one paw on her knee. She looked at him.

"I didn't *do* anything." Her voice sounded frail and small. "I just thought maybe that log, and it moved!"

Friend blinked.

"I thought I was being silly to try something like that." She closed her hand over the crystal. "How did I *do* that?"

Friend's tail twitched. He yawned and stretched gracefully, then began to clean a front paw. She reached absently to pet him, and opened her other hand to look at her crystal again.

"I'm not sure I like this." Colors jumped and ran across the cave walls, brilliant and swift. The crystal felt warm to her touch, like a live thing in her hand. She hurled it away from her in sudden panic.

Friend was on his feet in an instant to retrieve it. He brought it back in his mouth and dropped it into her reluctantly outstretched hand. It was undamaged, a gleaming, glittering chunk of tangible light in the palm of her hand.

By evening she had become quite adept at moving objects she wasn't touching. Once she was accustomed to the idea, it seemed a perfectly sensible thing to do.

26

When his giftmate was killed in a boating accident, Mahlo could have sought a new giftmate. He need not have whistled crystal with anyone new; his gift could have been happily mated with any of several others, to create different talents perhaps more useful in this age of Terran technology. But he had elected not to mate it again. He had playmates, workmates, and a lifemate to keep him company, and the lesser gifts did not require mating as Hawke's gift did.

Mahlo's lifemate Jorah had provided him with two sets of twins in close succession, so that his homelife was a happy jumble of child-oriented activities. His house was filled with all the Terran tools and toys he could buy. He was determined that his children would not grow up to be backward "natives," technologically ignorant and out of place in the Terran world.

He had known all his life that the future was with Terra: that seemed obvious. His own parents had been unable to provide him with an education that would have enabled him to make a place for himself in the technological world outside the reservation. To Terrans he was only an ignorant native: a fit subject for study by the Terran anthropologists who made periodic sorties onto the reservation like zoologists studying wild animals. They had been studying the People on the reservation since before Mahlo was born. They would be studying the People on the reservation after Mahlo was dead. Mahlo was going to get his children off the reservation.

He would have done the same for any children he could reach; his dream was that someday there would be no reservation. Someday all the People's children would have learned Terran ways and gone out to take their rightful places in the Terran world, till there was no one left for the Terrans to study and to exclaim over and to condescendingly aid. The People would not live in a zoo forever.

Arguments that the People's heritage would be irrevocably lost by his plan only angered him. The People's heritage was backward tribal superstition. It kept them at the "beads and baubles for the natives" stage when they should by rights have been joining the ruling classes. Terrans had conquered the galaxy: what was the superstition-ridden heritage of the People beside that?

It had taken Mahlo years to master Terran computers, but he had three of them in his home now, and saw to it that both sets of twins spent ample play time with them, painlessly learning through fun what he had learned through agonizing labor. Each day when he came home from the palace it was his habit to play with the twins, preferably using the computers or some other Terran technology in their play, while his lifemate had a parting chat with her workmates and greeted whatever couple had been invited to share their evening meal.

Tonight he and all four children were playing their new computer game "Space Chase," which was actually a thinly disguised course in astrophysics that the Terran salesman had had the temerity to suggest might be too difficult for children only five and six years old. Perhaps it would be, if the children in question were Terran. Children of the People were not so slow. Mahlo found "Space Chase" more difficult than his children did.

The five of them were sprawled on the floor in the family room with the computer when the Messenger from the palace arrived. She was one of Mahlo's workmates, and an old friend of the family, so Jorah brought her straight in to Mahlo, who rose to greet her. "Welcome, Nishka. You're in time for dinner if you want it."

The children squealed with delight and ran to

Nishka, demanding stories; she and her giftmate were storytalkers. Together they were one of many such couples whose gift enabled them to remember and recite the entire history of the People as wanted. Unmated, each was without any apparent gift at all; but a mated storytalker temporarily apart from his or her giftmate was still a talented storyteller: a sort of walking library, usually willing to oblige for entertainment. This time, however, Nishka fended the children deftly and shook her head at Mahlo, her pale brown curls glistening. "Business, Mahlo. Urgent."

He was aware, as always, how out of place Nishka seemed in a domestic scene, like a wolf in a toybox. Messengers were, of necessity, fierce warriors: the messages they carried were those too politically explosive to be sent by crystal or by telephone, and the tendency to destroy the Messenger who carried bad news was not limited to Terrans. Nishka looked her part.

She was of less noble blood than Mahlo and should have been larger than he, but a frail childhood had stunted her growth; she was nearly as small as royalty. But she was no longer frail. In spite of her size, she managed not even to look frail, and it wasn't only because she was invariably bristling with deadly weapons.

She was dressed like a warrior, in sturdy metal-reinforced leathers, and Mahlo knew that the visible weapons were not the only ones she carried, though he would have thought the visible ones would be adequate to nearly any occasion. She looked as deadly as her weapons; her face was gaunt and hollow, the mouth grim, the pale eyes cold. Even her smile was charged with an undercurrent of danger, although with children present she did her best to look as amiable as Mahlo.

Jorah, looking from Nishka to Mahlo, said sharply, "Children. Come, darlings. It's time to feed the cats." She threw an apologetic little grimace at Nishka as she led them away.

Mahlo absentmindedly administered one of his amiable smiles as Jorah left the room with the children, but his mind was already back at work. "What is it, Nishka?—no, wait, we'll talk in my office." He led the way, and closed the door behind them. "Well?"

Nishka moved past him with a flick of her cloak and settled comfortably in a chair beside his desk. "It's that Starling one that Tran is so sure of."

Mahlo went to his desk, but did not sit. "What about her?"

"Arkos is sending another man to interview the Starlings."

Mahlo sat down. "Damn."

"If Tran is right, the new man will find out."

Mahlo rubbed his forehead. "Who is it, do you know?"

She shook her head. "If Arkos has selected someone, he has not yet said. Only that it will be a Terran." She drew a gleaming steel dagger from a sheath up one sleeve and eyed it judiciously. "Does it matter? We cannot let anyone go."

"I know."

"He would know Tran lied."

"I know."

"He might guess that you have lied."

"I know." Mahlo's watery eyes seemed hypnotized by the dagger. "And even if Tran and Hesta go along again, what could they do?"

"Another unfortunate accident?"

Mahlo shook his head without taking his gaze from the dagger. "How many unfortunate accidents to people interviewing the Starlings could even Arkos be expected to believe? If no one he sends comes back . . ."

"Arkos is trusting, but not that trusting. I agree." Nishka polished the dagger briefly on one leather pant leg, then put it away. "And yet, if anyone he sent did come back . . ."

"I know." Mahlo blinked and looked away. "Damn. I had hoped he was satisfied."

"I could kill the Prince." Her voice held no emotion; it was only a suggestion, a course of action that seemed logical to her.

Mahlo shook his head sharply. "No. Not that."

Nishka smiled. "Too direct for you?"

He did not smile. "You always were too bloodthirsty to understand subtleties. Sometimes I think your memories of history have warped your mind."

She shrugged. "Perhaps. What, then?"

He thought for a moment. "We can't stop the new man, but we could delay him. Keep him from leaving, somehow. Maybe for as much as a week or two."

"What good would that do?"

"It would buy us time. I've started a plan that I think will work. If it does, Arkos will lose interest in the Starling, because what I'm going to do is convince him that I've found the Breaker elsewhere. I have someone in mind. If Arkos believes it, he'll forget her."

"How can you convince him that anyone else is the Breaker? Oh, I suppose you can convince Arkos, but only until Hawke meets the substitute. He would know. And then Arkos would know. And I doubt that either of them would believe that you made an honest mistake."

"Hawke would never meet the substitute." Mahlo smiled amiably.

"Never meet—? How . . . ? . . . Oh." Nishka matched his smile. "Anything I can do to help?"

"Not just yet." Mahlo steepled his fingers over the desk and let his smile broaden. "But I expect there will be a little something for you later on. Something right in your line of expertise."

They smiled at each other in perfect understanding.

27

Ugly spent most of the next afternoon working by hand with her tapa leaves, soaking and beating them to wear the pulp away. That left behind the fibrous skeleton which, when dried, would be a fine, soft fabric from which to make new garments. All the time she was working, she was aware of the crystal shard in her pocket, but she resisted the temptation to take it out and play with it. She had done enough of that when she first brought it back to the cave. She needed an afternoon of absolutely commonplace reality with no visions and no magic tricks. Work with the tapa leaves satisfied that. It was exhausting, dirty work, but when she quit at sunset she had amassed a respectable number of cleaned leaves, which she spread on the rocks to dry in the morning sun.

Friend greeted her at the mouth of the cave with a horned rabbit for dinner. Ugly cleaned and skewered it and put it over the fire to cook before she finally took out the crystal shard again. It caught the light of the fire and splattered it across the cave walls in brilliant reds and greens and purples. Ugly turned it slowly, watching the fragmented reflections on the faces of the facets: miniature flames leaping, Friend yawning, her own pale amethyst eyes staring back at her. . . .

The rabbit dripped hot juices onto the fire, and brief flames shot up, echoed in miniature in the crystal. One facet caught the light full on, splintered it, and hurled a scarlet swath of it directly into Ugly's eyes. She blinked against sudden dizziness. The reflections in the crystal swirled, misted, coalesced. . . . She was back at the crystal gully, looking at the crystal palace. But the crystal of the palace was changing into stone and wood. The prismed sunlight that had lighted the gully became flickering firelight and the occasional harsh blue light of an imported Terran fixture. The palace was neither underwater nor perched on a sunlit hill: it sprawled up one side of a steep, dark hill lighted only by torches and starlight.

As before, it was a world in microcosm, and Ugly could see it all at once and yet perceive every minute detail: the guards at the gate, grim in the torchlight, their weapons gleaming; the delicate tracery of lead flowers and vines on a stained-glass window of the palace; the white cloud of a horse's breath in the chill air of the highland night as it stamped its hooves impatiently outside a closed cottage door; even the ginger stripes of a tomcat taking his ease on the palace steps.

The scene was entirely silent, but Ugly could imagine the clatter of cartwheels and guards' boots against stone, the jingle of harness, the whisper of wind through the cracks and corners of stone and through the needle-sharp leaves of the yellow shower trees that flanked the main road to the palace. She could see into the palace, past stone and wood as if it were crystal. Without intention, or awareness of any particular goal, she moved swiftly along shadowed corridors in a soundless rush like a purposeful ghost, past doors and guards and flaming torches, up uncarpeted staircases, through bright chambers, till she reached the door of a certain room in a certain corridor. . . .

She did not enter, but could somehow see past the ornately carved wooden door, or through it, to the room beyond. It was a smaller room than most in the castle, and the only light was the fire in the stone fireplace that took up most of one wall. The furnishings were grand by Ugly's standards: a lacquered chest, a heavily carved chair, and a bed piled high with satin, velvet, and brocade bedding and pillows, deliciously soft and inviting. There was a cat asleep on the hearth, its tawny fur dyed orange by the fire. But what Ugly had come for, she knew, was to see the man.

He strode back and forth across the narrow room,

hands clasped at his back, head bowed: a brooding young man, in strange flowing garments, with a jeweled knife at his belt. Firelight glinted on the red-gold of his hair. His skin was a darker gold; he might have been cast of burnished bronze. His face was as elegantly modeled as if it had been done by a master sculptor, but it was beautiful only in terms of lines and planes, like a work of art made by a sculptor who liked to depict ugly things with beautiful lines. Like Ugly's, his face was too coarse for human beauty, the bones too evident, the eyes and mouth too large. Yet Ugly was drawn to him as she had never been drawn to any properly attractive human she had met.

She had felt the same despair that rounded his shoulders and pulled down the corners of his mouth. She was all too familiar with the compressed rage and anguish, aimless and implacable, that sent him pacing back and forth across that narrow room as if it were a cage. She knew too well what fierce longing for something unidentified knotted one's muscles like that, and shadowed one's eyes with the ghosts of all the big and little hopes that had died. He was as ugly as she, and he looked as lost and as sullen and as defiantly, desperately determined to survive as she.

Was he hated, too, by those around him, because he was a clumsy, unattractive misfit? She thought he must be; otherwise, why was he alone with his tormented misery? "You should run away," she said. "It's less lonely to be alone, and maybe your cat would go with—" She broke off, startled: at the sound of her voice, he looked suddenly and directly at her. There were blue smudges under his shadowed eyes. She had been right about his ugliness; it was perhaps even worse than hers. His eyes were a paler, even more disturbing shade of lavender than hers, and they seemed to stare right at her with the same wary hostility Friend had displayed toward her at first.

She must have made some involuntary movement, because the crystal image shivered and dissolved, and a new scene formed in its place: a different room in the palace appeared in the glistening depths of the stone. Here she saw two men, both older than the man she had seen in the other room, and both just as ugly as he: big-boned, light-haired, pale-eyed, they had none of the qualities of beauty recognized in Godsgrace. It had never occurred to Ugly to question the standards of Godsgrace, and it did not occur to her now.

The two men were dressed similarly to the younger one she had seen. The older of these two wore a circlet of gold set with chips of crystal around his head, rather like a simple crown. He sat in a chair much grander than his companion's, and had the unmistakable air of one long accustomed to power. This scene, like the last, was silent; but Ugly could see when the players spoke, and when the older man spoke, particularly to his servant, he was listened to very attentively, obeyed promptly, and honored with much ceremonious bowing. He was obviously a man of considerable importance.

He was also very possibly related to the younger man in the other room. There was something about the shape of his face, the gestures he made with his long, graceful fingers, even the look of his pale eyes, that reminded her of the younger man. This man could be his father. There was none of the son's half-wild look in the father's eyes, yet there was a strong similarity. The son had the hungry look of a predator. The father was well fed, but a predator still; serene, perhaps, in his age and his comfort, but dangerous to underestimate if one were his enemy.

Ugly felt an affection for him that almost made her smile. He could be a good father if he chose. It would be hard for him to find patience for someone as like him as his son, and harder still to understand such a one, but the love between them would be unquestioned and unquestionable. That was a good basis upon which to build understanding if they chose.

This man's companion did not belong in such a pleasant vision. She looked at his weak, watery eyes and his empty, affable smile, and she shivered. If the other two were predators, this one was a scavenger; cunning, sly, not too choosy, and all the more dangerous because he always smiled. She could not have said how she knew that. He looked like just a mild, middle-aged man of amiable disposition. Yet she was as frightened of him as she had been of the aircar search over the forest, or perhaps even more so. When he suddenly turned his gaze toward her, she reacted with a panicky start that shifted the crystal instantly, but not before she had seen the chilling blue of his eyes.

Now she was looking into a chapel. Not like the ones in Godsgrace, but unmistakably a chapel nonetheless, with an altar to the Crystal Goddess glittering with crystal sculptures, central of which was the Goddess herself.

The main part of the chapel was blue with the smoke of incense, shadowed but not gloomy, with tinkling crystal windchimes overhead and a dark-robed priest before the altar patiently lighting a great many stubby white candles. He looked up as someone entered the chapel, and Ugly clearly saw the play of expressions on his face as he saw who it was; awe, then impatience, then pity, and finally a politely assumed mask of impersonal friendliness. Ugly looked at the lean, shadowed figure that had prompted such a reaction.

It was the wild young man from the palace, with the tawny cat at his heels. Candlelight glowed yellow on the burnished gold of his hair and softened the harsh lines of his face. Ugly had no idea why his arrival had caused such an odd array of emotions in the priest, but she had recognized them all, and a passionate surge of protective affection for the pale-eyed stranger swept over her as she watched him approach the priest.

Perhaps the strength of her emotion made her hand tremble. Something shifted the crystal. It caught at the firelight and splintered it into dancing streaks and pinpoints all over the cave, and threw one blinding sheet of green into Ugly's eyes.

When she could see again, there were no visions in the crystal. There were only reflections, small, fragmented, and flat. After a moment she put the crystal away and turned the rabbit over the fire.

28

Hawke and the priest both looked up at the image of Lanalei just in time to see the green light fade from her eyes. "I thought someone was here," said Hawke. "Was it the Goddess?"

"She was here," said the priest. "And perhaps another." He looked speculatively at Hawke, wondering just how mad he really was. "You say you felt her presence, my lord Prince?"

Hawke was looking down at the tawny cat at his heels. "Go away. Shoo."

"She belongs with you, my lord Prince," said the priest.

Hawke looked at him in childlike surprise. "This cat does? Belongs with me? Why do you say that?"

The priest finished lighting his candles and stood back to survey the result with satisfaction. They made a very fine light that was reflected a hundredfold in the crystal on the altar. "Because it is true. Where did she get you?"

Hawke looked at the cat in confusion. "At . . . I don't know." He looked around the chapel. "Not here. But a place like this. There were windchimes. I know, because one broke while I was there."

"What broke?" The priest's voice was sharp. "A windchime? In a temple?"

"I suppose it must have been a temple. Yes, I'm sure of it." Hawke withdrew the shard of crystal from his pocket and held it out with the innocent trust of a child. "See? This fell, and I kept it." He blinked. "I don't know why."

The priest reached out to close Hawke's hand over the crystal and push it back toward him. "It was a gift from the Goddess. Put it away. Keep it safe. Do you understand me? It was a gift from Lanalei, my lord Prince."

"How do you know?" Hawke's voice held the sullen challenge of a scolded boy.

"I am her priest. I know what I know."

"That's no answer."

"Perhaps, but it is the best I have, my lord Prince."

Hawke put the crystal away. "Was the cat her gift, too?" he asked.

The priest smiled. "You may be her gift to the cat, my lord Prince."

Hawke made an indelicate sound. "A poor gift, then. An unmated Maker is of no use to anyone. Not even himself."

The priest's brows lifted. "I thought you understood: the Breaker does live. And as she is female, perhaps she will prove to be your lifemate, as well as your giftmate."

"Perhaps she will prove to be a figment of my father's imagination."

The priest shook his head. "No, no, my lord Prince, listen to me. Don't you realize why the Goddess has taken such an interest in you? I thought you understood. The crystal, the cat . . . She must have your giftmate under her protection. That's why I say the Breaker is female, you understand. Because Lanalei has taken her under her protection."

Hawke shook his head stubbornly. "The search is my father's fantasy."

"I have heard of the search. Aircars over the windward forest, a friend tells me. But there is no need for that, my lord Prince. The Goddess will bring you your Breaker when it is safe to do so."

"Safe? Why safe? Would it be unsafe for her to be here now?"

"Perhaps, my lord Prince." Could the Prince be so ignorant of palace politics? But perhaps he could; he clearly had only a very feeble grasp of reality. "Perhaps just now it is not quite safe for her to come to you."

Hawke shrugged the thought away. "Perhaps. And perhaps she isn't here because she doesn't exist."

"She exists, my lord Prince." Of that the priest was certain, now that he had seen Lanalei's gifts.

Hawke looked at him for a long moment, his amethyst eyes disconcertingly clear and penetrating. Then he shook his head and his gaze fell. "Aircars over the windward forest?" he said, and shook his head. "No . . . that was not my father's search. Not that." He looked up again, and his eyes were dull and confused, his expression uncertain. "Did you say I must keep the cat?" he asked with a child's reluctance.

A flicker of impatience crossed the priest's face, but his voice was gentle. "Yes, my lord Prince. You must keep her with you."

"Very well," said the mad Prince. "Come along, cat." The cat rose and stalked gravely out of the chapel with him.

29

At first light the next morning, Ugly returned to the gully of crystal. She did not know quite what she expected to find there; perhaps more visions, or some more comprehensible message from the Goddess. What she found was only a crystal-lined tear in the earth, bright as diamonds and cold as ice. She sat down, staring at the harsh beauty of its hard-faceted silence, and realized with a pang of terrible longing that what she had hoped for was another vision of the wild-eyed youth she had seen the night before.

His features were as clear to her in memory as if she were seeing him again in the crystal: the narrow face harsh with tension, the eyes bruised by shadows; the too-prominent cheekbones and the vulnerable width of his mouth; the dark line of his brows, sorrowfully slanted and angrily drawn together over the bridge of the sharp nose that was just slightly bent by some old break imperfectly set. . . .

She could see exactly the disarray of the red-gold hair; the way it had fallen almost across one eye and, on the other side, had been pushed back behind an ear just as much too pointed as hers. She remembered the bones of his jaw and chin, just as much too prominent as hers. She remembered every detail of his strange bright costume, from boots and tunic and belt to the swirling floor-length cloak tossed over his shoulders. Most of all, she remembered the fierce desperation in his amethyst eyes that should have seemed as startlingly unattractive to her as her own, but hadn't.

She had hoped for another vision of him, but the crystal remained still and silent, an enigmatic encrustation in a mountain gully, nothing more. She had been watching its bright, empty reflections in disappointed resignation for over an hour when Friend-appeared at her side with the gnawed foot of a squirrel in his mouth. He dropped it at her feet and stared expectantly up at her.

"Does this mean you want me to cook your lunch, or did you just want me to know you're a successful hunter?" she asked him.

He sat down, still staring intently.

"Well," she said, "I suppose there's not much reason to stay here; the crystal is just crystal. I guess the Goddess doesn't want to tell me anything more."

He rose expectantly.

"Okay, okay." She rose, and he led her back toward the cave. "How much do you understand, anyway, Friend?"

He glanced over his shoulder at her, his eyes wide with innocence.

It was during that trek across the valley floor toward their cave, with the waterfall misting blue in the distance and the sheltering green walls of the Mysterious Mountains towering overhead, that she realized she was going to leave the valley soon. She did not really want to go. She was happy here, at home in the cave that she had been preparing for long-term residence, with Friend for a companion and the deep mountain silence around them.

The thought of seeking a way through the mountains to Far Harbor was daunting, and the thought of entering that city's crowds was terrifying; yet that was what she was going to do. "Follow the crystal," the Goddess had said: "You must find your giftmate."

Ugly had no idea what a giftmate was, but the crystal had shown her strange people and places, and a young man with ghosts in his eyes. She believed she would find him, or perhaps her giftmate, whatever that was, in Far Harbor. For reasons she didn't even try to understand, that search was so important that she must accept the risk of being caught and executed as a murderer.

When she began packing after lunch, Friend didn't seem surprised at all.

30

The tawny cat accompanied Hawke into the High King's audience chamber with her nose and tail in the air and such an expression of regal superiority on her face that even if the guards had been inclined to challenge her, they might have thought twice about it. Hawke himself looked much less at home in their royal surroundings than the cat did.

King Arkos greeted the cat as soberly as he greeted his son. "Won't you introduce us, Hawke?" he asked.

Hawke looked at the cat. "I don't know her name." He took the seat next to his father and gazed blankly around the room. "Why am I here, my lord King?"

"Because I sent for you." Arkos held out a hand to the cat, who sniffed it disdainfully and then began to strop herself against his legs. Arkos stroked her and said regretfully, "I am too much alone since my Queen died. A cat would be good company."

The cat leaned against him briefly, then moved to Hawke's side and sat at his feet, looking back at the King.

"Of course I didn't mean *you*," said the King.

"A priest said the Goddess Lanalei gave me to her," said Hawke.

"Gave you to the cat?" asked Arkos. "I see. Did he say why?"

"I don't know. Why am I here?"

"I told you. Because I sent for you." Arkos was still entranced by the cat. There had been a time when, with Queen Lian, he could converse with cats. It had been pleasurable as well as useful. Lian had enjoyed their sense of humor. Arkos had never understood a cat's joke, but he had enjoyed Lian's enjoyment. How he missed her! He pushed the thought away impatiently and, to cover his momentary lapse, said the first thing that came to mind: "You must give her a name."

"She has a name."

Of course she had. But how did Hawke know that? Had he spoken with her? "What is it?"

Hawke shrugged, staring vacantly at the cat. "I don't know."

"Then how do you know she has one?"

"Everyone has a name." Hawke sighed, gazed at the far wall for a moment, and said suddenly, "Cat."

The cat looked up at him, ears perked, amber eyes narrowed.

"What's your name?"

The cat purred.

"There you are," said Hawke. "May we go now?"

"I didn't send for you to learn the name of your cat," said Arkos. "I didn't know you had a cat."

"I haven't. She has me."

Arkos poured a cup of tea and offered it to Hawke, who accepted it with a look of profound confusion, as though he hadn't the smallest idea what he was expected to do with it. Arkos poured himself a cup and sat back in his chair, smiling with tolerant affection. "Mahlo has found us your giftmate, Hawke."

Hawke spilled his tea. Bush appeared from behind their chairs to clean up the mess. Hawke put the teacup on a table beside his chair and reached down to stroke the cat. "Sorry, cat. Did I get that on you?"

"It's true, Hawke. I'm sure of it," said Arkos.

"The King That Was and Will Be never would," chanted Hawke. "The Prince that is and wasn't understood."

"I tell you, he exists, son."

Hawke looked at him sharply. *"He?"*

Arkos nodded. "His name is Petal, and he's in hiding somewhere in Town. His mother is Lady Sara: you've heard of her? A drunk and a disgrace, but noble-born. She is rabidly pro-Terran, which is why she has sent her son into hiding. I want you to find him. You know Town better than anyone."

"She sent him and he went? Just like that?" asked Hawke. "You claim he is my Breaker and he hides from me?" He shook his head in disbelief. "Ridiculous. Do you believe every scrap of nonsense Mahlo feeds you?"

Arkos didn't move, but his eyes flashed and his expression hardened and he was suddenly quite clearly the High King. "You forget yourself."

"Sorry, my lord King." Hawke tried unsuccessfully to look indifferent to the rebuke. He resented the awkwardness of the fact that his father could never wholly put aside his job; it was not only what he did, but also what he was. And he could grant extra leeway, in conversation, to the half-mad son he loved, but he could not permit mockery even from him; one does not mock the King. "I wish you were a shoemaker," said Hawke.

Arkos smiled. "Life would be simpler, would it not? Tell me, Hawke, why do you so dislike Mahlo?"

What could he say? That he, the mad Prince, thought he had heard Mahlo discussing treason with Tran? "I don't know," he said, and hated the sullen tone of his own voice. "The priest said my giftmate would be female."

Arkos nodded, well accustomed to his son's sometimes disconcertingly abrupt changes of subject. "And is that why you doubt that Petal is the one?"

"It is a reason." He sounded sullen, still.

"Not a very good reason," said Arkos. "Petal is homosexual."

Hawke didn't move. His expression didn't change. But there was uncertain and unwilling hope in his sudden, tense stillness. Homosexuality was not regarded with distaste among the People: one had an obligation to produce offspring, and most homosexuals dutifully fulfilled it. How they enjoyed themselves outside that duty was regarded as a private matter between them and their lifemates. Hawke swallowed hard. "Lanalei would . . ." He cleared his throat. "To her, a male homosexual would be much the same as a woman."

"Yes." Arkos smiled.

Hawke shook his head in sudden doubt. "No," he said. "No. The Breaker—if there ever was a Breaker —is dead."

"My lord King." Bush had materialized again at the King's side.

Arkos drew a breath, held it, then let it out slowly, staring in weary impatience at Hawke. "Yes?"

"A Messenger seeks entry, my lord King," said Bush.

Arkos closed his eyes. "Very well. Bring in the Messenger." Bush walked swiftly toward the great doors and Arkos looked again at his son. The interruption had dulled his anger. He had no trouble keeping it from his voice. "Why, Hawke?"

Hawke looked at him. Something flickered in his eyes: something dark and despairing. He did not answer.

The doors opened and the Messenger Nishka entered. Her brown curls were pulled back from her face in a style that made her look more gaunt and grim than ever. Her pale green eyes showed no expression at all as she glanced at Hawke, then swept back her cloak and knelt before the King. "My lord King." Her voice was as grim as her face.

"Rise," said Arkos.

She straightened gracefully, rose to her feet, and stood at attention, her gaze steadfastly meeting the King's, as was polite. "The Terran Igor McShane has agreed to accompany Tran and Hesta to revisit those Starlings as you requested, my lord King."

Arkos frowned. "Didn't Mahlo tell Tran I changed my mind about that?"

"He was uncertain, my lord King. It seemed best to proceed until you made your wishes known."

Arkos made a dismissing gesture with one hand. "There's no need to bother those Terran Starlings again. Their fosterling can't be the Breaker; Mahlo has found him in Town."

Nishka's eyelids flickered. "He has found the Breaker, my lord King?"

"We think so," said Arkos. "We're almost certain. Call off the Starling interview and thank the Terran McShane."

She bowed. "Yes, my lord King." She looked at Hawke, her eyes oddly hooded. "My congratulations to you, my lord Prince."

She had already turned to walk away when Hawke said suddenly, in a singsong voice, "My congratulations to you, lord Mahlo."

Nishka resisted the impulse to glance over her shoulder at him. She left the presence as swiftly as was seemly and released her breath audibly as the doors closed behind her. Then, aware of the covertly staring guards, she straightened and walked away, her face set. The Terran McShane had been spared a series of frustrating personal problems that would have delayed his trip to Godsgrace. Arkos was more fool than they hoped. But how much did Hawke really understand?

In the audience chamber, Arkos regarded his son with thinly concealed irritation. "Must you always do that?"

"What have I done?" The vacant grin was gone from Hawke's face as suddenly as it had come. "Have I offended you, my lord King?" He blushed in agonized embarrassment. "Oh, gods. I don't always know what I do. Did I do something wrong?"

Arkos sighed. "No, son. You've done nothing wrong. Will you go to Town to find your Breaker?"

"He is not my giftmate."

"How can you be so sure?"

"My giftmate would not hide from me."

"He was raised by a pro-Terran drunk who taught

him to hate our ways. You can change his mind about that when you see him, but meantime he is so much set against us that he *does* hide from you."

"The Breaker could not hide from me. I know it."

Arkos lost patience suddenly. "You know damned little. You are a self-indulgent, spoiled brat, and it's time you outgrew it. You *will* go to Town, and you *will* find your giftmate. That is my command."

Hawke shrugged, not quite insolently. "I will go to Town, my lord King, and I will find this Petal," he said quietly. "I cannot find my giftmate."

31

Ugly spent her last evening in the cave making a backpack of tapa leaves in which to carry her belongings. For an awl she used a splinter of rabbit horn, and for thread she used strong, dried morning glory vines. Once the pack was finished, she packed it with the rest of her prepared tapa leaves and dried vines; the few possessions she had brought with her from Godsgrace, plus two new bowls she had made from waterfruit shells and the spoon she had carved from driftwood; dried herbs, tea leaves, fruits, and berries she had been preserving; and splintered rabbit horns for more awls and straightpins. The skins of rabbits and squirrels that she had tried to cure were stiff, smelly failures, and she threw them away.

This time she was going to take an ample supply of water. She still had several unopened waterfruits, which she would carry tied to her belt, and before she left the valley stream she would fill her collapsible water jug as well. There would probably be springs and streams in the mountains, but she intended to take no chances.

She piled all those things near the mouth of the cave, together with a basket she had made from cattail leaves to use in foraging along the way. She and Friend spent the remainder of the evening sitting on the ledge outside, enjoying their last view of the desert, valley, and waterfall.

In the morning, Friend did not go foraging as usual. When Ugly woke, she found him waiting impatiently beside her piled belongings at the cave mouth. He seemed eager to begin their journey. Now that it was time to go, Ugly felt uncertain and almost frightened: the valley had become her home, and she had no idea what to expect of Far Harbor—if they could even find Far Harbor! Perhaps if Friend had seemed less eager, she would have decided not to make the trip after all, or at least not straightaway.

He sat beside her belongings, watching her alertly. Shouldering her backpack, she tied waterfruits and water jug to her belt, slipped the basket handle over her arm, and strode resolutely out of the cave and down the path to the valley floor. Friend, with a glance back to make sure she was following, set out toward the waterfall at a brisk pace.

Ugly followed, perhaps less eagerly but just as briskly. Her determination of the night before had faltered and turned to doubt, but she realized as they walked that she had complete confidence in Friend's decision. If he thought it was time to leave their valley, then it was.

The mist from the waterfall turned that whole end of the valley into sparkling mystery. The morning sun cast the east walls into shadow and highlighted the west walls in brilliant green. The stream was a band of silver set with diamonds in the distance; nearby, it was clear, rippling glass. The pebble bed looked like a path of rounded gemstones under the water. A grass-green frog with huge yellow eyes sat on a rock at the edge of the water and watched them pass. A family of doves, startled by Friend's approach, whirred up out of the grass and away, their yellow wings flashing in the sun.

Friend didn't hesitate all morning; perhaps during his hunting forays he had scouted the way. He led Ugly confidently past the waterfall, through the sun-sparked mist, straight to the ravine that led to the crystal gully: but he took turnings that led them away from the gully and slowly upward through increasingly narrow and difficult ravines and gullies till they stood at last, at noontime, on a shelf high above the valley floor, from which they could look back over the way they had come and over the valley itself. There Friend finally stopped and, throwing himself down in the shade of a small windchime bush that clung with tenacious roots to the sheer rock wall of the mountain, began to wash.

Grateful for the opportunity to rest after the prolonged climb, Ugly sat beside him and, removing her backpack, got out one of the waterfruit bowls in which to give Friend some water. He accepted it gravely and watched without apparent interest while she drank, then made herself lunch from the foodstuffs in her backpack and berries she had gathered in her basket.

After their rest, Ugly put the water jug in her backpack; tied to her belt, it had proved too awkward and had banged painfully against her hip. The waterfruits she left where they were. With several tied on each side, they balanced well, and they weren't heavy enough to be uncomfortable when they bumped against her. Friend seemed content to let Ugly lead the way on up the side of the valley and into a canyon that seemed to be going their way. They followed a rocky shelf that narrowed as they progressed till Ugly was afraid it would disappear altogether.

By midafternoon they were at least fifty meters above the floor of the canyon, and a howling wind had sprung up that tore at Ugly's hair and clothing and threatened to drag her off the narrowing ledge to her death on the rocks below. The basket that she had carried so comfortably on her arm all morning had become a deadly encumbrance that caught the wind and more than once nearly pulled her off the ledge. Even Friend was forced to move at a half-crouch, leaning heavily against the wall while his big kitten-paws tested each step before him.

When the ledge finally did narrow to little more than a toehold for Ugly, she could just reach another ledge above them that might supply a path on up the canyon. The only other option was to backtrack and try some other way, with no guarantee they could find one that was safer. Still, she was tempted to try that; the ledge they were on was so narrow, and the ledge above so high, that she wasn't sure she could climb from one to the other.

While she hesitated, clinging to the upper ledge with

her fingertips while she balanced on her toes on the lower one, Friend made the decision for her. With a low cry that gave her just warning enough to brace herself, he leapt suddenly and with agile cat-grace swarmed up her back to her shoulder and from there made one last effortless leap to the ledge above.

That leap very nearly undid Ugly. The force of it dislodged her left hand from its grip on the upper ledge. She leaned hard against the wall, toes digging into the lower ledge, right hand clinging with all her strength to the upper ledge. Friend sat on the rocks above her and peered curiously down into her face with apparently amused interest, as if wondering why she chose to hang there instead of following him up to safety. Her left toe slipped off the lower ledge.

Afterward she could not recall or imagine how she had kept from falling. There wasn't time to think about it; she had to act, and quickly. Her left side was swinging away from the rock wall. In seconds she would lose her right toehold if not her remaining handhold. With a fierce, twisting heave, she threw herself forward and upward, recovered her left handhold, and somehow scrambled straight up the rock in a frantic rush of motion that took her safely over the edge till she lay panting with terror and exertion beside Friend on the wide upper ledge. He watched this process with bemused fascination, then lifted a back leg to clean it.

The upper ledge was perhaps two meters wide, which seemed almost vast to Ugly after the lower one. When she could move again, she slid cautiously around till she could look over the edge the way they had come, and was very nearly sick at the sight of the fall she had so narrowly avoided. Hastily backing away, she kept going till she ran into the canyon wall and leaned against it, trembling.

Friend paused in his washing to observe these antics, then rose and, catlike, paced casually along the very edge of the drop for several meters, not even looking where he was going.

"Stop showing off." Ugly's voice was unsteady. "I

already know you're not clumsy. What you have to realize is that I am." She paused, and her eyes widened. "But I made it, didn't I?" She had lost her basket in the process and crushed one of her water-fruits, but she was alive.

Friend purred and sat down again, watching her. Ugly grinned at him.

"I'm not as graceful as you, but I did make it. I didn't fall. I don't know why not, but I didn't fall." In fact, grace and agility were natural for Ugly; and in solitude, with no one to make her self-conscious, she had acquired both long ago; as well as a much better ability to judge her own strength and to apply only as much as she needed for a given task.

Friend left the cliff edge to strop himself against her legs, and she stroked him absently. "The Starlings didn't like how strong I am; but if I hadn't been so strong, I'd be dead."

Friend purred and leaned against her.

"This is a nice place," she said firmly. "Safe. And it's late. Let's camp here tonight." There were woody shrubs for firewood and the wall provided partial shelter from the wind. She wanted to stay primarily because she was too shaky to go on, but it was a good place.

As usual, Friend seemed to understand her. Even before she had gathered her strength to begin collecting the resiny firewood available, he had disappeared in search of game. By the time he returned with meat for the evening meal, she had a cheerful fire on which to cook it. Performing "magic" with the crystal seemed easier each time she tried it. Lighting fires had become as simple a task as if she were using matches, and moving small objects was just a matter of imagining them moved. The Starlings had mocked her vivid imagination before: what would they think of it now?

They would be horrified and disapproving, of course. The thought of their disapproval no longer mattered to her. What she had learned to do might be "monstrous" and "unhuman," but she knew it was not wrong.

32

Mahlo had given Hawke several possible leads in the search for Petal, including the address of Lady Sara and possible addresses for several others who might know where Petal was if Lady Sara wouldn't say. Of course, Mahlo himself knew very well where Petal was, or at least where he was supposed to be; but telling Hawke where to find him, so early in the game, would have diminished the effectiveness of the whole plan. The longer Hawke had to search, and the more misleading truths about Petal he learned along the way, the more likely he would be convinced by the time he was allowed to find Petal.

Petal would be in no condition to disillusion him by then. Petal would be dead. He had been told he would be given fare to Freehold in exchange for his participation in the masquerade, but that would obviously be unnecessary, since his part wouldn't be completed until he provided a dead Breaker—himself—for Hawke to mourn.

Meantime, with any luck at all, Mahlo would surely have found the Starling Breaker, if she still lived, and seen to it that she would not embarrass him by someday showing up to giftmate Hawke. The affair of Petal should snap Hawke's feeble grasp on reality and render him totally and permanently unfit to inherit the throne, but Mahlo didn't like to take chances. Who knew what the discovery of the real Breaker might do for Hawke? The awesome power of a Maker-Breaker pair was legend. Terran rule on Paradise would be doomed by their mating: and with it, the People's hope of ever becoming anything more than a backwater stopover between planets of real importance in the galaxy.

* * *

It was only mid-morning when Hawke and his cat called on Lady Sara, but she was already well started on the day's drinking. She answered the door with a glass in her hand and invited Hawke in with a broad sweep of the same arm, thereby liberally sprinkling her carpet with amber liquid from the glass. It clearly wasn't the first time she had done that. The carpet had never been of the best quality, and the arc of stains near the door did nothing to improve it.

Hawke followed her inside reluctantly. His cat paused to smell the carpet, then went ahead of him into the apartment. Sara either didn't know who Hawke was or was too Terranized (or too drunk) to care. That in itself didn't bother Hawke; he wasn't always sure, himself, who he was; and he had often been too drunk to care. However, he was unaccustomed to dealing with others in that state, and he found to his surprise and dismay that he felt as embarrassed and disgusted by her drunkenness as others had often seemed by his.

It made him speak too abruptly, and his disapproval was evident in his tone. "Lady Sara, do you know where I can find your son?"

She had been about to gesture him into a stained chair in her untidy living room, which smelled so strongly of stale vomit and rotting kitchen garbage that it was all Hawke could do not to push her aside and open the window behind her for a breath of fresh air. Instead he waited, scowling, while she changed her mind about the chair and paused, swaying, to peer at him with bleary eyes. Her sudden, braying laughter startled him. "Petal's a big boy now. He doesn't report to Mama anymore."

"Then you don't know where he is?"

Her expression became sly. "What's it worth to you to know?"

He stared. "You'd sell him?"

She laughed again: a coarse, grating sound. "No, dearie, only his address. What's it worth?"

He hesitated, uncertain whether she was serious. "What do you want?"

She gestured expansively, spilling the rest of her drink. Hawke's cat, unnoticed, backed away, her ears laid back, and leaned against Hawke's legs. "As you can see," said Lady Sara, "I have very few needs." She lifted her glass, discovered that it was empty, and peered at it in confusion. "Odd." She promptly forgot it and gestured expansively again. "I'm of noble birth, you know. Untold wealth. Petal's of noble birth too, did I mention that? He's only a fosterling, but he's small. And he has peculiar eyes like your yours. Why, he's probably of nobler birth than I, and I'm a Lady. Did you know I'm a Lady?"

The Breaker would not necessarily be of noble birth. But still . . . "Tell me, Lady Sara, did Petal have an early Onset?"

"Of course he had. Why else would he be so small, you twit?" She poured herself a fresh drink from a bottle on the mantel, dribbling it across the hearth in the process. "It was terrible, I almost lost him, poor baby."

There were other royal gifts that, unmated, could kill. It needn't mean he was a Breaker. "Couldn't you mate him?"

She looked at him speculatively. "You ask a hell of a lot of questions, buddy. Why are you so interested in Petal, anyway? What's he done to you?"

"Nothing. I just—"

She interrupted suddenly as she noticed for the first time the tawny cat sitting patiently at Hawke's feet. "What's *that*?"

Hawke glanced down in confusion. "A cat. She's a cat, that's all."

Lady Sara stared at him in dawning horror. "Prince Hawke! You're the mad Prince Hawke!"

He admitted it, not really even noticing the adjective. He would not have objected had he noticed. It was true enough, though most people didn't say it to him so directly.

"Get out!" She spilled her drink again in her eagerness to push him toward the door. "Get out, you're not wanted here, there's nothing for you, get out!"

Mahlo's instructions to her had been to talk to Hawke, to encourage him in his search for Petal without actually leading him to the boy. Mahlo's payment for her work, however, had bought several bottles and produced a state of mind in which, even had she remembered his instructions, she could not have set aside her fear and hatred for the royalty that was, in her view, responsible for her own outcaste position.

Like Mahlo, Lady Sara wanted to destroy Prince Hawke and all he stood for. Unlike Mahlo, she did not have the patience necessary to forgo certain present satisfaction in favor of the mere probability of greater future satisfaction. She enjoyed his expression of dismayed resignation as she shoved him out of her apartment and slammed the door in his face. She was only sorry that the kick she aimed at his cat missed entirely.

The next name on Hawke's list was a Terran, a retired university professor who, according to Mahlo, had until recently shared an apartment with Petal. Hawke had no difficulty finding the address, though it was in the narrow, twisting streets of Old Town, a section so haphazardly arranged, so crowded, and so darkly stained with age and poverty that few outsiders ventured into its entangled avenues, and those who did almost invariably got lost in the first five minutes. Hawke knew Far Harbor too well to lose his way in any section of it. He might sometimes forget where he was going or where he had been, but he always knew where he was.

He nearly forgot why he was there when he found the door he wanted. The possibility that Petal might be his giftmate was becoming too real: early and severe Onset, unidentified and unmated gift, and he was homosexual, so the Goddess Lanalei would protect him. . . .

Hawke knew he ought not to hope. If he dared to hope again and was proved wrong, he would be lost. Yet the crystal in his pocket and the cat at his heels proved he *had* a giftmate, somewhere, didn't they? And if his giftmate lived, Petal was the best candidate in evidence.

Or not in evidence. That was the glaring inconsistency that kept bringing Hawke up short and restoring his bitter grip on reality: Petal was hiding from him. The Breaker would not, could not, hide from the Maker. That had to mean that Hawke was on a fool's errand of Mahlo's devising. . . . And yet, even if Mahlo were the King's enemy, why would he go to this trouble to create an elaborate, meaningless chase? For what purpose would he provide a false Breaker, when he knew that the moment Hawke met the candidate the truth would be out?

"Perhaps," he thought, "he hopes to drive me finally, wholly mad." Mahlo would still have to answer to the King. It didn't make sense. But the possibility enraged Hawke enough to clear his mind. He would search, but he would not hope. He would not lose what little he had left of life. He squared his shoulders and rang Professor Hirohito Jones's doorbell.

The interview proved no more useful than the interview with Lady Sara, and more disturbing: Professor Jones, being Terran, was poorly adjusted to his own homosexuality and seemed oddly unnerved by Hawke's failure to react to it in any way. Jones behaved normally enough at first, but became increasingly waspish in an apparent effort to provoke some reaction from Hawke. The only useful thing he said in the entire interview was that Petal had seemed to him an extraordinarily clumsy child, and that he himself had suffered innumerable minor misfortunes since Petal left him, almost as if Petal's clumsiness had been transferred to him.

Hawke had initially refused a seat in a ratty overstuffed chair by the room's only window. Now he sank abruptly into the chair and put his head between his hands, eyes closed, fingers tense in his tangled hair. "Professor Jones." His voice was harsh with strain. "Please, I must know. When you say Petal was clumsy . . ." He opened his eyes and stared at the professor, who was sprawled indolently on the battered couch next to him. "Is this truth, or are you just being . . ."

"Catty?" Professor Jones smiled, seemingly as relaxed as before, but there was a predatory gleam in his long-lashed dark eyes. "My dear, you have no *idea* how really unnerving it is when you look at a person like that. I promise you, your eyes are like *coals*. Glowing coals, in that positively *sculpted* face of yours, you simply can't imagine the effect. It's really quite devastating, I assure you it is. And that you ask, that you in all seriousness inquire whether the discarded lover might perhaps just possibly overstate by the teeniest margin his beloved's one major flaw—?" He waved one hand in an oddly dismissive gesture. "Well, I admit it. Perhaps I do exaggerate, by just the very smallest margin possible. Does it matter to you so very much? I assure you he's quite a good lover for all that."

"I don't care about that. But you say—"

Professor Jones interrupted him with an exaggerated show of surprise. "Oh, but really, I was given to understand this was some sort of job interview. You know that mad Prince of the giants? I'd heard he wanted to hire a lover of Petal's qualifications. And then I thought you said you were a messenger of his, of the Prince's, isn't that right? Isn't that why you're here? As a sort of royal procurer for the Prince?"

Hawke saw the malice in the professor's smile, and was quite well aware that Jones knew who he was, so he didn't bother to answer the question. Instead he said, "You say you've had a number of minor misfortunes since Petal left?"

Professor Jones shrugged negligently. "You might call them minor. I have not always lived, for instance, in such squalor. I doubt that Petal would have tolerated such a dwelling as this for five minutes; he puts on airs, you might as well know it. Fancies himself of noble birth, and, oh my, but he is expensive to keep!"

"The misfortunes?" said Hawke.

"One was the loss of my job, which explains my present circumstance. Of course it's only a coincidence. The university found out about my dismal perversions."

"Perversions?" asked Hawke, puzzled.

"Oh, *you* know." Jones made a limp gesture and winked provocatively. "I don't say Petal *told* them, I'm not sure he would have been quite all *that* vindictive, but the timing is interesting, wouldn't you say?"

Hawke stared at him in dismay. "You were fired for being homosexual? Is that what you're saying?" He shook his head. "I don't understand. What has that to do with teaching? I thought you were a teacher."

For the first time during the interview, Professor Jones seemed genuinely at a loss. He studied Hawke for a long, startled moment, judging the sincerity of Hawke's confusion; then he laughed. It was a hearty, unaffected, delighted laugh, and it transformed him: the cattiness and the effeminate mannerisms disappeared and did not return. "You really don't know, do you?" he asked in his normal voice. "That's what I like about you People: you're full of surprises." He hesitated, then said almost gently, "Let's just say it's not the Terran way to employ homosexuals, and let it go at that. Why did you want to know about my misfortunes, anyway? And what do you really want of Petal?"

"I—" Hawke hesitated, unwilling to put hope into words. "He—"

"Spit it out," grinned Jones. "It can't be all that bad."

"There's a—a small chance that he—that he might be my giftmate. Did he ever say what his gift was?"

Jones frowned. "No, he didn't. I don't know much about that stuff. I thought you People could pretty much pick and choose giftmates like any other mates. I mean . . ."

Hawke nodded. "Most can. Most gifts are common, and can be mated several ways. Not mine. And . . . perhaps . . . not Petal's."

Jones shook his head. "Well, I wouldn't know. I take it the person who has the gift you want would be clumsy, but that still doesn't answer the part about my misfortunes. Where does that fit in?"

"If he is an unmated Breaker, things would go well around him and badly for him . . . and badly for those who have become accustomed to his presence if he leaves."

Jones nodded. "Things don't really go wrong, they just quit going well, is that it?"

"That's it." Hawke's face was pale and set, his eyes bruised shadows. "Is that what happened to you?"

Jones nodded thoughtfully. "Yes, for the most part, I think . . . yes." He lifted a cautionary hand. "But look, don't get your hopes up on that account. I can see it's pretty important to you, so I have to tell you . . . Well, think about it. It's only natural. Any deserted lover—rejected—despondent—and believe me, I was all of that and more." He grinned suddenly, ruefully. "Petal is a very pretty, very capable boy, for all his clumsiness." He sobered. "Well, naturally, in a situation like that, you're going to start thinking that everything's going wrong. Things get all out of proportion. When you're depressed, you don't look at the world very clearly."

The hint of a smile pulled at Hawke's lips. "I know."

"Well . . . I'm sorry I can't be more encouraging, but I just don't know. And I don't know where Petal is; if I did, I'd be banging on his door, begging him to come back to me; where he's concerned, I have very little pride, more's the pity."

"You must have loved him very much."

"I did. I do." Jones shook his head, dismissing the sober tone. "I hope you find him, and I hope he's just what you're looking for. He may be, you know." He grinned again, fleetingly. "He was certainly just what I was looking for."

33

When Ugly and Friend finally climbed up out of the canyon they had been following, they found themselves on a high, sloping meadow under a lowering, slate-gray sky that had already swallowed all the more distant mountaintops and was trailing a curtain of rain toward the nearer ones. It looked to Ugly as though the plateau they had reached sloped gently right up to a narrow gap between two peaks past which they might actually see Far Harbor, but the rain would be upon them before they could cover the remaining distance, and the mountain air was too cold to make that prospect attractive.

"We'll have to camp here," she told Friend. "Maybe I could build some kind of shelter in those rocks over there."

Friend bounded past her at once toward the nearby tumble of boulders, tail in the air. She noticed again how much he had grown since they met: he was at least twice the size of the frightened kitten she had saved from a dunking in that forest pool not so long ago.

He wasn't full grown yet, but neither was he a kitten any longer, and for the first time she saw him for what he really was: an alien species; a creature different from her in every way, wild and unknowable. Her only companion in the world was an untamed predator.

As she neared the rocks, he leapt from hiding among them onto the one nearest her, and crouched at eye-level to stare at her. His eyes seemed alien all at once, with their wide vertical-slit pupils in the glowing amethyst irises. His face was a furry white mask set with unfathomable gemstone eyes, unreadable, expressionless, strange. She had no idea what he was thinking, what his real needs and feelings were, or even why he had befriended her. She could talk to him, but she could not communicate with him. She couldn't ever know or even imagine what went on inside his mind: he wasn't like her. The Starlings had called her unhuman, but how much more so was he! In that small, furry body, he couldn't even masquerade as human the way she could.

In the eerie light of the gathering storm she stared for a timeless moment into the cat-shadows of his eyes and was afraid. He returned her gaze with a cat's bland, unwavering stare. She thought suddenly, with a sense of the old, despairing misery, "What am I doing here, in the wilderness, alone with a dangerous wild cat that for all I know might attack me in my sleep one night? Or right now, for that matter?" At that moment, the cat yawned: a gesture that might have seemed reassuring if he hadn't thereby exposed quite such long, gleaming, white teeth. The needle-sharp milk teeth had gone the way of the triangular ears and tail. She wasn't taking care of a kitten anymore. She was setting up camp for the night with a carnivorous, half-grown cat.

The first misting drops of rain touched them and the moment passed: Friend was her familiar friend again, his gaze no longer sinister but only curious. He might be wondering why she was staring at him instead of finding them shelter for the night. She shook her head at her own nervous fantasies and moved forward to explore the tumbled boulders.

They were all sizes and shapes, tossed down from the slopes above in some great cataclysm in the distant past, piled across the meadow in a curving hill of broken stone and loose dirt and the skeletons of ancient trees, as if the face of the mountain had fallen. Wind had swept their surfaces clean, and rain had washed miniature gullies through the earth in which they rested. Changes in temperature had cracked their stone faces and piled chips and sand between them, only to be washed away again by rain and blown by wind. In places where the rocks left room, the resultant sandy mud had been washed out across the meadow: but where they were more tightly packed, it had acted as a form of crude mortar, cementing the boulders together to form partially enclosed rooms sheltered from the harsh mountain winds, where weeds and bracken had managed to find purchase for their roots and sun enough for their leaves.

In the thickening mist, Ugly selected one such room, carpeted with a minty, low-growing weed that cushioned the floor. The walls of rock leaned inward so far that they formed half a roof by themselves. Ugly completed it with hastily gathered bracken wedged in place and weighted at the edges by small rocks and piled dirt. When she was through, the little room was effectively sheltered from the storm and redolent of the mint she had crushed in the process.

She had left the room open on one side, away from the wind, and there she made a circle of loose stones for her fireplace. Firewood was easily gathered from the bleached-dry, dead trees she found among the boulders. Friend had taken shelter beneath the overhanging rocks as soon as Ugly had selected the room. Now he came out under her improvised roof and sprawled expectantly on the thick groundcover beside the fireplace to watch with solemn attention as she took out the crystal to light the fire.

She was well practiced at that by now. It no longer even seemed an unusual thing to do. She just held the crystal, looked at the dry wood, and made it burn. Then she put the crystal aside and looked in her backpack for dinner. Obviously Friend wasn't going hunting in weather like this. He was settled in by the fire for a good wash and didn't even look up when she offered him water. She drank it herself, then pulled off her boots and stripped off her wet jumpsuit, spreading it near the fire to dry while she snacked on fruit and roots from her pack.

Friend sniffed at the roots with bored curiosity and

decided they were inedible. She smiled at him as he
thrust one hind leg straight in the air for cleaning.
Only a cat could maintain his dignity in a position like
that—and even a cat couldn't look very dangerous
that way. She had just been feeling frightened and lost
and afraid of the gathering dark of the storm, and in
the isolation of her fear he had briefly become a
stranger. The same thing would probably have happened if he were a human instead of a cat; a frightened
mind played strange tricks. It was a lesson she would
do well to remember; second-guessing one's irrevocable decisions in a moment of crisis would hardly be a
productive way to behave.

When she had eaten, she checked the state of her
clothes. They were beginning to dry on top, so she
turned them. The boots were in good condition,
though old, but the jumpsuit was really falling apart
by now. It had already been badly worn when she left
Godsgrace, and it had been through a lot since then.
This evening of enforced inactivity would be a good
time to think about replacing it. She pulled out her
prepared tapa leaves and piled them beside her to see
how many she had. There were more than she expected: cleaned as they were, they had remarkably
little bulk for how strong and warm they were.

There were more than enough to make a new
jumpsuit, but if anyone were still hunting her, they
would have a description that included the jumpsuit.
Even a new one made of tapa leaves would be too
obviously a Godsgrace garment. It would be better to
wear something completely different when she arrived
in Far Harbor. Unfortunately, the only garments she
knew anything about were Godsgrace ones: jumpsuits
like her own, and the fancy dresses Megan had
sometimes worn. She didn't want to dress like Megan.
Not anymore.

There might be enough tapa leaves in her collection
to make a tunic and cloak like the ones worn by the
man she had seen in her vision—the young man who
had such wild, compelling eyes. . . . She couldn't

make anything as pretty as his; she hadn't had time to dye the tapa, and even dyed it would hardly compare favorably with his rich brocades and silks. But the leaves had dried to a soft, silvery sheen, not unattractive. She was sure she had enough for the long tunic, and if she patched them together carefully, she could surely manage at least a short cloak, too.

She hesitated, wondering whether she was planning a costume that only a man would wear. If so, she would stand out as badly in Far Harbor as she would in a Godsgrace jumpsuit. All she had seen in her vision were three men—no, four, counting the priest—and no women. What did the women of those people wear?

Then it occurred to her that those might not have been Far Harbor people, anyway. They might have been on the other side of the world—or nowhere at all outside her imagination. For all she knew, the people in Far Harbor wore the same plain, serviceable jumpsuits as the citizens of Godsgrace.

Well, it was a jumpsuit or a costume in imitation of a possibly imaginary man, and his was by far the prettier. Besides, she didn't believe he was imaginary. She would make a tunic and cloak like his, and if they weren't right for wearing in Far Harbor when she got there, then maybe she would just go somewhere else.

Satisfied with the decision even though she was well aware it was false bravado, she settled in to sew her tapa costume. She spent an hour with an awl of splintered horn, unruly morning glory vines, and tough, slippery tapa leaves before it occurred to her that the crystal might help her in this as it had with the fire. The people in the underwater vision had done things like sewing by looking instead of by hand. She put down the awl with a sigh and took up the crystal. It could do no harm to try. Friend began to purr.

It took her nearly another hour to get the knack of it, but after that the tapa and vines seemed to weave themselves together as if they knew what she wanted better than she did. She could somehow *feel* the cells in the leaves and, deeper than that, the swirling atoms that made up the cells of leaves and vines; and once she found just the right level to look at, deep inside the fabric, she could just *push* with her imagination, and the vines twined neatly through the leaf edges, parting the tapa fibers and then pulling them together again into seams that were barely visible once they were complete. The leaves bent and stretched and shaped themselves to fit with no waste at all. The garment took shape with only the briefest of hesitations when she became uncertain about a seam or a fold: memory of the shapes she wanted took form in the crystal's facets and danced in the splintered light till the tapa came together in perfect imitation of the vision, seam for seam and fold for fold.

When she finally lay down to sleep beside the dying fire, Ugly was wearing a tunic of shimmering silver green that fit her so smoothly it might have been made by a master tailor, and Friend curled up beside her under the warmth of her new tapa-fabric cloak. Outside their mint-scented little room the storm had abated. The air still held the sharp sweet tang of ozone and rain, but only an occasional drop still found its way through the bracken roof to sizzle in the fire or plop with damp finality onto the rocks. Ugly inhaled deeply of the rich odors of wet earth, crushed mint, burnt wood, and damp stone, and smiled to herself in sleepy satisfaction. She threw an affectionate arm across Friend, which he promptly dislodged in a fit of dignity, and fell asleep to dream of a sullen young man with eyes like molten amethyst.

34

All the People Hawke talked to about Petal reinforced, with anecdotes and descriptions, the idea that he might be a Breaker; nobody knew what his gift was, if that wasn't it. Nor did anyone know where he was. Some were telling the truth and some lied for politics or for profit, but Hawke was too shaken by hope to judge their stories rationally at all. His gift, had he been in control of it, might have helped him to discern the lies; but he had been fighting it too long to use it now. By late afternoon, he was convinced that he was actually on the trail of his giftmate.

What had puzzled him at first was why Mahlo, who was his enemy, would have put him on the trail of his giftmate: then it occurred to him that by showing Hawke that the Breaker existed, but contriving to keep them from ever meeting, Mahlo could destroy him more surely and more quickly than by simply getting rid of the Breaker without Hawke's knowledge. If that was Mahlo's plan, the fact of Hawke's hope could be a danger to Petal. He must not let anyone become aware of it. And he must not let the search drag out any longer.

If Petal was the Breaker, and Mahlo's plan was to keep him hidden from Hawke, the persons most likely to know where Petal was were Mahlo and Petal's mother. Obviously Mahlo would not tell Hawke, but Petal's mother might. When Hawke had seen her before, he had been daunted by her drunkenness and too willing to believe her ignorance, mostly because he had been anxious not to believe that Petal was his giftmate. Now that he dared to hope, he would see Lady Sara again. And this time, drunk or not, she would tell what she knew. He had that much power, at least, even if he was seldom sane enough to use it.

Perhaps soon he would be whole, the seemingly lifelong battle for sanity won at last. He only needed his giftmate. If Petal really was a Breaker . . . The hope of it dizzied him. To be whole, to be complete, to be giftmated! It was a concept almost beyond his ability to comprehend. Their gift was a powerful one. Nobody knew just how powerful, only that it was beyond anything the People had known in generations. But it wasn't the power they would wield that Hawke hungered for. That was almost a matter of indifference to him; he could not think in terms of the People, the kingdom, the power of a Maker-Breaker gift united. The power that he ached to know was the power that would bind them. With a gift like theirs, they would be nearly inseparable: only as giftmates would they ever feel whole.

He didn't even know what that would feel like. In childhood he must have been normal: he knew he'd had playmates like any other boy of the People. He must have felt whole enough then. But the awful, disintegrating force of a strong Onset that went unmated had blurred those memories almost to silence. Since Onset, he had known only isolation, loneliness, unrelieved *separateness* in a world of couples: a world in which he had no place: a world that for him had gone unexpectedly strange, distorted, unreliable, and frequently grotesque. He could not trust his own perceptions, and had no other means to survive. He was a half-thing, half-mad. But if Petal was a Breaker . . . !

He had intended to go directly to Lady Sara again, but found himself instead in one of Lanalei's temples, lighting incense for hope. To find himself in a temple when he meant to be elsewhere was not unusual. Often enough he found himself where he had not meant to be; and when it was in a temple, he sometimes lighted incense, though never before for hope.

What was unusual this time was that Lanalei responded with a vision.

At first he didn't realize what was happening. The altar crystals seemed suddenly brighter, and they cast out rainbow patterns across the room. He thought a beam of sunlight must have come in by the altar windows, to be broken into shards of vivid color and tossed back into the air; but the colors swirled and multiplied and grew brighter till they brought tears to his eyes with their blinding, brilliant beauty, and he could not close his eyes to shut them out.

He was aware of the cat at his heels, unexpectedly purring: a low, dry sound in the silence. The wind-chimes overhead were still. Blue incense smoke, sweet and crisp like a forest morning, created a delicate haze in the air that caught the light in all its shattered colors and carried it in shifting eddies up past the altar, swimming, changing. . . .

He saw figures on the palace stairs. Not at the new reservation palace, but at the old Crystal Palace in Town with all its rich gold and crystal decorations glittering like fire and ice in the light of torches set at intervals in the ancient stone and crystal of the walls. Terrans ruled there now, and the People were no longer allowed even to enter the ancient corridors; yet in his vision it was People Hawke saw on the stairs. His father the High King Arkos was preceding two other People down the time-worn stairs to meet a Terran delegation that waited like supplicants below.

Terrans always looked pompous and dark to Hawke, but these looked worried, as well. They wore mud-colored suits and dust-colored shirts. Their blank, black eyes stared round and empty from under brows drawn tight with something almost like fear. Their short, crisp hair was greased down against their heads like tarnished metal caps, and they smoothed it from time to time with nervous gestures of which they were wholly unaware.

The High King Arkos was in the full regalia of the High King: heavy robes of brocade, gold, and crystal;

the Crown that was reserved for the very most important of state occasions, because the weight of its massive beauty was more than a mere mortal's head could endure for long; the gem-encrusted scepter with its crystal head in the crook of his arm; and the King's Sword, as steeped in myth and history as it was carved and ornamented, its value incalculable, its power inexhaustible in the hands of the rightful King. Arkos moved with all the dignity of his office, with the dull fire of his half-forgotten gift burning in the pale, dangerous eyes that made his otherwise unremarkable face so startlingly predatory in moments of strong emotion. It was predatory now.

One of the figures behind Arkos was Hawke himself: a wild thing, chained by protocol and promise: a young man with eyes as ancient as the power that burned in them, glowing like coals in the sunken shadows of a lean, worn face that had somehow, in all the ravages of a brief and battered life, retained a certain untamed and untamable beauty, like a creature caught by forces it can neither control nor understand, but only endure and outwait—or outwit. His body, as heavily weighted with royal robes and trappings as his father's, still managed, under all the centuries of civilization that bounded its actions and attire, to give an impression of savagery in its lithe and patient elegance of motion. Never having seen himself as others saw him, he was startled at the impression his appearance gave, of something essentially uncontrollable that was nonetheless—at least for the moment—rigidly controlled.

The figure beside Hawke was robed and crowned as he and his father were, but was otherwise difficult to distinguish. The face was entirely in shadow, or blurred by the light. Hawke had the impression of dangerously glowing amethyst eyes, perhaps a shade or two darker than his own; and of a body even more lithe and elegant than his, with the unselfconscious and unintentional grace of a dancer or a cat. Beyond that he could see no details; not even whether the figure was male or female. The light of the crystals in their three crowns flared in the semi-darkness of the long, wide stairway like the light of power in their eyes.

The figure beside him must be his giftmate. It must be Petal pacing beside him, completing him, creating with him that power that had rekindled the light in his father's eyes and clearly disturbed the waiting Terrans. This was a vision of the future, and a promise. Petal was alive now and would still be alive when Hawke found him. Together they would form a coalescence of such power that even the Terrans could not overwhelm it with their weapons, their insidious technology, or their lies.

In Lanalei's temple a breeze caught at the crystals above Hawke's head, singing through the windchimes and breaking the vision. The rainbows receded. The palace stairs remained for a moment, outlined against the smoke, a glittering shadow; then it wavered and was gone. It didn't matter. Hawke had seen what he needed to know. The dream of a giftmate was real, and hope was justified. His giftmate lived. Hawke would find him.

The ghost of a smile pulled at his lips; it seemed he would, after all, end up with as many mates as anyone. With a homosexual giftmate, he would have to find also a lifemate with whom to produce heirs to the throne. With a giftmate, he would be able to take his rightful place at his father's side in affairs of state, and that meant workmates, which would lead to playmates, which would lead to a normal life. A whole life. A *real* life; no more shadowboxing with madness. No more lost, purposeless wanderings. No more wondering why he lived.

The tawny cat had ceased purring when the vision ended. Now she butted against Hawke's legs, recalling him rudely to the present. There would be time enough to rejoice when he was safely giftmated. First he had to find Petal. And for that, he must see Lady Sara again.

35

The morning after the rainstorm, Ugly and Friend woke to brilliant sun and a sky so blue and clear that it was difficult to believe in yesterday's sullen black clouds. Friend went hunting while Ugly was still drinking her morning tea and staring in awe at the panoramic view of the mountains they had climbed and the distant lowlands they had left behind. The air was so clear, the scene so radiant, there was an element of unreality to its beauty, as though she were looking at an artist's idealized conception in a crystal hologram.

The colors were as vivid as the rainbows thrown by a crystal prism. Distant details were clear and sharp: she could see the red-brown feathers of a hawk wheeling over a rock-strewn grassy pinnacle miles away, the delicate lines of his wings as finely drawn as the iridescent veins in a dragonfly's wings only a few feet away. She could see fields of yellow mustard blossoms swaying in the wind on a hillside beyond the valley in which she and Friend had so hopefully set up housekeeping in their comfortable little cave. She could see the white expanse of desert, the myriad greens of forest, and the stately progression of cliff-faced mountains that marked their boundaries. In the very far distance, shimmering into the lucent blue of the sky, she even thought she saw just one thin line of emerald ocean before the clarity finally dissolved into light and silence.

When she had finished her tea and rinsed her cup, Ugly turned for the first time to look the other way, up the sloping meadow toward the narrow pass in what might be the last major barrier between her and Far Harbor. That way was beautiful, too. The meadow was dotted with crimson daisies. The mountains were a sheer, verdant wall, with here and there a black or striated yellow outcropping of rock showing through the moss and lichen that elsewhere colored them such luxuriant green. They were a wall across the world, sharply outlined against the summer sky, with only one break in them at the top of the meadow: a gateway to another world, perhaps.

Now that the possibility was so near, Ugly found herself oddly reluctant to move on. By the end of the day she and Friend could be at the top of the meadow, in that pass if it was a pass, looking down on Far Harbor if Far Harbor really was just on the other side of the Mysterious Mountains. She thought in a kind of panic that they had a very nice camp here: perhaps they should stay a day or two; rest up from the long climb through the mountains. . . .

"Make up your mind," she said aloud. "You can be scared to stay alone in the wilderness, the way you were last night, or scared to go into Town, the way you are now, but you can't be scared of both."

After a moment's consideration she smiled wryly and said, "Oh, yes, I can!" Nonetheless she started packing her belongings for the trip up to the pass. When Friend returned from hunting, she was ready to go.

The walk upslope was an easy one, leaving her mind free to worry the problem of which option was more frightening: Town or wilderness; company or solitude? Out here, with only a cat for company, she was free and capable and happy . . . and any minor accident could prove fatal. In Town, in the company of people like the Starlings, she would be trapped once more within her own ugliness, her clumsiness, her general worthlessness. In case of accident or illness she would have help . . . but at any time she might be recognized and arrested for the murder of Emmett Starling.

Put that way, the wilderness sounded infinitely preferable, yet her steps toward the top of the meadow didn't falter. She liked being alone with Friend. She liked being the only judge of her own worth. She felt less clumsy and even less ugly when there was no one around to tell her that she was clumsy and ugly. But how could she judge herself to be of much worth when she had in effect retired from the human race because she had been told she wasn't good enough to be a member? Of what value was a person whose life benefited no one but herself and whose death would go entirely unnoticed?

She worried the problem—Town versus wilderness —all the way up the hill behind Friend, and it wasn't until they had paused for lunch and started on again that she thought unexpectedly of the young man the crystal had shown her. She knew from the look of his eyes that he had known the same despair that had driven her into the wilderness, yet he had not turned his back on humanity. In many ways he was as ugly as she—the same big bones, gaunt features, and hideous lavender eyes—yet he remained where he could be taunted and tormented. . . .

It was at that point in her reverie that Ugly realized for the first time how ugly all four of the men had been whom the crystal had shown her: all had the big bones and rough features for which the Starlings had named her Ugly. All had pale eyes, though only two, the young man and the older one who looked so much like him, had the really grotesque lavender color in theirs, the others' having been pure blue.

For a moment her steps did falter as she realized with dismay that the visions must after all have been only imagination. She had not realized till then how much she wanted them to be true. But it was ridiculous to think there might be so many others somewhere who were ugly in exactly the same ways as she. It had been a sort of wish fulfillment, then. Not that she would wish such ugliness on anyone. But she must have unconsciously been trying to create a world in which her appearance would be normal, not ugly.

Friend stropped himself on her legs and looked up

at her with narrowed eyes, and she realized she had stopped walking. She stood for a long moment looking at the creamy white of his fur, thinking of nothing. There were crimson daisies nodding in the wind beside him, their petals in brilliant contrast to their pale green leaves. The soil out of which they grew was hard-packed yellow clay scattered with black pebbles from the mountains above. A black beetle scuttled hurriedly from one pebble to another and disappeared in its shadow. Ugly watched it without interest, and did not move.

Friend opened his mouth. He had seldom spoken aloud since the day they met. Now he emitted a small, squeaky sound as though clearing his throat, then said, "Yow-ow?" in a big, hollow voice that left no question at all as to his meaning.

"Yes, all right," said Ugly. "I'm coming."

Friend leaned briefly against her knee, then lunged forward in a sudden kittenish rush through tall flowers, batting playfully at butterflies as he went. Pollen dusted yellow across his back and butterflies scattered. Ugly followed him slowly. A major reason for her decision to go to Far Harbor had been the desire to find the pale-eyed man of her visions. If he didn't exist—

She was suddenly, illogically, and completely convinced that he did. He existed, and she would find him. She felt the hard edges of the crystal in her pocket and smiled. One thing at a time. The way to survive was always to make the best plans one could, and then implement them, and no second-guessing without new information: just resolutely do what came next, one thing at a time. Right now, what came next was to find Far Harbor. She quickened her steps; they were nearing the top of the meadow.

An hour later they stood together between towering green peaks and looked down at Far Harbor's shining pastel buildings sprawled in crowded and colorful chaos between the mountains and the sunset-gilded sea. They had kilometers of wilderness yet to cross before they would reach the city, but they could see it now, and the sight was awesome.

Ugly had never before seen a settlement larger than Godsgrace. She had tried to imagine what a city would be like that was large enough to house a million people, but never in her wildest imaginings had she envisioned anything like this vast, tangled wilderness of streets and structures, steel and concrete and sheets of glass turned to molten gold by the setting sun.

She found a sheltered overhang in the rocks at one side of the pass, and she and Friend settled there for the coming night. He seemed as fascinated with the view as she was. They sat side by side with their backs to the mountain and watched the brilliant golds, reds, oranges, and lavenders of the sunset over the sea beyond Far Harbor; and then the changing, darkening blue shadows and sudden strings of jewels as night crept over the city and the Terran streetlights winked on.

36

When Hawke appeared at Lady Sara's door for the second time in as many days, her first impulse was to slam the door in his face and refuse to open it again. He was ready for that, with a booted foot on the threshold and one shoulder hard against the door. He didn't say a word: he just looked at her with those pale, mad eyes till she backed away so he and his cat could enter.

She preceded him down the hall into the shabby living room and poured herself a drink without offering him one. Still he didn't say anything. He just stood there, elegant and impatient, watching her. A fly buzzed against a window pane, a small, dry sound in the silence between them. Hawke's presence made the room look even drabber than it was. She wanted to hate him for that. Instead she felt suddenly, illogically afraid. "I don't know where Petal is," she said.

Something stirred in the dark of his eyes. For the first time she began to realize how serious the charade was that Mahlo had invented. This was the mad Prince, the Once and Future King, standing in her living room and looking at her with the pale amethyst eyes of the future and the past. She laughed nervously; he had been little enough in past, and would be nothing in future if Mahlo's plan succeeded. The so-called Once and Future King had never been and never would be King. That was a nursery rhyme, an old magicians' tale, a myth, an absurdity. But her laughter died under Hawke's unwavering gaze.

She turned away. "You're not the reincarnation of the Mad King Halkan any more than I am."

His expression didn't change except that one eyebrow lifted, and the glow of his eyes became more pronounced.

"I tell you I don't know where Petal is!"

"You know." His voice was curiously flat, as expressionless as his face.

She drank, refilled her glass, and put the bottle down so heavily it shook the table. "He's not your giftmate." She hadn't meant to say that. She hadn't meant to say anything. It was the power of his eyes and the sound of his voice, more like a King's than the High King's own. Lady Sara was an exile, but she was still of the People. Their legends were in her blood. Her mother had sung her to sleep with lullabies about the Once and Future King: he who was and who will be: the Maker, the demigod, the last frail hope of a conquered race: the mad Prince who would be giftmated to rule the world. Lady Sara drank again, afraid to meet his eyes.

After a long, silent moment, he said in the same flat voice, "If he is not, I will know when I meet him. Where is he?"

She was supposed to delay him. He wasn't supposed to find Petal nearly this soon. To be sure of destroying him, the process had to be dragged out till he really believed in Petal so completely that the truth, when he learned it, would break him. Then he would be destroyed, and the royal house with him; without an heir, Arkos would be only a quaint local figure permitted by the Terrans to play King. When he died, the lesser kings might bicker and squabble among themselves in an effort to put a new High King on the throne, but it would come to nothing; the Terrans would rule.

Lady Sara would be admired and respected for her part in saving Terran rule. Petal would be given fare to Freehold, where he could build a new life among the People there, who would not revile him for his homosexuality as Terrans did; and would not know, as the People on Paradise knew, how much of his life he had spent with Terrans. On Freehold he would be truly free. Neither he nor Lady Sara would be an outcast any longer. All Lady Sara had to do to assure their happiness was to put off Hawke for just a few days more.

She looked at him, at the fire of his eyes, at the hard stone features of the Once and Future King, at the bruised vulnerability of the boy's set mouth, and she told him the truth: "Petal is at 408 Makailani Street, apartment three. Ring twice, wait ten seconds, then ring twice again. He'll let you in."

Hawke nodded, unsurprised, expressionless. "Thank you." The catch in his voice was barely audible, but Lady Sara was a mother. She heard it.

She wished suddenly that she could kill him with her bare hands, slowly. She wanted, with the impassioned rage of the self-defeated, to reach out and destroy everything: Hawke, herself, the city, the planet, the universe. She said quietly, "You're welcome." She said almost gently, "Go away now."

Whether the Ugly People existed or not, Ugly was dressed in a copy of their clothing. She thought about it while she cooked and ate the meat Friend had provided for dinner: if they didn't exist, she would look ridiculous in their costume in Far Harbor. But she had already thought that out when she considered that they might not live in Far Harbor, and she had decided not to wear her Godsgrace jumpsuit anyway. The realization that the Ugly People might not exist at all didn't change the reasons for that decision.

After dinner she sharpened her knife, put it in the belt sheath she had made for it, and put it aside. Then she banked the fire and curled up in her cloak beside it, with Friend sprawled comfortably across her ankles, and stared down the mountain at the vast sprawl of Far Harbor. With any luck, she and Friend would be down there among those twisting streets and concrete corridors in only a day or two.

Lying in a mountain pass, listening to the wind and the nightlarks singing, it was hard to imagine being back among people again. From here, the city was a spilled jewel box of lights; but down there in its crowded streets it would look very different indeed. A pang of nervousness that was almost fear sent her pulses racing, and she had to resist again the desire to delay, to stay where they were, to wait.

Wait for what? There was nothing for them on a mountaintop. If they had a future at all, it was down there among the fairy lights of Town. *Do what comes next.* What came next was to climb down off the mountain. Tomorrow they would begin.

She fell asleep with the lights of Far Harbor in her eyes.

Makailani Street was deep in the welter of twisting streets and alleys, each only two or three blocks long, that made up the heart of Old Town. Hawke knew where it was, but it was one of the few he had never explored. He was mildly surprised at the condition of the big converted house at 408 when he found it; it was the best-kept house on a block where none of the houses were neglected. Rents here would not come cheap. From the condition of Lady Sara's home he had assumed that she and Petal were not well off financially. The discrepancy puzzled him only briefly; he was too near his goal now to concentrate for long on anything else.

From a window on the second floor of the house, Petal saw the mad Prince enter Makailani Street. His mouth twisted as he watched the lean, straight figure approach number 408. It was too soon. As usual, Lady Sara hadn't the courage of her convictions. She had given in too easily. The Prince should have been strung along for days more, and led through a succession of increasingly convincing witnesses to Petal's supposed gift, before being allowed to find him. The tantalizing unavailability of Petal, the difficulty of finding him, would in itself have helped to convince the Prince, if only because that which is difficult to obtain often seems more attractive than that which is easier to find.

If they failed to drive the Prince hopelessly mad, Petal would lose his chance to go off-planet. He considered refusing to answer the door when Hawke rang, but any delay thus achieved would be too short to be of value. The landlord lived across the hall from Petal and was a nosy busybody. Sight of the Prince would impress him so much, he would probably trip over himself in his eagerness to be what he liked to call "helpful." And he would know that Petal was home. He always knew what all his tenants were doing.

There was nothing for it but to let in the Prince and try to make the best of a bad situation. Maybe Hawke was already convinced enough. When you wanted something very much, you were easy to convince; Petal had often convinced himself of improbabilities without any help from anyone else. And he knew how much Hawke must want his giftmate. Petal's own gift would mate well with any of three others to form different completions; he could be priest, healer, or magician; but on Paradise he had found no one of the three willing to be giftmated with him, and he never would.

Too alien to fit in among Terrans, he was yet too Terran because of his upbringing to be accepted by the People. The burden of an unmated gift was not unfamiliar to him. His gift was far less than Hawke's, yet not easy to live with alone. With a gift so powerful that it had already driven Hawke half-mad, surely he would be easily pushed just that little bit farther over the edge that would make him clearly unfit to be King. Mahlo had sounded confident enough when he outlined the plan.

If Petal had known Mahlo's real plan, he might have been gladder to open the door to the Prince now, several days before he had expected to be found. As it was, he moved reluctantly in response to the bell and muttered a curse at his absent mother before he composed his face in the best imitation of amiability he could manage and swung the door wide.

His first sight of Hawke at such close range nearly stunned him into immediate and abject honesty. He had not known the Prince was physically so attractive. Pale amethyst eyes stared at him from a narrow, haunted face and he felt his polite smile slipping under their gaze. The movement of the landlord's door behind the Prince caught Petal's attention and brought him back to reality with a jerk. "Prince Hawke," he said, "what a pleasant surprise. Won't you come in? To what do I owe the honor of your visit? Has Mama got herself in some really serious trouble this time?"

Hawke and the tawny cat followed Petal into the luxurious apartment Mahlo had provided as a hide-out. Hawke didn't say anything; he just stared at Petal in blank astonishment. The cat sat down, tail twitching, and watched them both with grave attention.

"Would you like a drink?" asked Petal. "I've heard you like your liquor almost as well as my mama does." The remark was exactly the sort of flippantly callous comment he always made in difficult situations; it was a defense by offense that he had learned in a hard school, wending his way through the emotional pitfalls of growing up among Terrans. This time it had less effect on his victim than on himself. Hawke just continued to stare at him with a look of dazed idiocy. Petal felt suddenly like a murderer.

This is the way off-planet, he thought. It was the only way he knew; the only chance he had to find a world where he might fit in, learn to belong, acquire a giftmate, maybe even a lifemate, and with care and luck lead a normal life among People who accepted him. He would not give that up. "What'll you have?" he asked in his heartiest voice. "Gin? Whiskey? A glass of wine, perhaps?"

Hawke cleared his throat. "You're . . . you're Lady Sara's son? You're Petal?"

Petal had been standing at the bar with his back to Hawke, about to pour them both drinks. Instead, he turned and put his back to the bar, almost as if he needed the support. He met Hawke's gaze with careful disinterest. "At your service," he said. "What can I do for you?" He hadn't known it would be so hard. He hadn't known the Prince would be a regular person, attractive and pleasant and possibly kind. He hadn't known what it would be like to watch the light go out of those amethyst eyes like a fire dying: like a man dying.

Hawke's face was pale and his voice unsteady, but he held himself erect with a visible effort and said in an oddly hollow, distant voice, "You're Petal."

"That's right." Petal managed just the right cheerful inflection, but he was grateful for the edge of the bar at his back to steady him.

"You're not a Breaker." Hawke's voice was even more frail, more distant, like a voice shouted across a storm a million miles away.

"That's right." Petal's own voice broke, but Hawke didn't notice. He was past caring. Petal just managed to catch him when he fell.

39

It was near midday on the second day after they left the pass through the Mysterious Mountains when Ugly and Friend reached the first fringes of Far Harbor. To Ugly's inexperienced eye the buildings even here on the outskirts of the city seemed enormous: everyone in Godsgrace could have been comfortably housed in two or three of the larger ones. They were college dormitories: what Ugly and Friend had come upon was not actually Far Harbor, but Far Harbor University, which was in many ways a separate and distinct little city in its own right, but Ugly didn't know that. Nor could she realize that the first citizens of Far Harbor she saw, by whose example she would determine acceptable behavior and dress, were college students, a group notorious for their contrary and often antisocial ways.

By now Ugly was as capable of swift and silent movement as Friend was. She led him stealthily among the buildings, keeping safely concealed by trees and shrubbery, till they found a cluster of bushes from the center of which they could see a sidewalk, a roadway, and the entrances to two buildings, without being seen themselves. There they settled silently to observe the people in Town.

Ugly was relieved to see a few Terrans dressed in costumes similar to hers. There seemed to be a wide range of costumes considered acceptable, and very few of them resembled the Godsgrace jumpsuit. The new costume had been a good idea; she would be less conspicuous in it. It was true that she was still big-boned and ugly in comparison with these frail, beautiful people, but the cloak would help conceal even that.

They had been watching from their place of con-

cealment for over an hour when the first People
walked by, as big-boned and as ugly as Ugly, and
much larger. She watched them pass and went on
staring in their direction long after they were out of
sight. At first all she could think, in confused awe and
wonder, was that the Ugly People of her visions did
exist, after all. It was some minutes before she realized
that meant that the young man she had seen might
also exist, possibly right here in Far Harbor.

She did not know why it seemed so important to
find him if he did exist, and she had no idea how to
begin looking for him, but at least now she knew that
ugly people like him—and like her—did live here.
They were even common enough that none of the
normal people around them had seemed to take any
particular notice of their ugliness. She had been so
conditioned by the Starlings' ridicule that she didn't
realize even then that if her ugliness were a racial
characteristic, the race that shared it would be unlikely to consider it ugly.

In the hours that followed, a great many normal
individuals and three or four groups of Ugly People
passed the bushes where Ugly and Friend were hiding.
Ugly studied their clothes and mannerisms very carefully, and could see nothing about them very different
from what she had known in Godsgrace except clothing, which she had foreseen. She was sure her present
costume would pass.

The one disturbing thing she noticed was that the
Ugly People seemed never to go anywhere singly, but
were always in pairs or groups. She saw a lot of normal
people moving about singly, but no Ugly People. Did
that mean she would be noticeable as an Ugly Person
alone?

She knew the worry was just a way of stalling; she
was afraid to step out of hiding, and any little worry
was enough to keep her there. But Friend was growing
restless. And he was right: they couldn't hide forever.
She wouldn't go back to the wilderness, at least not
yet. That left very few options.

Even with Friend pacing reassuringly at her side, it

took all Ugly's courage to step out of concealment and walk nonchalantly down the road as if she had a right to be there. Her knees trembled so violently she was afraid she would fall. Her heart beat so rapidly she could hear nothing but its thunder in her ears. Her hands shook. Her eyes wouldn't focus. This was more difficult than anything else she had done since leaving Godsgrace.

She expected to be challenged at any moment, and she jerked convulsively when someone nearby shouted, but it wasn't directed at her. No one challenged her. No one paid any particular attention to her at all. A few of those she considered normal stared nervously at Friend, but the few Ugly People she saw didn't give him a second glance. They did look at her, and one or two smiled in passing. That was all. She was right out in public in the streets of Far Harbor and nothing happened.

After a while she relaxed enough to take more notice of her surroundings. They were moving downhill toward the center of Town, and leaving the university's landscaped open spaces behind them. Smaller plots of grass gave way to bare patches of earth crowded by smaller but much more numerous buildings. Laughing children played in dusty yards. Brown-eyed dogs watched Friend pass with their ears laid back. A dark-haired, dark-eyed man sweeping a porch looked so much like Emmett Starling that Ugly nearly stopped and stared at him, but Friend nudged her on. A woman taking clothes off a line turned to look at them, stared for a moment at Friend, then looked up and smiled cheerfully at Ugly. The laundry flapped in the wind, bright colors faded by sun and wear. Ugly returned her smile uncertainly.

A surface car hummed past, startling Ugly and Friend into brief immobility: neither of them had seen anything like it before. It was a small two-seater with a round, weary-looking man at the wheel and a thin, cross-looking boy beside him. Neither of them glanced at Ugly and Friend, and no one else on the street took much notice of the car. Ugly resisted the impulse to turn and look after it. They went on.

By now it was late afternoon, and Ugly had begun to feel increasingly aware that it had been a very long time since lunch. Friend could hardly go hunting for meat here in Town. If they found a place to sit down somewhere, Ugly could make a meal from odds and ends stored in the backpack she still carried in one hand under her cloak, but there was nothing in it for Friend. Also, they were getting low on water, and she hadn't realized how difficult that might be to replenish in Town.

Perhaps worst of all was that there would be no place to make camp when darkness fell. They could hardly camp on one of these small residential dust-patches. They might have to return to the wilderness to find a place to sleep, and food for Friend; but Ugly felt obstinately reluctant to do so. There must be some other option. There must be a reason they had been directed here. She felt sure the Goddess had wanted her to leave their valley and come to Town. Whatever the reason, she thought crossly that it ought to include food and a place to sleep.

A group of people in plain, worn jumpsuits like those common in Godsgrace crossed the street just ahead of Ugly and Friend and entered a small, square, drab, gray building that Ugly recognized at once as a church: the same sort of church she had known in Godsgrace. One of the people glanced at her and Friend, and it was all she could do to keep walking without any change in expression or pace; panic made her knees tremble again and made her hands shake so badly she nearly dropped her backpack.

If they recognized her . . . !

That was absurd. They couldn't recognize her. They weren't Godsgrace residents, they were just practi-tioners of the same religion. Nonetheless, she felt weak with relief when she and Friend were safely past the church and no one had called them back.

When she could think clearly again, she realized

that there must be churches of all kinds in a place as big as Far Harbor. There might even be one that belonged to the Crystal Goddess. If she could find one like that, she and Friend could surely rest there long enough to decide—or to be shown—what to do next. But how did one find a specific church, or anything else, in a place so large and strange as Far Harbor?

She could ask someone, but she didn't even know what the Goddess was named. She wouldn't know what to ask. Besides, the mere thought of actually approaching any of these strangers to ask directions was terrifying.

Friend seemed as weary as she was. He butted against her legs and emitted a single meek little meow in a questioning tone. Ugly glanced down at him and said, "I don't know," in a distracted way. He leaned against her, forcing her to stop, and looked up at her with narrowed eyes. "What is it?" she asked, glancing nervously around to see if anyone had noticed them. No one had. The few people in sight were all busy with their own concerns.

"Yee-ow?" said Friend.

Ugly shook her head crossly. "I don't *know*."

He looked at her a moment longer, then lifted himself effortlessly onto his hind legs in one graceful motion and put his front paws against her hip. With his nose, he poked curiously at the folds of her cloak, purring, till he found what he was looking for, and bit it. He also bit the hand she automatically reached out to smooth the fur on his head. His strong white teeth closed just hard enough on her flesh to pinch uncomfortably without breaking the skin. Then he released her and sat back down in front of her to wash one front paw.

Ugly looked at him in some confusion, and then at the little indentations on her hand where his teeth had pinched her. With the other hand she felt absently at her cloak to see why he had bitten that, too. Her hand bumped the secure little pocket she had made for the crystal.

"Oh, Friend," she said, "I'm glad *one* of us is intelligent, anyway." Smiling with relief, she drew the crystal from its hiding place and held it cupped in her hand to catch the light when she looked deep into its faceted brilliance. Beside her, Friend finished washing his paw and rose, ready to follow where the crystal led them.

40

The triumph that Petal felt lasted only an instant, not even as long as it took him to lower the stricken Prince gently to the floor. It seemed he had won his way off-planet, but at what cost? He stared for a moment at Hawke's pale face with its bruised smudges under the eyes; the skin drawn taut over sharp, high cheekbones; the mouth oddly vulnerable in repose. In an automatic, almost involuntary gesture he smoothed the tangled hair back from Hawke's forehead and gently traced with one tentative finger the hard curve of Hawke's jaw. Then he straightened and turned back to the bar. The tawny cat that had entered with Hawke put its paws on Hawke's shoulder and stared at Petal with solemn, jeweled eyes.

What sort of life could he build on this? The People on Freehold might not know his past, but he would. His Terran mannerisms and habits might pass for merely foreign on a new and distant planet, but he would know what they were and what he had done. His mouth twisted with bitter humor as he realized that this, which he had done in the hope of buying himself a place in a community of the People, was the most wholly Terran act he had ever performed.

He poured a glass of whiskey and knelt again by the Prince, who was showing signs of consciousness. The cat moved aside, watching solemnly. Lifting Hawke's head, Petal held the glass to his mouth and told him to drink. Hawke obediently drank, then choked, coughed, and sat up, sputtering. "That's better," said Petal.

There was color in Hawke's cheeks again, and the frail glow of fire in his eyes.

"Can you get up?" asked Petal. "It's not right for a

Prince to sit on the floor." He made a wry face. "At least, I suppose whatever a Prince does is right because he does it . . . that's the royal attitude, isn't it? But it doesn't *seem* right for you to sit on the floor."

Hawke looked at him without interest. The fire the whiskey had kindled was dying.

Petal sighed. "My lord Prince," he said gently but firmly, "get up."

Hawke struggled obediently to his feet and stood swaying, looking about him with dazed eyes. He saw the glass in Petal's hand and reached for it, but Petal drew it back before he could touch it. Hawke looked at him with the dull bewilderment of a hurt child.

"Prince Hawke . . . my lord Prince. . . ." Petal hesitated. If Mahlo's plan wasn't already successful, the application of plenty of liquor would surely do the trick. Hawke was either totally, irrevocably insane, or he was teetering on the brink of it. In either case a good drunk could finish the job. All Petal had to do was hand over the liquor. But he wasn't going to do it.

Hawke waited patiently, his eyes flat amethyst pools, pale and empty.

"You turned out to be an easier mark than we guessed," said Petal.

Prince Hawke didn't move.

"What a wimp," Petal said impatiently. "Sit down, why don't you?" He shoved the Prince into a chair.

The flat amethyst eyes watched without interest as Petal drank the whiskey he held, put the glass on the bar, and took a chair near the Prince. The cat settled bonelessly to the floor between them, watching the Prince.

"What does it take to make you angry?" asked Petal.

Hawke blinked.

"I've heard a lot about your drunken brawls. Don't you know how to fight when you're sober?"

Hawke smiled beatifically.

That was too much for Petal. He rose suddenly, with the fluid grace of a dancer, and stalked across the room to stand at the window with his back to Hawke. After a long moment he said, "Damn," very softly, and turned to face Hawke again. "I'm about to throw away the only hope of happiness I've ever had." His voice was hoarse with suppressed rage. "Maybe I'm throwing away my life, too, I don't know. I guess the High King Arkos will decide that. If you have the guts to get hold of yourself and *listen* to me, and then do something about it besides give up because life is hard."

He walked away from the window and absently picked up a ceramic statue from a niche in the wall. "I want you to know I'm not doing it for you. You're not worth it." His voice was shaking with rage and contempt.

Hawke's smile didn't falter.

Petal shook his head. "I can't believe I'm doing this." He thought about it. "Yes, I can. Not for you, not for your filthy royal house, not for anybody's damn politics: I'm doing it for me. Because I've always been like you are; I just sat around and let life hit me, and whined about how much it hurt; and I'm damned if I'll do that anymore. I wanted a place to belong, but I won't have it at this price." His mouth twisted. "Which means I won't have it at all."

He studied Hawke for a moment, wondering what was going on behind those pale eyes. The smile was gone, anyway. Petal's moment of furious contempt was past; he could see again Hawke's pain and potential, and he wanted somehow to reach past the barriers Hawke had built against the world; but how? On impulse he lifted the statue he held and hurled it directly at Hawke.

Hawke picked it out of the air with a lazy motion of one hand and went on staring at Petal.

Petal smiled, oddly drawn to the Prince again. "Well, that proves there's somebody in there. I think."

Hawke put the statue on a table beside his chair.

"You know you've been tricked," said Petal. "Deliberately tricked."

Hawke looked at the statue.

"You were deliberately led to believe I was your Breaker." At the sound of that word, a shadow of pain crossed Hawke's face, but Petal didn't falter. "It was supposed to take you several more days to find me, to be sure you'd let yourself hope enough so that the truth would destroy you."

Hawke nodded. "Mahlo." It was the first sound he had made since regaining consciousness, and his voice had a dry, papery quality to it, but it was strong enough for Petal to hear.

"Yes. Mahlo. You knew?" Petal stared, rigid with disbelief: how could Hawke have known? And if he knew, how could he have been so nearly destroyed? Or had Petal been wrong about that? What was going on? He had thought he was making a sacrifice, but if Hawke had known all along, then Petal had lost nothing: he'd had nothing to lose. "I'd swear you believed it," he said. "I'd *swear* it."

"I believed it." Hawke's voice was stronger now. "But now that I know it's not . . . you're not . . . I see how I was led."

"But how did you know it was Mahlo?"

"I knew."

Petal turned away. "I thought I was making a grand sacrifice, for once doing something brave and right and noble, maybe even . . . maybe *saving* you. . . . And you knew. You knew all along. You didn't need me."

"I needed you." For the first time, Hawke's voice held the authority of a Prince. "Never doubt that. I had dared to hope. The shock of another loss . . . I didn't even remember the vision the Goddess showed me. I gave up. I suppose I would have died if you hadn't bullied me." He said it as matter-of-factly as one might say, "I suppose it might have rained."

Petal looked at him fiercely. "I don't need your damn kindness."

Hawke smiled again, and it wasn't a beatific smile this time. It was a feral baring of teeth in readiness for battle. "I am not kind."

Petal could find nothing to say in response to that.

41

The temple that Ugly and Friend found by means of the crystal belonged unmistakably to the Crystal Goddess. The windows were crystal, there was a crystal sculpture on the stairs, and through the open front doors they could see the glistening crystal altar. They mounted the stairs together, Ugly somewhat cautiously, and Friend with his tail confidently in the air.

Afternoon sunlight streaked through the door and glowed through the windows, refracting through all the crystals inside and filling the air with rainbows. There were magnificent crystal sculptures and friezes everywhere. The ceiling was hidden behind a glittering mass of crystal windchimes that tinkled gaily in a gentle breeze through the door. The whole temple was a refined version of Ugly's beautiful crystal gully in the wilderness. And on the altar, her eyes glowing emerald green in the light, stood the Crystal Goddess herself, smiling a welcome at Ugly and Friend.

There was no one inside, neither keepers nor worshippers. After a moment's hesitation at the doorway, Ugly entered the temple and approached the altar, clutching her own crystal in one nerveless hand. As she had at the shrine in the wilderness, she felt drawn to the Goddess almost against her will. Aware of Friend purring audibly beside her, she walked along a carpeted path, through rainbows and the rich blue smoke of incense, to the circle of benches around the altar. There she knelt before the Goddess and stared intently up into the green, glowing eyes.

Friend seated himself gravely beside her, no longer purring. The only sound was the ceaseless, musical chime of the crystals overhead. The sandalwood scent of incense was almost dizzying, this near the altar. The brilliant splashes of rainbow colors that swirled in the air spun and sparkled and interwove themselves with blue swirls of smoke. . . .

She was looking at a flight of stairs made of stone so ancient it was worn into hollows where generations of feet had trod. There were flickering torches set at intervals in the walls, their light catching in myriad crystals, turning the air into a rainbow of fire and ice. There were people waiting at the foot of the stairs, pompous and dark and frightened. There were three Ugly People on the stairs, slowly descending.

Ugly gasped as she recognized herself on the stairs, with Friend stalking regally at her heels. The young man of her visions was beside her, with a tawny cat at his heels. His eyes seemed to glow with a fierce, frightening power as ancient as the stones of the stairs. It was, oddly, matched by a glow in her own eyes, as if together they formed something greater than human, a force or a focus of terrible power beyond understanding or imagination. No wonder the people at the foot of the stairs looked frightened. In the face of that power, Ugly herself was frightened, though in the vision she seemed to be a part of the force that frightened her.

Both she and the young man beside her were wearing heavy robes of brocade and gold, and glittering crowns encrusted with jewels and brilliant crystal; but the man preceding them down the stairs was even more magnificently enrobed and crowned. His eyes, too, glowed with a kind of power, though not as dangerously as Ugly's and the young man's. He seemed to be in charge, but it was toward Ugly and the young man that the people below them stared with such obvious and understandable fear.

One of the torches flared. Its light was caught in crystal and reflected, refracted, spun on smoke and rainbows till it glittered like broken glass. Ugly blinked reflexively. In that instant the scene shifted, so that she opened her eyes to the confusion of battle on a dark plain dotted with the dull red of campfires and swarming with soldiers engaged in battle. Shouts and cries and the sharp clang of steel against steel startled her. Sudden explosions and the whine of Terran weapons all but deafened her. The stink of death replaced the sweet incense of the temple. It was a nightmare scene of chaos and horror, in which she stood alone at the end of the world, momentarily forgetting the grim task she had set herself, while she gazed without interest across a darkened plain. . . . She saw the battle as if from a great distance: she watched two vast armies collide as relentlessly, as destructively, and as pointlessly as ocean waves crash against a vulnerable shore. Men out there were dying. . . .

Men were dead. She remembered her task and returned to it dully, grief and fear both blunted by a surfeit of horror: one cannot endure the end of the world forever. She examined every corpse she found, turning them when she had to, and they were many: she searched every ruin, choking on dust and smoke and the stink of decay: she looked in every gully, under every scrap of wreckage, behind every rock outcropping. Hawke was missing. Hawke was gone. Hawke was lost.

She might have been searching for days or for weeks or only for minutes. She had no sense of time, only of eternity. Hawke was missing. Without him, life was a barren plain, stretching as black and endless as the battlefield, as empty as death. She could not endure it.

If they had killed him, she would destroy them. She would destroy the world. She would destroy the gods. She glanced across the plain again: and wherever her gaze touched a smoldering campfire, flames shot up against the darkness, orange and yellow and deadly, and their light caught in the crystal, and a rainbow swallowed the darkness, and she stood in the sun again with Hawke at her side and Friend at her feet and a distant train of brightly dressed People approaching the palace, coming for the festival. She watched their approach for a moment, then turned to watch Hawke watching them.

It amused her that once she had thought him ugly. Every plane and shadow of his face was beautiful to her: every bone, every gesture, every line of his body was perfect: every expression, every tone of his voice, every look of his eyes was beloved. She smiled. He, aware of the smile, glanced at her with love and laughter. Where the gaze of their amethyst eyes met, a rainbow appeared in the blue smoke of incense and the crystals shattered it, scattered it, and she was kneeling in the temple again before the green-eyed Crystal Goddess and she knew that his name was Hawke. And she knew that she would find him.

42

Petal went willingly with Hawke to the reservation, to reveal Mahlo's plot to the High King. They made an odd pair, Hawke lean and predatory, Petal willowy and brave. It did not occur to them that they looked particularly dangerous, and they did not notice that everyone they passed on their way out of Old Town, People and Terrans alike, gave them a wide berth and stared after them in wary awe. Intent on their purpose, they barely noticed that they passed anyone at all. The tawny cat trailed, forgotten, behind them, ears erect, eyes bright, tail twitching.

43

The temple was just an ordinary place again, the Crystal Goddess just a statue. The room was beautifully decorated, the air thick with incense and splashed with rainbows, but it was just a room: the magic was gone. Ugly became aware of another presence and turned slowly, then rose swiftly when she saw the priest in his emerald-green robes waiting in silence behind her.

He was one of the Ugly People. He was, in fact, even uglier than she, and much larger. She took an involuntary step backward, away from him. Friend had not risen, but merely twisted his neck to look at the priest; now he said plaintively, "Yowrell?"

The priest responded in a language Ugly did not understand. He spoke directly to the cat as if answering a question, and waited politely when he had asked one of his own. Friend spoke again, and the priest looked at Ugly in surprise. "I must have misunderstood," he said. "Friend tells me your name is . . . Ugly?" This time he spoke Terran Standard, and she understood him perfectly.

She looked at him with surprise that matched his own, and nodded dumbly.

"But, my dear, you're hardly—"

"Friend told you? You can understand what Friend says?"

"Languages are my gift," he said modestly. "Oh my, excuse me," he added quickly when Friend butted him, "I've forgotten you didn't understand all I said to Friend." He bowed rather grandly, but with a mischievous smile. "My name is Stone. My giftmate Bela and I are priests of Lanalei. How may we serve you?"

"Meerrowl!" said Friend.

"Oh," said the priest. "Oh. Um. Miss . . . um. I simply cannot call you Ugly, my dear, it's so very inappropriate, don't you see? But Friend tells me that you've had a vision?"

"Yow-owr," said Friend.

"Ah, I see." The priest stared at Ugly in mild astonishment. "Oh, my goodness. Oh my!"

"What is it, what's the matter?" Ugly took another step away from him and came up against the altar rail. "Why are you looking at me like that?" If there had been room to pass between him and the benches, she would have bolted. She glanced to one side, toward the next break in the encircling benches, and to her horror saw another priest approaching, this one female and just as large as Stone.

Following her gaze, Stone smiled happily and said, "Ah, Bela. I wasn't sure you'd heard me. Would you call the police for me, dear? This young lady—"

Ugly didn't wait to hear the rest. She turned frantically away from them both and hurled herself desperately toward the next opening in the benches. She didn't make it. Neither priest moved, but Friend did. She thought he was leaping up to run with her. Instead, he tangled himself in her feet and then slid gracefully out of the way to watch her fall.

She landed hard and banged her head painfully against a bench. The blow dizzied her and the fall had knocked the breath out of her, but in spite of that she tried to rise, to run again. All she achieved was an awkward scrabbling motion, half-crawl, half-fall, but she had to escape. They had recognized her. They knew what she had done. They would call the police, and the police would kill her, and it was no more than she deserved, but she wanted to find Hawke, she needed to find Hawke, she couldn't die before she found Hawke. . . .

Gentle hands lifted her and set her gently but firmly on a hard wooden bench. The universe lurched sickeningly with the movement and she could not focus her eyes. Someone was speaking to her from a great distance, but all she could hear at first was the roar of blood in her ears and her own voice, dazed and childlike, saying in a thin, frail, wondering tone, "My head hurts."

"And no wonder," said Bela. "Friend, you could have been more careful."

"Meow," said Friend. He rubbed himself ingratiatingly against Ugly's knees.

"Well, what's done is done," said Stone. "My dear young lady, really you must listen to Friend, really you must. You know he is your friend. Trust him. He knows we mean you no harm."

"The police?" Her voice still sounded frail and small and oddly distant.

"Oh, my dear, what did you think? Surely you couldn't imagine . . . ? There would be no reason . . . ? Oh my, oh my. We must call them, you know. To escort you to the reservation palace. To be sure you'll be safe on the way."

The palace? Did they take murderers for execution to the palace? She wondered dizzily why she needed to be safe on the way to her execution. She had no intention of going anywhere with the police. She must find Hawke. She said in her thin little child's voice, "I will go alone."

"Oh, my dear, my dear, we could hardly risk that, really now, I'll warrant you're from one of the villages, yes? Not from Town. You don't know your way around. I don't like to say it's dangerous, but don't you know, it *is* dangerous, at least some sections of Town are, there's no getting around that, where you have so many People and Terrans together. . . . And what if something happened to you on the way? Oh no, no, you must let us help you. Really you must. The police will escort you, and see that no harm comes to you. We must be sure you get safely to Prince Hawke without further mishap, now, mustn't we?"

Ugly's vision was clearing. She stared up at Stone in wonder. "Prince . . . Prince Hawke?" The shock of the title momentarily drove all else from her mind. She should have guessed, from the costumes and the crowns, but it simply hadn't occurred to her. She wondered dully whether a Prince would even notice her. "*Prince* Hawke?"

Stone didn't seem to notice the emphasis. "Of course, my dear. Lanalei told you his name, didn't she? Now you rest here while Bela calls the police. Oh my, this is exciting. Bela, do light an extra candle on your way past. Oh my, oh my." He smiled complacently at Ugly. "We had heard that Lanalei was protecting you, my dear, but to think that she would lead you to our own little temple! To be instrumental in such a wonderful event! Oh my!"

Ugly blinked at him and wondered vaguely what he was talking about. It didn't really seem to matter; she knew now that she must still be dreaming, watching crystal visions. He had said they would take her to Hawke. Nothing in real life could be so simple. She smiled up at the priest and waited with calm, detached interest to see what would happen next.

44

Petal and Hawke stood before the King, their expressions identically wary in the face of his towering rage. He had been silent except for an occasional terse query since they began their tale. It was impossible to know what he was thinking. His initial frank disbelief had given way, slowly, to killing anger, but with whom? They had finished their story minutes ago. Since then, none of the three of them had spoken. A servant moved slowly through the room, replacing guttering candles. A moth hurled itself ceaselessly against a window, seeking the light. Hawke's cat, seated comfortably at the King's feet, watched it with the alert gaze of a hunter.

Arkos clapped his hands so suddenly and so sharply that Petal and the cat both jumped in fright. Bush appeared at the King's elbow. "Yes, my lord King?"

"Bring me Mahlo."

"Yes, my lord King." Bush hurried from the room, shutting the big doors carefully behind him.

The moth moved to another window. The servant who had been tending candles finished his work, put the basket of candle stubs and fresh candles over his arm, and left by a smaller door into the King's private chambers. Arkos scowled at Hawke and Petal. "Sit, both of you." He gestured toward chairs. "We will wait."

45

The police were kind to Ugly. The priests had told them very little, not even her name: only that she must be brought safely to the palace with the sealed message they had given her, which she was to deliver personally to the King. Two policemen came to pick her up, in a groundcar painted bright red with a flashing red light on top. They were what she thought of as "normal" people, not ugly, but they were very polite to Ugly and the priests and, after their initial surprise at the sight of him, were reasonably polite to Friend, as well.

The trip with them through Far Harbor to the reservation beyond would always remain vague in Ugly's memory. Too much was happening too quickly, and she could not take it in. She sat patiently clutching the sealed scroll the priests had given her, staring through the car's smoky windows at a blur of bright lights in the sudden night outside, exhausted and trying not to be frightened. Beside her, Friend sat erect in his seat, amethyst eyes narrowed, watching through the front windshield with total concentration, as though he were driving.

The bright lights thinned and then ended. For a time they traveled in total darkness, the outside world compressed into the twin cones of the car's headlights. The reservation lights must have been visible from a distance, but Ugly didn't notice them until the car passed through the decorative gateway onto the reservation, and the torchlit palace loomed suddenly before them.

The policemen handed her and Friend politely over to ornately robed guards on the palace stairs. The guards were Ugly People. The policemen waved at

Ugly, and one of them smiled. They drove away while the Ugly People opened the great doors into the palace. Suddenly Ugly and Friend were standing inside, at the foot of a long flight of wide wooden stairs, facing the amiable enemy she had seen with Hawke's father in her visions days ago.

He bowed politely and held out his hand to her. She looked at it, uncertain what he wanted. He produced one of his affable smiles and said something pleasantly in a language she didn't understand. Beside her, one of the guards from the stairs outside said something to him in the same language, and the affable smile faded somewhat as he stared at her with an odd intensity; but his voice was pleasant enough when he spoke again, this time in Terran Standard: "My name is Mahlo. I am chief advisor to the High King. In fact"—here the smile became a wry grin and the weak eyes blinked owlishly—"as you might guess, I've just been summoned to him." He nodded meaningfully toward another man whose presence Ugly had not noticed. "So you see, if you'll just give me the message you're carrying—it is a message for the High King?—I can take it directly to him for you." He held out his hand again.

Ugly stepped back involuntarily and put the scroll behind her back, like a child concealing a forbidden treat. "No!" Her voice squeaked. She cleared her throat and said again, more quietly, "No. I was told to give it to no one but the High King himself."

Mahlo studied her for a moment, and abruptly seemed to lose all interest in her. He shrugged and said crossly, "Very well. Let us at least show you the way. Come along, Bush." He started up the stairs before Ugly and raised his voice to say without turning his head, "Have you brought this precious message all the way from your village?"

Ugly followed him and his silent companion up the stairs, with Friend pacing regally beside her. "No. How did you know I'm not from here?"

"From where? The reservation? My dear, quite

aside from the fact that you don't speak our language, your quaint country costume—tapa leaves, isn't it?—and your accent. Unmistakable. Which village are you from?"

She didn't hear the question; she was looking down at the swirling folds of her cloak in grim resignation. "Is my costume wrong, then?"

The silent man whom Mahlo had called Bush glanced at Ugly in startled amusement, but she didn't notice that any more than she had noticed his longer gaze of startled admiration when they first met at the foot of the stairs. Mahlo laughed aloud: a small, rippling, artificial sound. "If you meant it to make you look like one of the People, then you've failed dismally. However, I really don't think you ever need worry whether your costume suits you."

It was a compliment, but Ugly had no way of knowing that; she had never heard one before. She nodded gravely, aware that her ugliness would transcend even the finest of costumes, and said with weary resignation, "I suppose not." She didn't notice the puzzled looks both men gave her at that.

They reached the top of the stairs and proceeded down a long, dimly candlelit hall. "Does the King know you're coming?" Mahlo asked.

"No." Ugly looked at the two men in sudden fear. "The priests seemed so sure it would be all right. The ones who gave me the message. He . . . the King . . . he'll see me, won't he?" Her voice sounded childishly defiant.

"Ah, a message from a priest," Mahlo said without interest. "Well, we'll see."

Bush had been studying Ugly speculatively from behind a veil of lowered lashes. Now he looked away, as if suddenly satisfied, and said in a confident tone, "The King will see you, don't worry." Mahlo glanced at him in surprise, but Bush merely looked enigmatic and led the way toward the King's audience chamber.

Friend began to purr in anticipation. It was a startlingly loud sound in the silent corridor.

46

Ugly and Friend were let into the High King's audience chamber, but held at the door while Mahlo and Bush went forward to meet the King. Ugly hardly noticed what they did; she was staring in awe at the room itself. It was enormous, almost as large as the temple of Lanalei where she had met the priests, and it seemed larger because of the tapestries hung on the walls. At first glance, they looked like doorways into exotic worlds, as if the room had no walls but only dark windows onto the real night outside, and between them, broad openings onto strange and beautiful daylight places where laughing people and wondrous animals played in deep forests and wide sunny fields.

When she looked away from the tapestries, at first she could see nothing but candles glowing: hundreds of candles set in alcoves and niches, on tables and pedestals, in tall candlesticks and short ones, singly and in bunches. Their light picked out the gold threads in the tapestries and caught in the crystals set in the designs. Even in the temple of Lanalei there had not been so many candles all lighted at once. They gave the room a bright golden air of festival and turned the little scene at the far end, where the people were gathered, into a stage play acted in silence, because she could not hear the actors' voices from where she stood.

She stared at them idly, feeling oddly disassociated from the entire situation. They were deeply involved in conversation, and the one called Bush, who had promised to bring Ugly's presence to the attention of the King, was obviously going to have to wait for an opportunity: the King was at present ignoring him completely.

There had been two people already with the King when Bush and Mahlo joined them. At this distance Ugly could not clearly see their faces, but one appeared to be a pale young boy in not-quite-shabby garments, with long pale hair that he kept flicking nervously out of his face. The other was Hawke. He was dressed more elegantly than his companion, but not as well as the King.

The resemblance between Hawke and the King was even more evident, now that she saw them together. At first all Ugly People had looked pretty much alike to her, but now she had begun, as in her last vision, to see past their ugliness and, in fact, to find them not really ugly after all. She liked the prominent high cheekbones of Hawke and his father, and the big-boned lankiness of their bodies, evident even under the heavy brocade robes the King wore.

Mahlo and the boy beside Hawke seemed to be arguing. None of them had noticed Ugly and Friend except the big tawny cat who had been sitting at Hawke's feet: she rose when she saw Friend, and started across the room toward him. He promptly slipped past the disconcerted guards to meet her halfway. The guards, apparently deciding Friend was not a danger to the King, returned their attention to Ugly, who should in their opinion have been made to wait outside.

Bush had insisted she be brought through the doors to wait while he asked the King to see her; he had guessed what she was, and did not want any risk of losing her now. When there was sufficient pause in the confrontation between Mahlo and Petal, Bush whispered to the King and gestured toward Ugly. It brought her to the attention of all four of them when Mahlo, who did not hear the whisper but had seen the gesture, said indifferently, "Ah, yes, the priests' waif. She claims she carries a message for you, my lord King."

Mahlo had been trying to discredit Petal by any means available, and had met much stronger resistance than he had expected. The King was too willing to believe the mad Prince and the half-Terran hireling. Perhaps the lovely Terran waif would provide sufficient distraction to give Mahlo time to think of a new angle of attack.

Petal wasn't much interested in the girl; he had just been shocked into silence by the realization that Mahlo must almost certainly have meant to kill him. It would have provided a much more traumatic shock to Hawke than the truth, and it would have been cheaper and easier for Mahlo than sending Petal to a colony. It was Petal's sudden silence at that realization that had provided Bush with the opportunity to speak of Ugly to the King.

Arkos was briefly irritated at Bush's interruption, till he saw the look on his son's face as Hawke looked toward the girl. Only then did Arkos realize what Bush had said: "I think the priests have sent us a Breaker."

Hawke knew her at once. He stood up slowly, not aware of moving at all. It was as if her presence wiped away all the years of loneliness, loss, uncertainty, insanity: he was whole again, and as full of joyous energy as a child.

Ugly never noticed when the guards ceased to block her way to the King. Once Hawke's gaze met hers, she would have gone to him through barriers far more substantial than a pair of palace guards. She had not known why she felt a compulsion to come into the city and to find this man, but she knew when their eyes met and the shock of his power, of his being, of his need, met the strength of hers. She moved past the guards without seeing them; without seeing anything but the man whose gift matched hers.

Mahlo, believing the Breaker safely lost in the windward forest, did not at first understand what had happened. He was still framing possible refutations to Petal's story when the King looked at him in sudden contempt and said in a cold and deadly voice, "This is the Starling child, Mahlo. I recognize her from the hologram they sent. So Petal's story is true after all, isn't it, my old friend?"

"My lord King—"

"Silence!" The King signaled the guards and looked away from Mahlo's anxiously ingratiating smile, back toward the beautiful young Breaker who had come to restore his son's sanity and his life.

In that instant Mahlo, realizing he could salvage nothing from the situation, struck his last and most desperate blow against the King and his heir. Before the guards could reach him, he had his crystal in his hand, and had begun to sing the one song a crystal singer could sing most effectively alone: the Death Song. He thought of his children growing up in a zoo when they could have been rulers, and he poured his rage and frustration into the power of his gift, and he sang for freedom, for hope, for life . . . and for death.

Ugly didn't know what Mahlo was doing, but she felt his power. There was a tenuous and tender sense of connection between her and Hawke, as if each held one end of a fragile crystal thread stretched across the space between them. Mahlo's song plucked and pulled at that thread as painfully as if he struck Hawke and Ugly physically. Where there had been rainbows there were fire and ice: where there had been joy there was killing grief: where there had been the first frail awakening of love there was the unexpected violence of sudden loss. Hawke staggered back, his new assurance viciously undermined, and Ugly could not reach past the glittering notes of the crystal song to comfort him. The shrill and brittle melody pierced her heart like a flashing sword and tore at her mind, shattering her courage and her strength.

She was Ugly Starling again, clumsy and stupid, a waste of food. A murderer. *Can't you do anything right?* The voices echoed in her mind, as fierce and fresh as if she had never left Godsgrace. *What is the matter with you? You're a monster; a clumsy, ugly, horrible monster. You're not even human. You're noth-*

ing but a waste of food. Monster! Useless space garbage! You've killed, you've killed, you've killed . . . !

Through sudden tears she saw Hawke stumble away from her, eyes closed, hands pressed hard against the sides of his head, and she thought he could hear the voices too. He had not known she was a murderer. He had not known she was useless, a waste of food. He would not, could not, want her now. . . .

She should never have come here. She had been happier in the wilderness. No one, there, had been offended by her appearance or her past. Why had she ever imagined there would be a place for her here? Why had she dared to think that Hawke would accept her once he knew what she was?

Friend butted anxiously against her leg and she remembered her fear of him that night in the wilderness. Dear Friend, her only friend, and she had seen him as a stranger, dangerous and wild. . . . She should have stayed out there with him. He butted her again, harder this time, and she remembered her own voice saying, "A frightened mind plays strange tricks." *It was a lesson she would do well to remember: second-guessing one's irrevocable decisions in a moment of crisis would hardly be a productive way to behave.*

She blinked. Hawke *had* wanted her. He had seen her, seen how ugly she was, and in spite of that he had somehow reached across the space between them to touch her with gentleness and love. She stared at him, torn by despair and fragile hope, and in sudden defiance chose hope.

She could not have said exactly what it was that she had done, except that she *reached* for Hawke somehow, in a way that was similar to what she did to light fires or to move objects with her crystal: similar, but much more powerful. With Hawke and the hope of life so near, her need was greater than ever it had been before. She could see him, she had felt the touch of his mind, and that moment's joy had been greater than she had known could exist. She would not give that up without a fight.

The sinuous and deadly melody of Mahlo's song tunneled fiery violence through her determination, but she fought it now. She would *not* be nothing. She would *not* be a waste of food. She would *not* be a monster. And she would *not* see Hawke destroyed because she was a murderer. He had stumbled backward, nearly fallen, and grasped the back of his chair to hold him upright. Mahlo's song was as bad for him as it was for her. It was killing him. She could not undo the murder she had done, but she would not pay for it with Hawke's death. First things first. She would save him—somehow, she would save him—and afterward she would face whatever reckoning she must for the murder she had done.

Dazed and dizzy and unaware of tears streaming down her cheeks from eyes that blazed with brilliant amethyst fire, she gathered all the strength she had found in the wilderness, and all the courage she had found in solitude, and she offered it up whole to Hawke in a desperate, aching, anxious effort of reaching, wanting, giving, needing. The air between them seemed to crackle with the sheer energy of her hope. When she had given him all she had, she would be helpless and hopeless, prey to Mahlo's song; but Hawke would be saved, and that was all that mattered now. . . .

She did not see that the King, too, was ravaged by Mahlo's song. She did not see Petal and Bush backing away, torn by mindless fear and killing agony, bruised by the crystal notes. She did not even see Mahlo, with his twisted smile and his eyes so dark with hate and the desire for death that they were bottomless pits of black shadows into which a universe might have fallen and died without hope. She saw only Hawke.

The lines and planes of his face were more familiar to her than her own. She knew the despair that had almost won him over, and she fought it with all the hope she could summon. She knew the slow, grinding pain of self-loathing that had worn him down and smudged the shadows under his eyes with blue, and she fought it with all the confidence she had ever felt or could imagine. She recognized the weary rejection of hope that closed his eyes against her, and with all her strength she willed him to open his eyes, to look at her, to hope, to live, to accept the gift of her life. She offered it gladly, in exchange for his.

The crystal Death Song battered her with fear, despair, defeat, self-loathing, and a terrible yawning emptiness; loneliness that perhaps no other of the People could have resisted; but she was Terran-trained to withstand all of that, and worse. She had endured as much at the hands of the Starlings. She could endure it this much longer: long enough to bequeath her strength to Hawke. Once, she would have fallen under the first onslaught of Mahlo's song, but not now. Not after the isolation of the wilderness, the friendship of Friend, the hope of Hawke.

He opened his eyes. They were battered and black, the amethyst fires reduced to dying embers, but they looked through the killing void of Mahlo's song to her, and in that instant she knew they had won.

Afterward she never fully remembered that terrible, silent battle of wills. Once Hawke had accepted the strength of her hope, he accepted the burden of the battle as well. He became a focal point through which her energy could be channeled against Mahlo: and then he gathered his own strength, added it to hers, and together they built such a towering mirror of resistance that Mahlo's song could harm no one but himself.

In the last instant before the song killed him, Mahlo knew what had happened. He knew he had lost. He knew he had not killed the Maker-Breaker pair nor stopped their bonding; and that together, they would destroy Terran rule on Paradise. Perhaps, in that moment, knowing the futility of it, he could have stopped his song before it killed him. He did not.

47

"I am Ugly, my lord King," said the Breaker. The tawny cat and the white cat sat side by side at her feet, their raspy purrs humming like miniature motors, their wide amethyst eyes staring intently at the King.

"No, my dear." The King's smile was as much relieved as amused: the battle had been fierce and the outcome by no means guaranteed.

"I beg your pardon?" said the Breaker, her face a study in uncertainty and something like fear.

"You are not ugly, my dear. You are, in fact, quite beautiful."

She looked startled, looked at the cats, looked at Hawke, and forced herself to look at the King again. "I am?"

He nodded, still smiling.

She absorbed that, her gaze moving from him to Hawke and back again in wonder. Then the uncertainty returned, and the fear, and a determined courage. "Yes, my lord King," she said obediently enough, but without conviction. "Still, it is my name."

"Then we shall have to find you another name," said the King. "That one will not do. I doubt it is the one you were given by your parents."

"I have no parents. I . . ." She hesitated, swallowed, and looked away. "I had foster parents."

"Nonetheless, you did have parents once," said the King. "They were killed in the earthquake on Freehold: that much we know. I suspect you must be the daughter of the King of Freehold; she was never found. We shall see; the magicians will know. It is their gift. If I am right, I assure you that you could hardly have a nobler background. King Leaf was a loyal subject of mine, and a great friend. I was sorry at the—"

"My lord King." She had straightened her shoulders and moved just perceptibly away from Hawke, and her face was pale and fierce and lonely.

One does not interrupt the High King. However, when one has just saved his life, his heir, and quite possibly his kingdom . . . "Yes, my dear?"

"I am also a murderer, my lord King." Her voice was firm and strong and absolutely toneless.

Arkos stared. "You are what?"

"A murderer, my lord King."

He studied her gravely. "I see."

"I didn't mean to kill him, my lord King." There was more life in her voice as she said that, but it was gone when she added bravely, "Still, I did."

"Who is it you killed?" asked the King.

"I killed my foster father, sir. Emmett Starling. I just pushed him, they were hitting me and I . . . I shouldn't have fought back. I never did before. I don't know why I did then, but . . . I did. And I killed him. They . . . they weren't very strong, I think. The Starlings." She glanced at Hawke again, confusion evident in her face. "They said I was a monster, but . . . I've seen so many people as ugly as I, since I came here . . . some bigger and stronger . . . I don't understand." She looked again at the King. "But I know I killed him."

"Was this when you left home?" asked the King.

She nodded, not trusting her voice.

To her surprise, he smiled again. "No, my dear. You are no more murderer than you are ugly. Emmett Starling is alive and well."

She stared. "You *know* that?"

"Yes, child. As well as I know that you belong with my son, as well matched as the pieces of crystal that Lanalei gave you." Ugly and Hawke had put their shards of crystal together, and the two pieces had fit as perfectly as if they had once been a whole. "And as well as I know, my child, that you will one day be Queen of my People."

"I?" Her eyes went round and startled, like a wild thing just ready to take flight. "*I* will?" Her voice cracked.

"You will."

As imperceptibly as she had moved away from Hawke, she moved back to him, as if he were a source of strength for her. As perhaps he was. "And . . . I'm not ugly?"

"You're not ugly," Hawke said firmly.

"Oh." She ventured a tremulous smile. "Then I will need a new name, won't I? You could hardly call the Queen 'Hey, you!' "

48

They said her name was Emerald. They showed her holograms of two people they said had been her parents. There were holograms of a baby girl, too, that they said were of her, taken in the palace on Freehold before the earthquake. They said she still had relatives there on Freehold: aunts and uncles, a cousin, and some others whose relationship she didn't understand, because it was by gift rather than by blood. The People had names for a complex variety of such relationships, but they didn't translate into Terran, and she was not yet fluent enough in the tongue of the People to make any sense of them.

They gave her a dozen rooms in the palace, her own private rooms, with servants to tend to them and to her every need. Hawke moved into a suite across the corridor. The sense of total immersion in each other's life and mind that they had experienced during the battle with Mahlo had so frightened them both that, drawn as they were to each other by the awesome power of their gift, they fought it and stayed apart and made tentative, nervous advances like adolescents in the throes of a forbidden infatuation.

The tawny cat had a name now, too. In the battle, King Arkos had somehow regained some use of the gift he had shared with his Queen—someone had said that the Maker-Breaker power had acted as a catalyst, but she didn't know what that meant—and when it was over he had talked with the cats. She could do that, a little, with Hawke's help, but Arkos had done it that night and had told them with satisfaction that the tawny cat was named Amber and that Amber and Friend were lifemates. The two cats had a room of their own in what Arkos called "Princess Emerald's apartments." They visited Hawke more frequently than he visited her. They both had more experience at friendship than either she or Hawke had.

And that was the trouble. She and Hawke were singletons. They always had been singletons. It was all they knew. An entire nation depended on their ability to be something they were not: a pair.

At least Hawke fit in these surroundings. He looked elegant in brocade and velvet and silk. She felt encumbered and rather silly, like a child playing dress-up with the wardrobe of a princess. And she was useless: there was no work for her here. Servants cleaned and cooked for her, dressed and bathed and tried to entertain her, selected her costumes and combed her hair and plumped up cushions for her to sit on and would not let her so much as pour a cup of tea for herself. Hawke was accustomed to all that; he grew up in this palace. He had always been a prince. He might be as unnerved as she was by the strength of their attraction to each other, but he dealt with it in familiar surroundings. He knew the correct social behaviors for the circumstance of being heir to a throne. She didn't.

She had not even accepted, emotionally, that she actually was a princess. It was too like a fairytale to be real. Intellectually she understood that the magicians had established her heritage beyond doubt, but emotionally she still felt like the monster fosterling of the Starlings'. A waste of food, not a princess. And Prince Hawke was expected to accept her as giftmate, as lifemate; *Prince* Hawke. She, Ugly Starling, was to marry Prince Hawke, whom the People called the King That Was and Will Be. . . .

She was aware that in some ways Hawke was as ill-at-ease as she was. He was accustomed enough to his rank, but she knew he still heard the unspoken adjective: the mad Prince. He no longer looked or behaved like a madman, but he could not feel certain of his sanity. He, like she, had been too long alone. A nation of couples depended for its salvation on two people who knew only solitude.

Thus it was that she found herself, three weeks after the battle with Mahlo, pacing the sumptuously decorated rooms of her apartment in a flowing green silk gown that trailed the carpeted floor and repeatedly tripped her silken-slippered feet. Anxious servants followed her with tempting trays of the kingdom's tastiest delicacies, and a hairdresser rushed fretfully at her side trying to place one last gem-encrusted pin in her hair, and a dressmaker stood looking after her with straightpins in his mouth and an unfurled tape measure dangling from his fingers. Sunlight cast arched parallelograms of gold across the floors from the open windows that maidservants kept closing when she wasn't looking. Somewhere in the distance outside a lark sang, the trilled notes heartbreakingly clear and sweet on the still morning air.

"Princess Emerald, you must eat something," said a maid, thrusting a tray of steaming, buttery rolls and sugary buns into her path and nearly tripping her.

"Princess Emerald, just let me pin this one last curl in place, do," said the hairdresser, grasping at her hair.

"Princess Emerald, I cannot design the gown to fit if I'm not allowed to measure," called the dressmaker, his tone accusatory.

"Princess Emerald, you shouldn't leave these windows open; you'll catch cold."

"Princess Emerald, you've been up since dawn; you must rest. Sit here, Princess Emerald."

"See how soft the cushions are, Princess Emerald."

"Just taste this starberry tart, Princess Emerald."

"Or the baked thrush, Princess Emerald."

"Or these sweetbreads, Princess Emerald."

"Princess Emerald."

"Princess Emerald."

She put her hands to her ears and wondered rather wildly what would happen if she screamed. Instead she said very quietly, very calmly, and very clearly, "Go. All of you. At once. Leave me. Go away. *Go.*"

For a long moment no one moved. Then the dressmaker, shrugging, began to pack away his pins and fabrics. A maid looked at her tray of delicacies, looked at the Princess, and said hesitantly, "Princess Emerald—"

"—Leave the tray if you must, but leave! Silently. Now." Her voice was not quite steady. When the hairdresser made one last fretful lunge at her hair, Princess Emerald nearly slapped her aside. "*Go!*" The hairdresser went, looking aggrieved. One by one all the other servants departed, with many a backward glance and murmur of distress, till she was alone. For a long moment she didn't move. She just stood there in a parallelogram of sun, with glittering gems in her hair and the green silk of her dress badly wrinkled from much unpracticed lifting of the skirt to keep from tripping. The matching green silk slippers pinched her feet. Sighing, she stepped out of them and walked slowly to the nearest window, bunching the hated skirt in an awkward tangle over one arm to leave her feet free.

One of the servants had closed the window. She opened it and sat tentatively on the edge of the wide, velvet-cushioned window seat. First she leaned back, twisting her body so she could see the carefully tended gardens below, riotous with cultivated flowers in every color. Then she straightened and turned back to the two rooms of her apartment visible from there. They were like the garden: riotous with cultivated beauty. The room she was in was carpeted from wall to wall with luxurious furlike fabric woven in a rainbow of colors of abstract design. The neighboring room had a polished stone floor with thick rugs at intervals, their plush fabric and tasseled ends perfectly designed to trip anyone unaccustomed to walking in the flowing gowns of a princess.

The pale stone walls were hung with tapestries depicting landscapes in improbable colors, with stiffly posed wildlife and gold-threaded flowers. The furniture was all heavy, black, lustrously polished wood, carved intricately with the shapes of fierce birds, stalking cats, rearing horses, and other animals all so lifelike that their gemstone eyes seemed to glitter with malevolence and pity. The chairs and couches were deeply piled with pillows in every color and texture. The tables were inlaid with crystal and precious metals, and burdened with gem-encrusted boxes, gold and silver flagons and bowls, slender crystal sculptures that glittered full of rainbows in the light, and massive bouquets of heavy-scented garden flowers in ornate ceramic vases.

Even the trays on which the servants had brought such tempting delicacies for her meal were of precious metals encrusted with glittering gems set so thickly that they ought to have looked merely gaudy but were, instead, graceful and lovely. They might suit the Princess Emerald. The whole apartment might suit the Princess Emerald. It did not suit Ugly. She wanted her cave in the wilderness. She remembered it suddenly and with such fierce longing that her throat constricted and her eyes burned with unshed tears.

"Emerald?"

She did not consciously recognize the voice and had no real intention to respond at all: it startled her as much as it startled Hawke when she cried out in rage and anguish, "My name is *Ugly*!"

With anyone else there might have been some confusion as to whether she meant that the name Emerald was ugly or that she was named Ugly, but Hawke knew. The moment he entered the room he knew, too, that he should have been there sooner, and more often. He saw the room through her eyes and for one brief moment saw, too, the beloved sand-floored cave with which she compared it. "You want to go back." It was not a question.

She stared at him with huge, haunted eyes. "I can't go back." It was not a denial.

He wanted to hold her. Instead he stayed where he was, ten paces from her, and waited. Their gifts, the mysterious connection between them that was lodged in their minds or their bodies or their genes, created a nearly tangible tension between them, like a rubber-band stretched taut, almost to breaking. Hawke resisted the tendency to lean physically against it, away from her; it felt as though, if he did not, he would fall not just toward her but somehow through her, drowned in the fearsome power of their united gifts.

She leaned away from him and said in a small, hoarse voice, "I don't know how to be what I am. I don't know how to be a giftmated princess." After the battle, she had erected barriers against him that she did not understand or intend: in the same way that she had used the crystal for lighting fires and moving objects, she had used the power of it, in her mind, to build a wall between them. She did not know why she had done it, any more than she knew how she had done it; she only knew that she had done it, and that now she was trapped inside a crystal cage of her own devising, separate from the man she had come so far to find.

"I shouldn't have left you alone so much," he said. "I thought it was what you wanted."

"It was what I wanted." Her voice sounded hollow, even to her own ears.

He shook his head: a brief, curt gesture that dislodged his hair from behind one ear and let it fall across his forehead, veiling one eye. He shoved it back impatiently. "It's not that easy."

She sighed and turned away from him to look down into the gardens. The crumpled fabric of her skirts rustled audibly in the stillness of the room. "Nothing is easy."

"Quitting is easy." There was an unexpected note of harsh mockery in his voice. "Giving up is easy."

She thought the mockery was meant for her, and did not even wonder whether it was justified. "Sometimes it is also wise." Her voice sounded old.

He shrugged, though she was not looking. "Not now. Not between us." He hesitated, while the pull of their gifts tore at the crystalline structures of the barriers between them. He did not know which of them had built what barriers; only that the barriers were there. "*Can* you, Emerald? Can you quit?"

"My name is Ugly."

"You could bear it? You could . . . leave me?"

"It would be a kind of death. I know that." She did not take her eyes from the gardens. "But it would not be so very difficult, really."

He moved then, involuntarily; jerkily, like a puppet in inexperienced hands. When he was almost within reach of her she made a fending little gesture that stopped him as if he had come up against a solid wall between them. He did not reach toward her, though he wanted to. "Emerald, what is it? I can feel it: there's more than I understand. It isn't just habit, or loneliness, or . . . what is it? Let me help you."

She shook her head. "There's nothing." It was all she could do not to reach for him: to keep whole the barriers against her need for him. "There was a valley in the wilderness. Friend and I lived there. We were happy." She paused, and the silence pressed at her ears. Outside, a lark trilled gaily, and a fountain splashed, and the metal of a horse's harness chinked against itself; but inside the palace, between her and Hawke, there was silence so sharp and hard it was like a physical presence. She spoke only to banish it, unaware of what she would say till it was said. "Then the Goddess—I saw her, in the crystal, and she told me to find my giftmate, and I didn't know what that was."

"Emerald—"

She shook her head again, briefly, still not looking at him. "I did it, though. I crossed the mountains and I came to Town and the Goddess said I would find you and I found you. And it was important. You needed me, against that man Mahlo. I know that. I know what we did."

"And you know what we are meant to do: what we will do. She showed you that, too."

"The stairs in the Crystal Palace, and the Terrans waiting, and us in all those fancy clothes." She looked at him, and her eyes were flat amethyst pools, unreadable.

"That's important too, Emerald."

She smiled faintly. "I know that. You think I don't know that? You think I don't realize that this whole nation of Ugly People depends on *us*? Nobody else, just *us*?" She shifted impatiently. "Oh, I get cross at nothing to do, and I hate it how they all *hover* all the time, trying to do things for me, but I know it's because they expect us to practically save the world for them, so I can hardly complain that I don't have anything to do." She smiled again, without amusement. "Not when I have a whole world to save."

"Not just you. We. Together."

She closed her eyes. "Neither of us knows how to do anything together with anyone. Haven't you noticed? We're *not* together. We're both too separate."

"We don't have to be."

"We—I—don't know any other way to *be*!" It was almost a cry of pain.

"You do. Emerald, you do. You did it. You—when Mahlo sang—I would have given up, but you didn't let me. You gave me your strength, and we stopped him. *We* did it. Together." He was watching her closely, but she did not move. "Emerald." Her face twisted just visibly at the sound of her name. He said it again: "Emerald."

She turned her face away, her body rigid.

"Emerald, we can do it again. You know we can. The barriers between us are of our own making, and we can break them. We *will*. The Goddess showed us that. We—"

She jerked away suddenly and curled into a small, shivering ball, eyes closed, face hidden by a veil of hair. "Don't," she said helplessly. "Don't."

Bewildered, he touched her shoulder, but she pulled away. "Don't what? What's wrong? That vision—the two of us and my father the High King, and the Terrans humbly waiting—that will happen, Emerald.

The Goddess showed us. We'll confront them, and we'll *win*."

She straightened suddenly to face him, and he was startled at the rage and pain in her eyes. "But at what cost, Hawke? *At what cost?*" Then she *reached* for him, and the barriers cracked, just enough for her to show him the vision she had seen in the temple. In her anguish she thrust it at him so suddenly there was no time to adjust to the new point of view; he was simply immersed in her memory. One moment he was with her in the palace: the next, he was standing alone at night, looking out on the confusion of battle on a dark plain dotted with the dull red of campfires and swarming with soldiers engaged in war. Shouts and cries and the sharp clang of steel against steel startled him. Sudden explosions and the whine of Terran weapons all but deafened him. The stink of death clogged his nostrils. It was a nightmare scene of chaos and horror, in which he stood alone at the end of the world. . . . He saw the battle as if from a great distance: he watched two vast armies collide as relentlessly, as destructively, and as pointlessly as ocean waves crash against a vulnerable shore. Men out there were dying. . . .

Men were dead. She remembered her task and returned to it dully, grief and fear both blunted by a surfeit of horror. One cannot endure the end of the world forever. She examined every corpse she found, turning them when she had to, and they were many: she searched every ruin, choking on dust and smoke and the stink of decay: she looked in every gully, under every scrap of wreckage, behind every rock outcropping. Hawke was missing. Hawke was gone. Hawke was lost. . . .

He fought his way up out of the dark with an effort, finding his own identity in the depths of her despair and pushing free enough to say, "I'm here, Emerald. I'm here." In one quick movement he took her in his arms, lifting her to her feet and holding her, and she pressed her face hard against his shoulder, trembling with weariness and fear. "I'm here," he said. "It's all right, Emerald. . . ." But the vision of chaos was permanently etched in his mind.

She said dully, "You saw the cost. How can we, Hawke? How can we do that? Is freedom from the Terrans as important as that?"

He tightened his arms around her, uncertain what other response to make, and the force of his sudden love and pity crumpled the last barriers between them. The arms around her were her own. The body he held against his was his. The past was a mad jumble of bright scenes impossibly tangled: he remembered the peace of the wilderness valley, the excitement of the waterfall, the security of the cave; she remembered the confusion and dread of wandering the streets of Far Harbor in search of a giftmate she dared not believe existed. They stood at the edge of the crystal gully and saw the Goddess Lanalei, and drowned in the sea-green smile of her eyes. *I* remembered *my* childhood in a palace/in a village; as a prince/as a monster; as a beloved son/as a despised burden; always alone.

That was the touchstone, the mirror in which the *I* became *we*. Each knew that solitude for his/her own and found in it the separation required to sort all the other memories, so that *he* could remember *her* growing up in a village while *she* remembered *him* in the palace. Without that recognition of individuality, they had been, briefly, one mind stumbling perilously near the edge of irretrievable insanity, the power of their joined gifts an awesome but directionless force lost on the brink of chaos. Then the Goddess smiled and whispered, her voice the silver breath of wind in a crystal windchime, the words incomprehensible except for that one word: *alone*.

It gave them back to themselves and made of them both less and more than they had been. As one mind, they had been an almost incomprehensible power that was at the same time rendered powerless by confusion. As two, together, each deeply aware of the other and yet each a discrete individual voluntarily lending strength to the other, they were perhaps less powerful than the mad thing they had briefly been as one; but they were yet infinitely more than either alone, or even than the sum of their two evident gifts. For a fraction of an instant they knew what they were. Then that awareness, too, was thrust beyond them by the hypnotic swirl and eddy of the sea-green Goddess's smile.

The world fell away into a rushing distance and became a spinning crystal gem in an endless sea of space. Galaxies tumbled their glittering, faceted, crystal stars against a velvet silence. Starships rode the skirling winds in the darkness. Multitudes sang, fought, and marched to meet their varied destinies, and died, and were reborn in greater numbers on an ever-expanding number of jeweled worlds in the darkness. Strange suns lighted alien landscapes. People and Terrans and other races indistinct at this distance met and worked together and loved and fought, lived and died, met individual eternities in the brief red flashes of half-seen wars and longer outbreakings of peace. . . . The universe expanded and contracted and sang to the crystal wonder of stars. . . . A single nightlark sang, sharp and sweet in an eternal silence. A perfect amethyst orchid opened waxy petals to greet a dewspun dawn. A meteorite cut a swath of crimson across the lightening sky over the Mysterious Mountains. The Goddess Lanalei said softly, "I can reach you now." And the world fell back into place.

They were two people standing together in a palace room. Emerald drew away enough to look into Hawke's eyes, and saw the stars just fading. He managed a shaky smile and clung to her, more for his own support than for hers. They were two ordinary people again . . . and they would never be two ordinary people again. The Goddess Lanalei had touched them with something more than visions. They were more than just two people, more than either of them could understand, more than they could even imagine. Together they were not just a couple, not just a joined pair, not even a unit, but a power, a force, as inexorable as gravity, as bright as sun, as enduring as legend, as powerful as love.

"I think . . . ." Hawke cleared his throat. "I cannot argue with *that*."

She shook her head slowly. "Nor I. We must do what must be done. *She* would not ask us to pay a price higher than the goal deserved."

"That battle, though . . . It wasn't what we thought. I don't know what or when it was, but . . . I think it comes *after* we confront the Terrans at the Crystal Palace."

"It doesn't matter so much, after all; we must do what me must, and trust her about the cost. But . . . yes. And . . . maybe we can find a way . . . Maybe we could avoid it yet, if we manage well enough with the Terrans at the Crystal Palace. . . ."

He smiled down into her face that was still bright with the afterglow of galaxies. "Which we can't do at all till we get them to let us back *into* the Crystal Palace."

She smiled, amused at herself. "Yes. First things first."

He said gently, "And the first thing is: I love you."

She said it, too, and they laughed because it was so much like saying it to oneself; but for the two of them, that was quite a first step in itself. Then they stopped laughing, because they were ready for the next step. Past, future, and possibilities mattered not at all just then.

Afterward, among the tumbled cushions of the bird-carved couch, they laughed again for sheer joy, and talked a little even though words were superfluous, just because they liked to hear each other speak; and then they slept, cradled in each other's arms, where they belonged. The world could wait a little longer to be saved.

THE BEST IN SCIENCE FICTION

THE TOR DOUBLES

Two complete short science fiction novels in one volume!